Exit Wounds

Also by Neil Broadfoot

No Man's Land
No Place to Die
The Point of No Return
No Quarter Given
Violent Ends
Unmarked Graves

Neil
Broadfoot

Exit Wounds

CONSTABLE

First published in Great Britain in 2025 by Constable

Copyright © Neil Broadfoot, 2025

1 3 5 7 9 10 8 6 4 2

The moral right of the author has been asserted.

All characters and events in this publication, other than those clearly in the public domain, are fictitious and any resemblance to real persons, living or dead, is purely coincidental.

All rights reserved.
No part of this publication may be reproduced, stored in a retrieval system, or transmitted, in any form, or by any means, without the prior permission in writing of the publisher, nor be otherwise circulated in any form of binding or cover other than that in which it is published and without a similar condition including this condition being imposed on the subsequent purchaser.

A CIP catalogue record for this book is available from the British Library.

ISBN: 978-1-40871-879-7

Typeset in Minion Pro by Initial Typesetting Services, Edinburgh
Printed and bound in Great Britain by Clays Ltd, Elcograf S.p.A.

Papers used by Constable are from well-managed forests and other responsible sources.

Constable
An imprint of
Little, Brown Book Group
Carmelite House
50 Victoria Embankment
London EC4Y 0DZ

The authorised representative
in the EEA is
Hachette Ireland
8 Castlecourt Centre
Dublin 15, D15 XTP3, Ireland
(email: info@hbgi.ie)

An Hachette UK Company
www.hachette.co.uk

www.littlebrown.co.uk

For my parents, John and Sheila Broadfoot,
who didn't let a little thing like dying get
in the way of looking after me

CHAPTER 1

It was no different from any other city alley – litter strewn across the dirty grey concrete, graffiti on the pitted walls, some artistic, some profane. Stench of piss, vomit and stale beer. Above, the sky was a sullen, numb grey, a watercolour of indecision threatening either rain or sleet.

Connor Fraser glanced around again, trying to see something that would explain why he was there. He turned slowly, looked back to the opening of the alley and the street beyond, caught the eye of a woman walking past. She paused for a moment, appraised him with the kind of dipped-beam gaze he knew all too well. Intellect dulled by hash, booze or something stronger, something that left her arms puckered and bruised, her brain rotted. She shrugged, as though dismissing him from her thoughts, then started walking again.

Connor peered into the void she'd left, watching life go on. A typical afternoon on the Falls Road, the low rumbling moan of traffic, the occasional shout, people getting on with their lives. It looked so normal. But this was Belfast, and the awareness of violence was imprinted on the collective consciousness, a traumatic memory. No one really spoke about it, but everyone knew that violence was only ever one wrong turn away.

He sighed, took one last look around the alleyway. Was damned if he'd check behind the overflowing rubbish bin wedged against the back wall. It seemed welded there, barricaded behind forgotten bags of rubbish. Whatever he was meant to find eluded him. He reached into his pocket, made the call.

'Connor?' The tone was a mixture of question and surprise. 'What's up, big lad?'

'I'm here,' Connor said. 'Now, you want to tell me what the hell I'm meant to be looking for?'

'Here?' Simon McCartney asked, the alert wariness in his tone giving Connor's stomach an oily clench. 'Where's here?'

'The alley behind the Old Dog on the Falls Road, like your message said.'

'What message?' Simon asked, concern hardening his voice.

'The message you sent . . .' Connor trailed off, the realisation hitting him like a hard left hook. 'Shit,' he whispered, more to himself than Simon. 'Your phone's been cloned. I'm burned.'

Simon's response was immediate, so loud that it stabbed into Connor's ear and seared into his mind. 'I'll get to a secure line. RUN!'

CHAPTER 2

Connor dropped the phone and stamped on it, cursing his stupidity. Simon was a known associate of his: it was only logical to exploit that knowledge to get to Connor. After all, it was what he would have done.

He started back down the alley, towards the road, planning to get lost in the afternoon hubbub. Stopped dead when he saw a car draw up, sleek and black. Retreated into the alleyway, ducked behind a refuse bin, cursing himself for not bringing a gun. Seemed like a no-brainer at the time – the PSNI didn't take kindly to people walking the streets with a firearm, former officer or no.

Now it seemed like another stupid mistake. Potentially a fatal one.

The passenger door of the car opened, and a man unfolded himself from it. About six foot two, squeezed into a suit just expensive enough to be forgettable. His shaved head caught the weak afternoon light, seemed to absorb it somehow. When he straightened, Connor could see dark, empty eyes set in a face that was as forgettable as the suit he wore.

He turned, leaned back into the car, said something Connor couldn't make out to the driver, then started to walk into the alley. As he moved, he drew a gun from his suit jacket.

Connor gave a silent curse. Swallowed the sudden surge of adrenaline that turned the saliva to thick acid in his throat. He looked around for anything he could use as a weapon. Grabbed for a beer bottle beside the bin with a hand that wasn't quite steady.

The man inched closer, his steps like glass-filled drumbeats on the grimy alley floor.

Connor held his breath. Waited.

One more step. Then another.

Connor exploded from his hiding place, swinging the bottle at the man's temple as hard as he could. It shattered on impact, the blow juddering up Connor's arm. The man staggered back, cursing, blood exploding from his temple. Connor closed on him, grabbed for the gun in his hand. The man twisted, dropping to his knees and pulling Connor forward, directly into the rabbit punch he had aimed at his temple.

A blinding explosion of pain and Connor felt the world lurch. He bit his tongue, forced himself not to release his grip on the man's gun hand. Instead, pulled him in, then drove his free elbow up into the bottom of the man's jaw. Felt teeth grind together and snap as the man's head was thrown back. Connor jabbed his fist into the man's exposed throat. He crumpled, hand releasing the gun as he clawed at his neck, gasping for breath. He crashed to the ground, lips already turning blue, and Connor knew he had crushed the man's windpipe. He took a half-step back, felt the world lurch sickeningly as blood, warm and sticky, oozed down his face.

He reached for the gun his attacker had dropped, closed his grip on it as he heard a car door slam at the end of the alley. Looked up to see another man walk around the car from the driver's side. He was as broad as his partner was tall, wearing the same anonymously expensive suit, holding the same gun. The gun he was raising to Connor as he walked.

Connor darted to the side, felt another wave of nausea at the sudden movement. No choice. He raised the gun, pulled the trigger. The recoil of the shot made the pain in his head roar, almost drowning the screaming from the street as the approaching driver's head exploded in a mist of blood, bone and brain.

Connor cursed, forced himself to breathe. Took a moment to turn back to his first attacker, check his pockets. Nothing. Not even a handkerchief. He stood, hurried back up the alley. People were running on the street, either to get away from the gunshot or to find out what was going on. Across the road, a group of men emerged from another pub, their faces telling Connor this was just what they had been waiting and hoping for.

He paused for a moment at his second attacker, checked his pockets as well. No ID or handkerchief, but something more useful. Car keys.

Connor grabbed for them with numb fingers, hurried to the car. Saw the men across the road start towards him, raised the gun and they froze. Message received.

He ran to the driver's side, hoped the ringing in his head and the dimming of vision in his left eye would let him drive. He started the engine, wondering where to go. Somewhere he could disappear, just another face in the crowd, somewhere he could think. Only one answer, really.

Connor put the car in gear, drove away.

Welcome to Belfast, he thought abruptly, stifling the sudden urge to laugh.

Welcome home.

CHAPTER 3

He turned the car, making for central Belfast. His first instinct had been to head out of town, towards the Divis Mountains or the Colin Glen, get away from the network of cameras the police would undoubtedly try to use to track him. But being in an isolated location worked both ways: it gave him solitude, but deprived him of resources.

So town it was. Time for a little shopping.

He drove as slowly and anonymously as he dared, the urge to dump the car and walk an almost physical presence. But the sickening bayonet of pain in his left temple and the way any sudden reflection or flash of light from another car stabbed into his brain told him he was in no condition to walk. Knew the signs well: he had concussion. Hoped it wasn't a bad one. He didn't have time for it.

Saw the shop he was looking for ahead, same faded green and gold awning over the door, unchanged since he had walked this beat with Simon years ago. He pulled in, killed the engine. Closed his eyes, grabbed onto the steering wheel and leaned forward, ignoring the wave of nausea that brought tears to his eyes. Tried to think through the pain and the spent adrenaline. They'd cloned Simon's phone, used it to lure him to a trap in the Republican heart of Belfast. Two men, guns standard police and military issue, Glock 17. So something really was going on after all. What Danny had made sure he was given was important in a way he didn't yet understand. But what did . . .?

The sudden blare of a horn made Connor gasp, sit up straight. He peered out of the windscreen, saw a car parked nose to nose with him, engine giving a whining growl in the way only a tuned turbo could.

Shit, Connor thought, looking up at the frontage of the shop. O'Connell's Convenience. What the sign didn't tell you was that, for the right price, that convenience could fall on either side of the law. Which made the owners a little nervous about who visited, so they had guards stationed around the shop, looking for faces that didn't fit. And one was now nose to nose with Connor.

The driver of the car in front of him, a blue Subaru Impreza, killed the engine and got out. He was big, all gym-sculpted muscles and buzz-cut hair, but Connor could still see the echo of Miles O'Connell in the man. It was in the eyes, so brown they were almost black, and the way his mouth twisted into a sneer that he probably thought was a genuine human smile.

Like father, like son, Connor thought.

He sighed, patted his jacket. Gun still there. Hoped he wouldn't have to use it. Got out of the car. Last thing he needed was to be in a confined space.

''Bout ye?' he asked, as he stood up, wishing he had a pair of sunglasses.

'Cannae park there, pal,' the driver said as he approached. 'Customer parking for my da's shop. And you sure as fuck aren't a regular.'

Connor took a deep breath, felt a wave of exhaustion roll over him. He needed to get off the street now. 'So you'd be who? Rory? His eldest, I'm guessing?' Connor said. 'And how is old Miles anyway? He out now, or is he still inside for using this place as a front to launder drugs cash for Malky Tomlinson's crew on the Falls?'

The man in front of him stepped forward, hands bunching into fists as the colour drained from his face. Connor could see a tattoo ripple over the muscles in his left forearm, could tell by his stance he was a southpaw. 'Just who the fuck are . . .'

'Easy,' Connor said, lifting his hand. 'Didn't mean anything by it. I used to know your dad back in the day. He was a good sort, despite his, ah, off-the-book activities. Made sure nothing got too out of hand. Kept civilians as far away from trouble as he could. Never let Malky deal to kids.'

'That why you're here?' Rory spat. 'To pass on your respects? Well, yer a bit fucking late. Now piss off. Don't give a fuck if you knew my da. Peelers aren't welcome around here. And you reek of peeler.'

'Really? And the woman at the store told me it was Armani,' Connor said, regretting the words as soon as he'd said them. The last thing he needed to do was wind up Rory. But even as he thought it, he heard his father's words: *That Fraser temper. Watch it, son. It'll get you into trouble one day.*

Rory took a step forward, one hand reaching behind his back. Connor sighed, dropped his head. Looked over Rory's shoulder to the car he had just got out of. Nice car. Four-wheel drive. Fast. And not connected to a shooting on the Falls Road less than an hour ago.

'Your da still make sure all the security cameras are out around here?' Connor asked.

'Wh-what?' Rory asked, hand freezing behind his back as he instinctively glanced up to the eaves of the shop, confusion crumpling his features.

'Aye, thought so,' Connor said. 'Tell me, son, you got a phone on you?'

Rory jerked, as though Connor had slapped him. 'What the . . .? Ack, naw, fuck it, you just need to . . .'

He lunged forward, the knife he produced from behind his back glinting in the sun. Connor stepped into the arc of Rory's swing and pivoted, tucking his fist into the side of his head and driving his elbow into Rory's forearm. The knife sailed through the air, a slash of quicksilver in the late-afternoon sun, then clattered to the ground. Connor kept moving, ignoring the agony screaming through his head and the churning of his stomach. He dropped his knee, shouldered Rory in the chest, then followed through with a hard left hook to his jaw. Rory staggered, eyes rolling back in his head as he lurched to the left and slammed into the side of his car. Connor stepped forward, grabbed him, then slammed his head off the bonnet of the car, the shock of the blow tearing new pain loose in his head.

He stumbled back, took a deep breath. Then he bent down, found the car keys on Rory and threw him into the back seat. Found a phone in a cradle stuck to the dashboard, said a silent prayer of thanks when he realised it was unlocked, a playlist of music scrolling across the screen. Dialled a number only he and Simon knew, a number they had prepared for a day just like this. Waited.

'Big lad,' Simon said, after the second ring. 'Jesus Christ. You okay? What the hell is going on?'

Connor took a breath, bit back another wave of agony. He needed to rest. 'Later,' he said, starting the engine of the car and pulling away. 'I've an errand to run. I'll get some burners and call you back. Can you arrange a place for me to lie low?'

Simon whistled. 'You don't ask for much, do you?' he said, his tone just the right side of mocking. 'Okay, give me twenty minutes then call me back.'

'I'll make it twenty-five,' Connor said. 'It'll take me that long to get to the Shankill and dump some rubbish.'

'Shankill?' Simon said. 'Christ, Connor, what the hell are you planning?'

Despite himself, Connor smiled. It cut through the pain and the confusion, made him feel like himself again.

'Just a little old-fashioned mischief-making,' he said, glancing in the rear-view mirror. Talk soon.'

CHAPTER 4

Simon looked down at the phone in his hand, muttered a curse. Knew he should have been on the first plane to Belfast the moment Connor had called him two nights ago with that list of names. Instead, he had stayed in Stirling, cementing his new life with Donna. The thought of her sent a shudder of panic arcing through him. Donna Blake. Lover, soon-to-be fiancée if he asked the question right, and reporter. Hard-nosed, ruthless reporter who would just love to know all about whatever shit storm Connor had stirred up in Belfast, then tell the nation about it on one of her regular Sky News slots.

Question was, what had Connor stepped into?

It had started a week ago. Connor and Simon had been wrapping up a training session at the gym, which basically entailed Connor lifting unfeasibly heavy weights, then chasing Simon around a boxing ring and grappling him into submission. Since his problems with his girlfriend, Jen, Connor's focus on training had taken on an almost obsessive quality, as if he was punishing himself physically for the problems in his relationship – and his inability to fix them.

They were just taking off their gloves when Connor's phone had buzzed. He took the call, and Simon watched as a maelstrom of emotions flitted across his friend's face in less than two minutes. The creased brow of confusion at an unfamiliar number, the smile as he recognised the voice at the other end, the dropping of the shoulders and the darkening of the brow as bad news was delivered, the whispered promise to get in touch soon. When the call ended, Connor stood there, head down, phone forgotten in his hand. Despite his physical presence and massive shoulders, he was more like a little lost boy than the man who had rained blows down on him in their sparring session.

'You all right, big lad?' he asked, trying to keep his tone light, casual.

'What?' Connor blinked, almost as if he was surprised to see Simon there. 'Oh, yeah, yeah. Sorry. Just a bit of bad news is all.'

'Want to tell me about it?'

Connor shrugged, as though he was processing the information and struggling to frame it. 'That was the mum of an old friend from Belfast, Danny Gillespie.'

'Don't think I've heard that name before,' Simon said.

'You wouldn't have. Before we met. Danny was in my psychology classes back at Queen's. Good lad. We hung about a lot. Drinking at Lavery's, weekends down in Cork and Galway, you know, usual stuff. I joined the police, and he went on to take a lecturing job in London. Just kind of drifted apart, you know how it is. The odd text, an email now and then.'

How many of his friends were just acquaintances now, the bond between them on life support via the odd text or a crappy forwarded joke? Simon wondered. Didn't much like the answer.

'Anyway,' Connor had said, straightening as he tossed his phone back into his bag, 'that was his mum. Seems he was visiting her in Dunmurry, went out for a drink one night, staggered onto the road after one too many and . . .' He had lifted his hands, dropped them, helpless frustration on his face.

'Jesus, I'm sorry, man,' Simon said.

'Thanks,' Connor said, almost reflexively. 'Funeral's next week. Mary wants me to be there, one of the pall-bearers.'

Simon frowned. 'Bit odd,' he said. 'I mean, from what you said, you weren't close any more, and pall-bearing is a family job normally.'

Another shrug. 'Danny was an only child,' he said. 'And the rest of the family is scattered across America and Canada. Besides, I don't really mind. Be good to get away for a bit.'

Simon nodded, not wanting to poke at the elephant in the room. The death of Jen's father, Duncan MacKenzie, almost a year ago had driven a wedge between Jen and Connor. A wedge that had widened with Connor's investigation into MacKenzie's death, which had brought some uncomfortable truths about the man to light. Truths that had tarnished Jen's view of her father – and Connor. They were trying to move forward, aiming for the home Connor had bought for them before Duncan's death, but still the distance remained, a yawning chasm that neither seemed able to cross.

'You want some company?' Simon had asked. 'We could hit a few of the old haunts, get into a wee bit of trouble in Belfast for old times' sake?'

Connor laughed. 'Christ, no,' he said. 'Can you imagine the crap Donna would give me if I dragged you off for a lads' jaunt to Belfast? She'd kill me.'

'Aye,' Simon said. 'Fair play.'

So Connor had left for Belfast, and life had gone on. Simon had lost himself in transferring to Police Scotland from the PSNI, moving into Connor's now-vacated garden flat in Park Circus and stalking jewellers in the area until he found the perfect ring for Donna. But then, on the night after the funeral, Connor had called.

'Connor, 'bout ye?' Simon asked, relieved to hear from him. The thought of him alone, brooding, as he stalked the streets of Belfast, wasn't a comfortable one. 'How did it go?'

'Not bad,' Connor had said, in a cold, distracted tone that made Simon uneasy. 'Interesting crowd. Listen, can you do me a favour? Track a few names down for me, current location, movements et cetera?'

Simon agreed, his unease hardening into dread as Connor gave him three names that could only mean trouble. Trouble that now seemed to have landed squarely at Connor's door.

He shook himself. Time enough for introspection later. Right now he had to find somewhere safe for Connor to lie low until they figured out what was going on. He thought for a moment, then smiled. Only one option he could come up with. He began dialling the number, paused. Looked at the phone. What was it Connor had said? *Shit, your phone's been cloned.*

Simon didn't like what that told him. Whoever they were up against, they were professionals. Technically proficient. Highly resourced. And gunning for his friend.

He put the phone down, walked through into the bedroom, reached into the cupboard, and pulled out a battered leather sports bag. A throwback to his previous life, when being targeted by terrorists was a real possibility and the ability to get out of town fast was literally a matter of life and death. The bag held money, a couple of fake IDs, a gun and, most importantly, a burner phone.

He unwrapped it, inserted a fresh SIM card, switched the phone on, got dialling. Waited.

'Gemma,' he said, when it was answered. 'Simon McCartney. Look, I need a wee favour. And I need it to happen now, okay?'

At the other end, Gemma sighed, a familiar sound. Comforting. Gemma Arthurton made everything sound like a chore. But the truth was, she was the most professional fixer Simon had ever met.

'Tell me what you need,' she said, accent pure west Belfast. 'And then tell me how you're going to pay me back for this.'

CHAPTER 5

Connor stayed off the motorway, instead threading the car through the back roads and suburbs that led him north from the Falls Road to the Shankill Road. He drove slowly, the rumble of the car's engine seeming to resonate with the snarling agony in his head. Spotted what he needed soon enough, and smiled.

It sat at the turning into a small, residential street lined with red-brick terrace houses, which faced onto what looked like allotments. Connor indicated, pulled into the street, bumped the car up onto the pavement and looked over his shoulder into the back seat. Saw Rory O'Connell lying there, his face already turning a dark, angry purple, his breathing noisy and liquid. Connor felt a brief pang of guilt at the knowledge he had broken the kid's nose.

That Fraser temper, son. Watch for it.

Shook it off. Didn't have time for it. He got out of the car, looked up at the sign bolted to the bricks in front of him. It dominated the wall, dwarfing the awning for the taxi company on the corner of the building. White star on a blue background, Red Hand of Ulster held up in a *Stop* sign in the middle, crown above it. VANGUARD BEARS, DEFENDING OUR TRADITIONS, read the text that looped around the star. Connor looked to his right at another sign bolted onto the harled wall above a small, battered door. *Ulster Volunteer Force, 1913*, the sign read, emblazoned over the sepia-orange-stained image of men in military-style outfits and bunnets. You didn't really need the

Union flag bunting criss-crossing the street to work out this was a Unionist area, but it was a nice touch.

Connor blipped the central locking on O'Connell's car, making sure the alarm was armed. Then he wiped the key, as he had the steering wheel and everything else he had touched in the vehicle, and dropped it into a drain as he walked away. He didn't know how long Rory would be out, but when he woke up, his movement would set off the car alarm. And Connor guessed the alarm, parked where it was, would draw some Vanguard Bears or other Loyalists, all of whom would be very interested to know why the son of a noted dealer and money launderer in the heart of Republican Belfast had dared to step into the Union-loving Shankill Road. Questions would be asked but, more importantly for Connor, it would cause trouble between certain less law-abiding citizens of the Republican and Loyalist communities. And that type of trouble would demand police attention, which would otherwise be trained on him and his activities on the Falls Road earlier in the day.

He walked back onto the main street, checked his watch. Still five minutes until he was due to call Simon back. Five minutes when he didn't want to be a sitting target. He got moving and, on instinct, started walking back towards the Shankill Leisure Centre. A few years ago, a small-time thug called the Librarian had been run over not far from the leisure centre. At the time, Connor had wondered if it had been more than a tragic accident. Ironic that, years later, he was thinking the same thing about Danny Gillespie. Instinctively, he tapped his breast pocket, feeling the items Danny's mother had given to him at the funeral.

'Danny would have wanted you to have these,' she had said, her face set and pale, blue eyes, so like Danny's, hard and defiant despite the tears that shone from them. Connor looked down, saw she was pressing an old wristwatch and what looked like a prayer book into his hands.

What did it mean? Were they just treasured keepsakes she wanted her son's friend to have, or were they something more? Something that would give Connor a clue as to what was going on, and why he now had Simon chasing ghosts.

A few moments later, the phone Connor had stolen from Rory O'Connell chirped. He took it from his pocket, answered.

'How you doing?' Simon asked before Connor had time to speak.

'Honestly? Been better,' Connor said, rubbing his left temple as he did. He could feel the swelling there, as though a tennis ball was being inflated under his skin. God alone knew what it looked like. 'But I'll survive. Anyway, thought I was meant to be calling you.'

'What can I say? I got tired of waiting. First, do you need a hospital?' Simon asked, his clinical tone telling Connor he wasn't talking to his friend now but the professional police officer.

'No,' Connor said, wondering if the lie was as obvious as it felt on his lips. 'Took a bit of a crack to the head, but I'll be grand after some rest and time to think.'

'Okay,' Simon said. 'You always were a hard-headed bugger. Got an address for you on Glencairn Street. Remember that?'

'How could I forget?' Connor said, recalling a residential area beyond the Shankill on the road out to the Black Mountains.

'Good,' Simon said, then gave him the house number. 'Get there. We've arranged a bolthole for you, all the supplies you need to patch yourself up, clothes. Dump this phone when we're done with this call. Contact me when you get to the house. We've left instructions there.'

Connor was about to ask who 'we' were, then thought better of it. To turn something like this around so quickly, he must have gone to Gemma Arthurton. She had worked with the PSNI back in the day, coordinating security for high-value informants and witnesses. When she had been pensioned out of the service after one bad day too many, which had involved a pipe bomb, and a near miss that had left her with one leg four inches shorter than the other, Gemma had discovered that her skill in creating anonymous boltholes for those who didn't want to be found was a highly sought-after commodity.

'Okay,' Connor said. Five-minute drive if he still had a car, or a twenty-minute walk. Question was, could he face stealing another car? Two in one day seemed a little excessive, even for him.

'Be safe, Connor,' Simon said. 'We'll talk soon.'

'Thanks,' Connor said, relief washing through him. 'One last thing. Those names I gave you the other day. Any luck? This has got to be connected to them.'

Simon sighed. 'Depends what you mean by luck after the day you've had,' he said. 'Get yourself safe. Then we'll talk.'

Before Connor could say anything else, the line went dead. He took the phone from his ear, looked at the dead black screen. Could see a dimly distorted reflection there, was glad it didn't show too much detail. Heard the first shriek of a car alarm behind him as he took the phone in both hands, snapped it in half then threw it into the gutter.

As he started to walk, he smiled at the thought of Rory O'Connell waking up in the back of his car. At least he wasn't the only one having a bad day.

CHAPTER 6

'So, Paulie,' Jen MacKenzie asked, 'just how much shit am I in?'

The question hung in the air, seemed to turn the atmosphere in the office into an almost physical presence that bore down on them. Across the desk, in a comically ill-fitting chair and squirming like a naughty schoolboy who had been hauled into the headmaster's office, Paulie King wrestled with the question, his face a picture of embarrassed confusion. Whether it was caused by her swearing or the obvious answer to her question, Jen couldn't decide.

They were in an office at MacKenzie Haulage, the business Jen's late father, Duncan, had built over more than a quarter of a century. When Duncan had died the previous year, the victim of a killer bent on revenge, the company, along with everything else her father had owned, had passed to Jen. But, as she had quickly found, keeping Scotland's third biggest haulage and transportation business afloat wasn't simply a matter of trucks on the roads and happy customers.

Far from it.

Paulie picked up a sheet of paper from the desk and studied it intently, as though all the answers to his problems were written there. Tossed it aside with a frustrated sigh. 'Look, Jen,' he started, tone tentative, the bearer of bad news he didn't want to deliver. 'Maybe I'm not the best person to be talking to about this. Maybe try Argyll. He knows the books better than I do.'

Jen snorted. John Argyll was the senior accountant with Argyll and Mathieson, the company her dad had used since he had founded MacKenzie Haulage. A small, slender man whose sallow skin was marred with acne scars, Argyll was, Jen had to admit, excellent at his job. He knew the business inside out, from contracts with house builders to move materials around the country, to contracts with government to ferry stationery supplies between office buildings. What he couldn't explain was why, with all the contracts continuing uninterrupted after Duncan MacKenzie's death, the business was suddenly suffering cashflow problems, overheads now dwarfing turnover.

But Jen knew, or strongly suspected. And the look in Paulie's eyes told her he knew the answer too. 'Fine,' she said, taking the piece of paper Paulie had discarded. It was a list of the client contracts, and their worth, that MacKenzie Haulage had been involved in over the last six months.

Worthless.

'Look, Paulie,' she said, ignoring the warning flare of pain from her hip as she shifted her weight, 'we both know this is about as much use as a sheet of used toilet paper. This tells me about the contracts we've got, the ones on the books. What it doesn't tell me is which contracts we've lost. You know, the ones Argyll never gets troubled with.'

Paulie opened his mouth, closed it. Gave her a pained look. If he'd had a hat, he would have been wringing it between his massive hands. 'Look, Jen, I'm not sure your dad would want me talking to you about—'

'To hell with my dad,' Jen snapped, the anger in her voice resonating with the flash of grief that roiled in her chest. 'He's gone, Paulie. And if I'm going to keep his business alive, I need to know the full picture. And that means the contracts off the books, the less than legal ones. I need to know what we've lost and . . .' She paused, feeling as though she was at the edge of a cliff. '. . . what we have to do to get them back.'

Paulie's eyes darted to hers, something at once predatory and sympathetic flashing behind them. He ran one huge hand over the bristle on top of his head. 'I'm no' sure you can,' he said at last, his tone low.

'What do you mean?' Jen asked.

Paulie shifted his bulk, the chair squealing a soft protest. Reached into his jacket pocket, then stopped. Jen smiled despite herself. No matter how stressed he was, 'Uncle' Paulie would never smoke one of his cheap cigars in front of her. It was one of his unwritten rules.

'Well, you're right,' he said, dropping his hand into his lap and trapping it under the other. 'When your dad died, most of the, ah, off-the-book contracts just . . . stopped. No one knew what was going to happen with the business, and these folk aren't exactly the type who can hang back and see what happens, so they made alternative arrangements.'

Jen studied Paulie, felt the cliff edge loom in front of her again. Did she want to do this? Could she? With her dad gone and her life as a personal trainer ended, thanks to being run over, almost killed, outside her workplace, what choice did she have? If she let MacKenzie Haulage fold, what had her dad's life been for – his sacrifice, the long, hard hours he had put into building a future for her? No. She needed MacKenzie Haulage to survive. No matter what.

'Alternative arrangements for what?' she asked.

Paulie looked up to the ceiling, as though he was blowing imaginary smoke from the cigar he hadn't lit. He shook his head, as though making a decision, then levelled his gaze on her. 'Biggest deal was bringing product down from Aberdeen and distributing across the Central Belt,' he said, voice all business now. *Not the only one who just jumped off a cliff, am I?* Jen thought.

'Product? What does that mean?' she asked.

'Drugs,' Paulie said, voice flat. 'Coke. Heroin. Speed. Ecstasy. Some hash. The dealers up north had a supply link with Europe. They bring it into Aberdeen harbour, and your dad would arrange distribution around the rest of the country.'

Jen felt something cold and bilious slither through her gut. She had always known her dad had worked on both sides of the law, but to hear Paulie talk about it so casually brought home the harsh, ugly reality. No wonder Connor had hated the man.

Connor. She stopped, took a deep breath, forced away the cascade of thoughts that flooded her mind. Her father's death had driven a wedge between them, and what she was doing now was hardly likely to bring them closer together.

'How much would that kind of work be worth?' she asked, forcing herself to focus.

Paulie blew air between his teeth. 'About four mil to your dad, I think,' he said.

Jen rocked back in her seat, the pain in her back cutting through the shock that screamed through her mind. 'Four million . . . a year?' she whispered, her lips numb.

Paulie nodded. 'Now you can see why we're in trouble. Using the business to launder that cash was the way your dad worked it, but the truth is, the haulage business isn't as profitable as it once was. Crackdown on emissions, rising fuel prices, tariffs relating to Brexit. It's a loss leader, and the legal side of things is bleeding cash.'

Jen blinked, tried to organise her thoughts. Four million a year? Jesus.

'So what happened?'

'Like I said, when your dad died, the dealers up north found different ways to move their product around the country. Not as effective as your dad's method, but you know drug-dealers – where there's a market, there's a way.'

A news report she had read flitted into her mind. Something about a rise in crime in deprived areas as the cost of drugs soared due to scarce supplies. Now she knew why.

'You know the people Dad worked with in Aberdeen?' she asked.

Something like fear crossed Paulie's face, tightening his cheeks, as though he had tasted something bitter. 'Now hold on a minute, Jen,' he said. 'Telling you about all this is one thing. You own the business now. You have a right to know the full picture. But getting you involved in it . . .'

'It's my choice, Paulie,' she said, her voice harsher than she'd expected. 'All I'm asking is you set up a meeting. I promise I'll let you know everything that's going on. Hell, I'll even take you with me.'

'Really?' Paulie said, his voice tinged with hope.

'Course,' Jen said, gesturing to the crutch that was propped up at the side of the desk. 'After all, you're not expecting me to drive all the way to Aberdeen like this, are you?'

Paulie smiled, whatever he was about to say in reply cut off by the ring of the phone. He frowned, grabbed it, his meaty paw making the receiver look like a toy.

'MacKenzie Haulage,' he barked. He listened. 'Who's calling?'

Silence again. Something in the way the furrows on his brow deepened as he listened made Jen uneasy.

He looked up at her, holding out the handset. 'For you,' he said. 'Someone from Montrose House care home. They're trying to get in touch with Fraser, can't reach him. You're listed as next contact for his gran, Ida? Say they need to talk to you, now.'

CHAPTER 7

Connor opened his eyes slowly, squinting warily at the morning light streaming in through the blinds of the room.

After his call with Simon, he had made his way up the Shankill, stopping in the first shop he could find to buy a pair of sunglasses and a baseball cap. It made him feel like an extra from a bad spy movie, but he needed the sunglasses' help with the pain the waning daylight sparked in his head, and the baseball cap provided additional shade. He loosened his shirt and zipped his jacket – just another wage slave heading home after another day in the office.

He took a circuitous, looping route despite the exhaustion that made his legs tremble, heading up the Shankill, then ducking into Woodvale Park, a large municipal area crammed with landscaped flowerbeds, a bandstand, football pitches and a children's play area. It was a good place to get lost, and to spot anyone following him. When he had lived in Belfast, Connor had come to the park to train when the weather was good, slipping on a weighted vest and doing interval sprints up and down the length of the football pitches. Satisfied he wasn't being followed, he stepped out of the park onto Ballygomartin Road. From there, it was a short walk to Glencairn Street, a narrow canyon of terraced and semi-detached houses. Cars were bumped up on the pavement, and Connor scanned them as he walked, checking for anyone watching him.

Satisfied he was alone, he stepped into the front garden of the house

Simon had told him about. Punched in the code Simon had given him for the key safe bolted to the wall next to the front door, then stepped inside. He was confronted by a steep staircase and a door to his right that led into what looked like a living room. He turned to close and lock the front door, felt a rush of relief when he saw the three deadbolts sitting at the top, middle and bottom. He slid them home, the heavy clunking sound massaging away the tension in his shoulders.

The living room was small, narrow, a couch against one wall, a TV on the other. In front of the couch was a coffee-table with a Post-it note on it. Connor approached, discarding his hat and glasses, and picked up the note: 'Supplies in fridge. Courtesy of SM, who says you're not being let out of his sight again. Make contact with him in morning. Comms are under this table.'

Connor smiled then crouched. Found a box with a half-dozen basic mobile phones in it. Burner phones or, as Simon called them, condom comms. Good for one use only. He made his way to the end of the living room, stepped through the door into a perfunctory kitchen that held the essentials – kettle, microwave, sink and hob. There wasn't much room for anything else. There was a door on the opposite wall, the same deadbolt set-up as the front door. At the far end of the kitchen he saw the fridge, and made for it. Inside, he found a full medical kit with antiseptic dressings, bandages, suturing kit, surgical glue, painkillers and even two syringes of adrenaline. On the top shelf there was an array of sandwiches, bottles of water and, Connor saw with a smile, a half-bottle of whisky. Only Simon would think it was okay to keep a bottle of whisky in the fridge, and tell Gemma to leave it there for him.

He took the first-aid kit back into the living room, found a small mirror, and started to patch himself up. Mostly his injuries were superficial, and the pain in his head was starting to recede, either from encroaching exhaustion or because the concussion wasn't as bad as he'd feared. He didn't know.

As he worked, he tried to put together what had happened. He had attended Danny Gillespie's funeral at Danny's mother's request. The service had been held at Milltown Parish Church in Portadown. Milling about outside, waiting for the hearse to arrive with Danny's coffin, Connor had felt a bolt of recognition at some familiar, unwelcome faces. Key figures from both sides of the paramilitary divide, the Provisional IRA and the Ulster Defence Association. Faces he knew from his time as a police officer with the PSNI, faces he had been trained to spot and treat with extreme caution. He had called Simon that night, listing the names of Bobby McCandish, Colm O'Brien and Brendan Walsh, wanting to check if it was merely his imagination running riot or the need to find some meaning in his friend's death. Why would senior paramilitary figures be at the funeral of a psychology lecturer working in London? A lecturer who, as far as Connor knew, had had no connection to the Troubles?

But then he had received the message from 'Simon'. He had found something, had arranged for an information package to be dumped by a police contact in the alley behind the Old Dog pub on the Falls Road.

And then all hell had broken loose.

He put aside the first-aid kit, reached for his jacket. Found the prayer book and watch that Danny's mother had given him. Flicked through the book, found nothing out of place, not a bookmark or a slip of paper jammed between its pages. Put it down and studied the watch. It looked vintage, the black face faded with age, the gold numerals aged and dappled. At the bottom of the face, under the numeral 6, an arrow pointed up towards 12. He flipped the watch over, but saw nothing, the back of the casing covered by the worn leather of the watch strap. NATO, he thought randomly. This type of watch strap is NATO-style.

Reflexively, he flicked his wrist a couple of times. It was a move he had learned as a child watching his father getting ready to leave for work. As he paced the house, preparing for the day, he would hold his watch, the stainless-steel band catching the light and clinking gently as he flicked it, then spun it round his finger, twirling it, like a cowboy spinning his pistol. It was, he told Connor once, to wind the watch, which was automatically wound by movement.

Connor stopped flicking, looked at the watch. No joy. The second hand was still frozen. He considered, then spotted the small crown on the side of the watch. Twisted it a few times, the ratcheting click of the motion surprisingly satisfying. And then, sure enough, the second hand moved smoothly as the mechanical movement kicked in.

He put the watch down, sank back into the couch, tried to stop the thoughts crashing through his mind. Paramilitaries at a civilian's funeral. Connor set up by what looked like professional killers carrying government-issue firearms. A prayer book and an old watch. What the hell did it all mean?

He sighed, closed his eyes. Wasn't sure if he had fallen asleep or passed out, but the next thing he knew it was morning, and he was squinting warily at the light of a new day. He checked his own watch: 7.13 a.m. He leaned forward, wincing at the stiffness in his neck from sleeping sitting upright on the couch. Rolled his head, grateful that the pain behind his eyes had receded, now little more than a gentle throbbing reminder of an old wound. He headed to the kitchen, grabbed a bottle of water from the fridge, drank half in one slug, then settled on the couch, grabbed a burner phone and dialled Simon.

'Jesus,' Simon said, by way of a greeting, 'didn't you know that fugitives on the run are meant to sleep late? It's why they call it lying low.'

Connor chuckled. 'So that's what I am? A fugitive?'

'I don't know yet,' Simon said, his voice serious now. 'I checked into those names you gave me, and all three have kept their noses clean, though it's an open secret that they're still moving in paramilitary circles in their respective communities. But there's nothing to indicate any link to your pal Gillespie, or why they would feel the need to turn up at his funeral.'

Connor sighed, rubbed his eyes. Of course it wouldn't be that easy. 'Anything on our friends of the Falls Road?' he asked. 'Any chatter on dark ops ongoing in Belfast or the surrounding areas?'

'Nothing's been made official,' Simon said slowly. 'And no reports of your activities on the Falls Road have been filed, not that that means anything. Folk can be awfully blind when they want to be. You sure they were pros and not enthusiastic amateurs who'd seen *Men in Black* once too often?'

Connor thought back to the alley. To the clinical, almost detached movements of his first attacker. The way he had absorbed Connor's attack and turned it back on him. The targeted blow to the temple, designed to confuse and incapacitate, not kill. And then there were the guns. Police and government issue. And the way they'd held them . . . 'No, they were pros,' he said. 'I take it running the plate on the car I stole from them didn't get us anywhere.'

'Oh, it got me somewhere, all right,' Simon said, the soft whisper of pages being turned leaking down the line as he spoke. 'It got me to the address of a Mr Tommy Bell of Grimsby, the registered owner of a Volvo S40 with that exact licence.'

Cloned plate, Connor thought. *Another tick in the professionals' column.* 'Okay,' he said. 'So what's next? You said something last night about getting me home. But I think I need to stay here, Simon. Whatever is going on, the answers are here.'

'Aye, but . . .' Simon hesitated, drew a breath as though he was about to keep speaking, then exhaled.

'Simon? What?' Connor asked. 'Am I missing something?'

'No,' Simon said, just a little too quickly for Connor's liking. 'No, it's fine. You're right. You staying there is the right move. For now. But keep your head down, for God's sake. Just because I can't find any police reports about firearms being discharged and two men being killed on the Falls doesn't mean the police aren't looking into it. Which means they, and whoever else is involved in this, will be looking for you.'

Connor thought about that. About the blow his attacker had landed. A blow to incapacitate, not kill. Which meant they needed something from him. Question was, what?

'Okay,' he said, snapping himself from his thoughts. 'This safe-house you've set me up in, is it secure for a couple of days?'

'Yeah,' Simon said. 'Should be, long as you keep your bloody head down.'

'Scout's honour,' Connor said.

'Connor, I . . .' Simon stopped.

'Simon? Look, I'm sorry. I appreciate this, I really do. And I'm sorry for dragging you into it. Whatever the hell it is.'

'Hey,' Simon said. There was something Connor couldn't recognise in his voice. 'What are friends for?'

Connor opened his mouth to reply, but it was too late. Simon had ended the call.

CHAPTER 8

Simon tossed the phone onto the coffee-table, glared at it. Stood up and went around the breakfast bar to the kitchen, busied himself making coffee. Was aware of movement at the other end of the breakfast bar, saw a pair of unblinking green eyes surveying him coolly.

'What?' Simon said to Tom, the stray cat that had adopted him as her own when he had moved into what had once been Connor's garden flat. 'Let me guess, you think I should have told him? And what would that have accomplished, other than him burning a path from Belfast to here?'

Tom said nothing. Simon sighed, felt guilt twist in his gut. The call had come from Jen last night, asking where Connor was and explaining why she needed to get in touch with him urgently. She explained that Montrose House, the care home Connor's gran was in, had called her, saying Ida Fraser had 'taken a turn for the worse'. As Jen wasn't technically family, the nurse who had called her had been vague on what had happened, but it was bad enough that they needed to contact Ida's grandson as soon as possible. Simon had ducked Jen's questions as well as he could, saying only that Connor was away on business, as she knew, and he hadn't heard from him. The lie sat badly with him. He liked Jen, wanted to see her and Connor get over whatever was driving them apart, but he knew he couldn't tell her the truth. And, besides, what would he say? 'Don't worry, Jen. Connor's running for his life in Belfast. I think he's killed two people in the last twenty-four hours, but fear not, I'll have this wrapped up, get him home to his gran's bedside before you can say "shadowy conspiracy".'

Hardly.

The timing of it bothered him, though. Just hours after Connor had slipped out of an elaborate trap in Belfast, Jen gets word that his gran was ill? Yes, Ida Fraser was an old woman, and the dementia that was ravaging her mind and robbing her of her present had been getting worse over the past few months, but her sudden 'turn for the worse' was a little convenient, wasn't it? After all, what better way to flush Connor out of whatever bolthole he was in than to get word out that his gran was ill? That they had cloned Simon's number to lure Connor into a trap meant that whoever was after him knew his background, who he was close to, the pressure points they could squeeze.

And for Connor Fraser, no pressure point would get a stronger or more immediate reaction than his gran. If he found out she was ill, nothing would stop him rushing to her side and, potentially, straight into the arms of the people who wanted him.

Guilt twisted in Simon again, needling him into action. He busied himself making coffee, trying not to think about the lie of omission he had just told Connor. The answer, of course, was obvious. He would go to the care home in Bannockburn. Either he would find that Ida was suffering some form of medical issue or, if his suspicions were correct, he would have a cosy little chat with whoever had staked out the care home and was waiting for Connor to turn up.

It was, he thought, as he poured his coffee, a meeting he was looking forward to. Whoever was after Connor had lured him into a trap using Simon's number, then hurt him and forced him into hiding. No one did that. Not to Simon McCartney's loved ones. It was a rule he lived by. He knew that, in his work as a police officer, people would try to hurt him, kill him even. That was fine. Part of the game, a risk Simon accepted. But to use him to try to get to the people he loved?

Fuck. That.

The chirping of a phone dragged him from his thoughts. He looked across to the coffee-table, momentarily confused when he saw that the phone sitting there was dark and lifeless. Then he cursed his stupidity and walked to the couch to retrieve his daily-use phone, not the anonymous one Connor was using to contact him.

He picked it up and smiled when he saw the name of the caller.

'Morning, darlin',' he said, as he answered. 'Let me guess, you've decided to pull a sicky from the hourly bulletins. Going to run away with me for a day and a night of debauchery?'

Donna Blake laughed, the sound almost musical. The thought of the engagement ring he had hidden in the bedroom flashed across his mind, then faded, like the afterglow of a camera flash.

'Hardly,' she said. 'Just wanted to let you know I might be a little late for dinner tonight. Seems the government is planning to make a statement on prisoner numbers or something this afternoon so I'm being sent to Edinburgh to cover it.'

'Ah, okay,' Simon said, careful to keep his tone neutral. After everything that had happened with Connor, he had forgotten about his planned dinner with Donna that night. And, if he was honest, her being stuck in Edinburgh for a while meant he didn't have to make excuses about why he was creeping around a care home in Bannockburn.

'. . . okay with that?'

'Huh?' Simon said, cursing himself. 'Sorry, Donna, say that again. I've not had my full dose of coffee yet today.'

'It's nice to be with a man who's so attentive,' Donna said, playful sarcasm frosting the edges of her voice. 'I said I'll call you when I'm leaving Edinburgh. My mum is getting Andrew from school and keeping him tonight, so I'll just head straight to the flat.'

'Not a problem,' Simon said. 'I'll have dinner and wine waiting for you.'

'Meaning,' Donna said, 'you'll stick your head into Morrisons for some wine and dust off the takeaway menus.'

'Like you said, ain't it grand to be with a man who's so attentive?'

Donna laughed. 'Idiot,' she said. 'Got to go. See you tonight. Love you.'

'Love you too,' Simon said, then ended the call. He held the phone for a moment, staring at the screen. When he had originally come to Stirling to visit Connor and help with a case, the last thing he had expected was to meet the woman he wanted to spend the rest of his life with. But now here he was. Moved from Belfast to Scotland, standing in the flat he'd bought from Connor when he'd moved into the house he had bought for him and Jen. A house he had spent months renovating to accommodate Jen's mobility issues after her accident. A house that now stood cold and empty.

A thought flitted across Simon's mind, and he bounced the phone in his hand. Let the idea solidify and take shape, then smiled. It could work. He thumbed a quick text, hit send, then powered down the phone and retrieved the burner. Then he went into the bedroom and grabbed his leather bag from the cupboard. From it, he took a fresh SIM card, a set of lockpicks and a gun. As a former PSNI officer, Simon was technically allowed to carry a firearm for his own protection, and he had a gun in a locker at Randolphfield Police Station that could be signed out at any time. But this gun was different. An old memento from Belfast, its serial number had been filed away long ago and there was no paper trail that would ever link the weapon to Simon. It was, effectively, a ghost gun.

Simon checked the magazine and chamber, then placed the gun in a pancake holster he clipped to the back of his belt. Grabbed his keys, made sure Tom had food and water, then left the flat.

Climbing the stairs from the garden flat to the street-level parking bay, Simon was confronted by two cars, Connor's sleek Audi coupé, all sweeping curves and quiet, restrained power, and his own little pocket rocket, a Renaultsport Clio that was all front-wheel-drive power and over-revving aggression. He thought for a moment, smiled. Fished the key Connor had left him from his jacket pocket, then headed for the Audi. Got in, started the engine, then typed 'florists' and 'Bannockburn' into the satnav.

After all, it wouldn't do to turn up empty-handed for a visit with Ida Fraser.

CHAPTER 9

Connor chewed mechanically on one of the sandwiches he had retrieved from the fridge, not tasting it as he replayed his conversation with Simon. Something about the call, the tension in Simon's voice, bothered him. It was, he supposed, perfectly natural. Connor had called him, neck-deep in shite and asking for help after being targeted by what seemed to be professional hitmen, whose deaths had not been reported, officially anyway, to the PSNI. Simon had moved heaven and earth to arrange a safe-house for him at the drop of a hat. So, yes, some tension in his voice was understandable, almost to be expected.

And yet . . .

Connor finished his sandwich. Now that he had eaten and rested, he could feel his energy return. Problem was, with renewed energy came the irresistible desire to act. He got up, toured the upstairs of the house, which he had neglected the night before. At the top of the steep stairs he found a bedroom, smiled when he spotted a pile of T-shirts, two pairs of jeans, underwear, socks and trainers sitting on the small double bed pushed up against the back wall of the room. All in Connor's size.

Typical Simon. Always ready.

Opposite the bedroom, a bathroom contained a sink, toilet and shower cubicle. Above the sink a small shelf was stacked with toiletries. Towels sat on the closed toilet lid. Connor gratefully peeled off his clothes and stepped into the shower.

Standing under the piping hot water, letting the heat and steam ease his aching muscles, Connor ran an inventory of what he had left in his room at the Grand Central Hotel in Belfast. It wasn't much different from what Simon had supplied for him here: toiletries and clothes. The only thing missing was his work laptop, which was linked to the secure server at Sentinel Securities. Connor leaned against the wall, letting the water massage his neck. If someone was after him, as the confrontation in the Falls indicated, it was reasonable to assume they would be casing out the hotel, waiting for Connor to return to collect his belongings. But the laptop was the only item that held any real value for him, and as that was secured and monitored by Sentinel, there was nothing on it for any third party to glean. The conclusion was simple: abandon the room at the Central, forget about his belongings and the laptop.

Which meant Connor had one immediate task. Go shopping. The question was, how? He still had his wallet and passport, but using any of his cards when he had exhausted the emergency fifty pounds in cash he kept in his wallet would be an instant red flag to anyone looking for him. So what to do?

He finalised the plan as he dressed, smiling as he silently thanked Rory O'Connell for the idea. Briefly wondered how O'Connell had fared when he woke up in his car on the Shankill. Felt an all-too-familiar pang of guilt at the memory of O'Connell's broken nose, the sound his head had made as Connor had slammed it off the side of his car.

That Fraser temper, son. Watch for it.

He found a jacket hanging in a cupboard in the bedroom, wasn't surprised to find it was, as with the other clothes, in his size. Made his way downstairs, arranged three of the burner phones in his pockets, then added the Glock he had taken from his attacker. Paused at the coffee-table, looking down at the watch and the prayer book Danny Gillespie's mother had given to him at the funeral.

Danny would have wanted you to have these.

Outside, it was one of those fragile mornings when the sky was a deep, clear blue, marred only by the thin chalk line of an aeroplane's jet trail, but the air still carried the threat of a cold snap. He put his hands into his pockets, dipped his head, started walking. It would have been quicker to get a taxi or a bus, but Connor wanted to walk – it would give him a chance to think and, if anyone was following him, being on foot would give him options on how to react.

He walked east, down the Shankill and into town. About forty-five minutes later, he was approaching North Street, in the city's Cathedral Quarter. While it had been years since Connor had lived or worked in Belfast, he kept track of what was going on in the city, like a wary parent watching his child making their way in the world once they had left home. Belfast, like many cities, was gripped by a chronic drugs problem, fuelled by a surge in homelessness and a lack of facilities to get the vulnerable off the streets. Driven by addiction and desperation, many of those sleeping rough would pay any price for something that would make them forget reality for a while, so they turned to class-A drugs, heroin, crack cocaine, ketamine, and, of course, booze. Connor remembered one article saying that North Street, and a lane that connected it to Writer's Square, had become 'a hotspot indicative of the city's war with drugs and addiction'.

Which made it perfect for his needs.

He strolled down the street, a patchwork of vacant shops, nail bars, barbers, a car park, a pub. Stopped when he came to a junction, the old art-deco grandeur of the abandoned Bank of Ulster sitting there, white stone and green flashing daubed with cheap graffiti. Crossed diagonally and stepped into the lane, walking slowly, head on a swivel. It didn't take him long to find what he was looking for. Just off North Street, down a small lane that led to a park in the shadow of a block of flats, he spotted a car. Not as flash as Rory O'Connell's Subaru Impreza, but still low, sleek and powerful. Looked up, saw that the security cameras on the walls were conveniently angled away from the parking bay. Connor smiled to himself, then walked back onto North Street, where he found a coffee shop. Five minutes later he was back in the park, coffee in one hand, paper in the other. He found a bench and sat on it, watching the car over the top of his paper.

Sure enough, it wasn't long before the first person approached. Oversized jacket, skinny jeans so tight you could almost see the wearer's bony knees, baseball cap, sallow skin, small, feral eyes that seemed to dart everywhere at once. The passenger-side window slid down smoothly as the figure approached, then leaned in, almost as if giving the occupants directions. They leaned forward momentarily, then were off.

Connor shook his head. It was an age-old method. Put a network of dealers out on the streets, getting hits to regular customers, the rough sleepers, the power drinkers, the lost. But dealers who worked in such areas were normally users themselves, so you didn't trust them. Better, then, to give them just what they needed to make a couple of deals, then resupply them while pocketing the cash they had made. That way, you were controlling supply and making sure you weren't ripped off. And, to make sure you could get away in a hurry, you drove a car. Something fast, powerful but forgettable. Something you parked, say, in a disabled bay where the security cameras were angled away.

Connor watched for another ten minutes, saw another three visitors to the car. Looked at his watch. Just before 11 a.m. The early-morning shift was almost over, plenty of customers woken by their addiction and needing another hit. Hits that the dealers buzzing around the car, like bees returning to the hive, would be more than happy to sell them.

Time to make his move.

He folded the paper, tucked it into his pocket. Thumbed the lid of his coffee cup as he walked. Approached the car casually, swung round to the passenger side, dark eyes watching him from behind the windscreen. Saw the passenger and the driver exchange a shrug as Connor rapped on the window.

The passenger's voice drowned the whir of the window mechanism as it slid down. 'Whatever it is, pal, we're no' interested. So just fuck off down the road and we'll—'

The man's voice dissolved into guttural sputtering as Connor threw the coffee into his face. It was tepid, but still enough to shock, which was what Connor was counting on. Connor reached in, grabbing the back of his head and throwing it forward, the car rocking slightly as it cracked off the dashboard. In one fluid movement, he drew the gun from the back of his jeans, pinned the passenger's head to the dashboard, then trained the weapon on the driver.

'What the fuck is this?' the man whispered, the paleness of his skin a shocking contrast to the lurid, fiery ginger of his beard.

''Bout ye?' Connor said with a smile. 'I'm collecting for the Salvation Army, doing the Lord's work. She told me you lads would just love to make a donation.'

'Fuck off!' the driver spat, as the passenger tried to raise his head. Connor slammed it back into the dash. 'You any idea who we work for? The type of shite you're in?'

Connor shrugged, pushed the gun further into the car. 'Could be Mickey Mouse, could be Donald Trump,' he said, letting the emotion bleed from his voice. 'Both equally dodgy bastards, as far as I can see. Doesn't really matter, though. What matters is your boss isn't here but I and my extremely big gun are. So, you've a simple choice to make. Give me the cash you've collected this morning, or I'll see just how much of a mess I can make of your windscreen and head with one shot.'

The driver grimaced. Reached into his jacket pocket. Connor kept his eyes locked on him. *Don't fucking try it*, his gaze said. The man produced a fat wad of crumpled notes. Connor nodded, let go of the passenger's head and stood back, gun still pointed into the car. 'Pass it over your mate,' he said.

The passenger leaned back as the driver leaned across him, and Connor could see blood pooling around a nose that was clearly no stranger to being broken. He reached forward, took the notes, felt only the briefest moment of resistance.

'You're fucking dead,' the driver hissed.

'Aye, maybe,' Connor said, with a shrug. 'But not now, and not today.' He backed off, allowing the outside world to bleed back into his awareness as he concealed his gun. Nothing to see, just Belfast going about its business as usual. 'Do yourselves a favour,' Connor said, as he took another step back. 'Don't follow me. Don't get smart. Tell your bosses you were jacked by a lunatic with a gun. A lunatic with no connection whatsoever to Rory O'Connell.'

It was as if the name had electrified the car's seats. Both men jerked to attention, studied Connor as though for the first time. He tipped them a salute, then walked off. Wondered if the Cash Converters near the CastleCourt shopping centre was still in business.

Only one way to find out.

CHAPTER 10

Simon eased Connor's Audi into a parking space outside the care home, tyres crunching softly on the gravel as the car came to a halt. No sign of any pursuers on the drive from Stirling, and he had kept his pace steady, making sure it wasn't too hard for him to be followed. Now, scanning the car park, he saw nothing out of the ordinary, just the usual smattering of cars and SUVs, the care home on a hill, like some grand old lady sitting on a throne and surveying her kingdom.

Simon knew Montrose House and its grounds had once been the home of the Montrose family, which had made its money from the barges and coal ships that once sailed the canals that wound through central Scotland, delivering supplies where they were needed. The family's fortunes had dwindled along with the appeal of the canals as a form of commercial transportation, and the house, along with the lands had been sold off and modernised to serve as a care home for the elderly. Bracketed by two apartment-style blocks that were attached to the main building by gleaming umbilical cords made of glass and steel, the grandeur of the original Montrose House was still clear to see in its imposing Victorian-style sandstone façade and twin picture windows – huge eyes that bracketed the main reception door.

Simon took one last look around the car park, then reached for the oversized bunch of flowers he had collected on the way. Getting out of the car, he discreetly palmed his gun, covering it with the bouquet. If there was going to be trouble, he didn't want to waste time fumbling it into his hand.

He climbed the steps to the home, went inside. The black-and-white marble floor and wood panelling in the reception area were the only remaining hints of the house's history. The rest of the area had been overtaken by calming pastel landscape prints, sofas and chairs, and low tables with neat racks of leaflets advertising Montrose House's services.

Simon crossed to the reception desk. A vaguely familiar woman, with dark hair, pale skin and a professional smile, greeted him, light dancing off the lenses of the gold-rimmed glasses she wore..

'Hiya,' Simon said, grasping for a name to connect to the face. 'I'm here to see Ida Fraser.'

'Of course,' she said, the professionally detached smile intensifying. 'And you would be . . .'

'Simon McCartney,' he said. 'Friend of the family. I got word that Ida had taken a wee bad turn, wanted to check in on her for her grandson.'

The smile on the face of the receptionist – *Sandra,* Simon thought – faltered, then dissolved. She sat up straighter in her chair, a teacher about to admonish a wayward pupil.

'Mr, ah, McCartney, as you're no doubt aware, we are unable to discuss confidential medical information with anyone apart from immediate family. I'm afraid . . .'

Simon held up a hand, smiled. 'I know that, Sandra, I know. But I'm a friend of the family. Connor, Ida's grandson, is a close friend and he asked me to pop in on Ida, make sure she was okay while he was away on business. He asked me to deliver these flowers to her and his personal assurance that he'd be in touch as soon as work commitments allow.'

Sandra's eyes darted between the flowers and Simon's face, torn. She needed another push.

Simon was about to speak when another voice interrupted. 'Can I help, Sandra?' A tall, slender woman approached the desk, adjusting thick-rimmed glasses as she did. If her cool, unbroken gaze didn't say this was her domain, her no-nonsense, almost severe business suit did.

'Ah, this is Mr McCartney,' Sandra said. 'He's a family friend of Ida Fraser and was asking about her condition. I was telling him we can't discuss medical matters with non-family members.'

Simon switched his focus to the woman now standing in front of him. 'Ah, Ms . . .?' he said, raising his eyebrow along with his tone.

'Black,' she said, extending a hand. 'Aileen Black. I'm the manager.'

'Ah, grand,' Simon said, shaking it. 'I was just telling Sandra here that Connor got word that his gran had taken a turn, and he wanted me to check on her. Your records will show I've visited more than once before. All I'm going to do is deliver an old woman some flowers and a hug from her grandson. No confidences broken. Any medical assessments I make will be mine alone, nothing that's come from you unless you talk to Connor directly. Where's the harm?'

A glance between the flowers and Simon's face, Aileen chewed her bottom lip. 'Fine,' she sighed at last. 'Mrs Fraser is in the day room. I take it you know the way?'

'I do,' Simon said, jutting his jaw down the long, wide hallway beyond the reception desk. 'It's the room at the end, looking out over the gardens. Ida loves it there.' Black gave a smile as tailored to the moment as her suit. 'Go on, then,' she said. 'But . . .' She paused, uncertain for the first time.

'But what?' Simon asked.

Aileen hesitated. 'Just take it easy, Mr McCartney. She has taken a bit of a turn for the worse. Not physically but, well, you know . . .' She flicked a hand, as though wafting away smoke.

Simon nodded. Connor had arranged for his gran to go into care because dementia was slowly eroding her memory, robbing her of her sense of who and where she was. He had done his best to ensure she was comfortable, making sure the flat she had in the home was full of furniture and mementoes from her former home in Stirling, visiting as often as he could, but fighting dementia was like fighting time. Ultimately, the clock ticked one way, and nothing you could do would stop it hitting midnight at some point.

He murmured his thanks and headed off for the day room. Found Ida sitting in a chair on a small balcony looking out at the manicured gardens, blanket pulled over her knees. She seemed smaller than Simon remembered, frailer. Her snow-white hair was now a dull yellowish grey, and her skin had a sickly, waxy sheen. But what drove the dagger home, making Simon want to call Connor there and then and get him home now, no matter the consequences, were her hands. Simon remembered Ida Fraser pouring tea on previous visits with Connor, marvelling at the elegant dexterity of her long, thin fingers. But now they were disfigured, twisted and swollen like the thin, desiccated branches of a dying tree. On the backs of her hands, a knotted network of veins protruded, almost black against her pallid skin.

He took a deep breath, stepped forward and knelt beside the chair. 'Ida?' he said softly. 'Ida, it's me, Simon. Thought I'd come to see the prettiest girl in Montrose House.'

Ida started slightly, as though jerked from her thoughts. She turned slowly, her once-vibrant eyes now rheumy, sunk into the wrinkled eye sockets.

'Connor?' she said, her gaze strafing Simon's face. 'That you, son? What did you do to your hair?'

Simon felt something hot loosen and churn in his chest. 'No, Ida. It's me, Simon. That big lug of a grandson of yours is away on business. He asked me to visit you instead. He was worried when the home called, saying you'd had a wee bit of a turn – wanted me to bring you these.' Simon proffered the flowers, careful to stow the gun as he did.

Ida's eyes flicked over them, and her smile intensified. Instead of comforting Simon, though, the gesture disturbed him. It was as though she was seeing them with no idea of their context or meaning, beyond some ingrained reflex that smiling was how she was meant to react.

'Thank you, son,' she said. 'Would you mind putting them on the table? My hands.' She lifted them in jerking slow motion. 'I have a wee bit of a time holding things at the moment.'

'No problem.' Simon laid the flowers on a small table at the side of Ida's chair. On it sat a plastic tumbler, a jar of water and a copy of *The Times*, folded to the crossword. He smiled. Ida had always liked her crosswords.

'So,' he asked, as he hunkered back down beside her, 'the nurses said you were feeling a wee bit poorly. How you doing now?'

'Nurses?' Ida said, confusion turning the frown lines on her face into deep creases. 'What nurses? Honestly, Connor, you shouldn't haver so much, son. I'm fine. It's your mum we have to worry about. She's the one who needs the nurses just now.'

The hot thing in Simon's chest lurched. Connor's mum had died a few years before, her body ravaged by a cancer that no amount of radiation, or drugs, could stop. As Connor told it, Ida had been instrumental in nursing Claire Fraser through her final, agonising days. And now, here she was, dragged back by dementia, worrying about a dead daughter-in-law and confusing Simon with her grandson.

'Aye, sure enough,' he said, trying to sound more upbeat than he felt. He had done the wrong thing in keeping this from Connor. He should be here now, and if that meant killing anyone who got in his way, so be it. The helpless anguish Simon felt roiling through his chest demanded some form of retribution, and whoever dared threaten his friend and kept him away from Ida deserved it.

'Now,' Ida said, gesturing again with her hands. 'More important things. Did your friend, Simon, manage to get in touch with you?'

Simon blinked. 'Sorry, Ida. It's me. I'm Simon. Connor is away on business. He asked me to look in on you, make sure you were okay.'

'Ah,' Ida said, something flashing in her eyes as the bleariness lifted a little. 'Simon! Of course. How are you, son? How's that nice girl of yours, Diane? I see her on the TV all the time. Very, very pretty girl, Simon. Very pretty.'

'Donna's fine,' Simon said, hoping the correction wasn't taken as an insult. 'We both are, Ida. I'll have to bring her with me the next time I visit.'

'That would be nice. Tell me, son, did you manage to catch up with Connor yet?'

Simon took a deep, steadying breath. 'Aye, I did. All good,' he said, patting her hand. The skin was warm, smooth, almost feverish, despite its ghostly pallor.

She nodded, the answer seeming to satisfy her. Gave his hand a surprisingly firm squeeze, then looked back out into the gardens, face slackening. Simon wondered what she was staring at – the gardens as they were, or some dimming, confused memory only she could see?

He waited, letting the soft sounds of the day room flood the moment. Then he stood slowly, put his hand gently on her shoulder. 'Right, Ida,' he said, as her head turned back to him. 'I'll away. You take care of yourself, okay?'

'Okay, Connor, son,' Ida said, a smile as empty as her eyes creasing her face. 'You take care of yourself. And remember,' she twisted to the table and picked up the newspaper, offering it to him, 'don't forget to take Simon's number with you. He wrote it down. Seemed important. Might be something to do with that girl of his, Diane. Pretty, pretty girl. Tell him I send my kind regards, will you?'

Simon said nothing, just took the newspaper. Felt his blood run cold and the air suddenly escape from the room as he read what was there. In the empty section of the paper below the crossword, where readers usually scribbled their thoughts about the clues, a message had been written. A simple thirty-four-word message that made Simon suddenly very aware of the exposed view the window gave to the day room, and the weight of the gun at his back.

> We can get to your gran, Mr Fraser. We can get to anyone. We know what you have. We want it back. Do it, or things will get very ugly.
> You have 12 hours.

Below the message was what looked like a mobile-phone number, scrawled in angry black slashes.

Simon cleared his throat. When he spoke, his mouth seemed full of sand. 'You mind if I keep this, Ida?' he said, lifting the paper.

'No problem, Connor,' she said, concern pinching her face, making her voice a taut, urgent whisper. 'But you get in touch with Simon, okay? He left that number for you. I don't want to be the one responsible for you not getting him. You phone him, today, okay? Nice boy, Simon. Got a pretty girl now, too. Diane, I think.' She nodded to herself, then flicked her eyes back to Simon, something close to panic flashing in them. 'You call that boy, promise me, Connor? He left that number with me so it's my job to make sure you get it.'

Simon reached forward, put what he hoped was a reassuring hand on Ida's, glanced at the note on the newspaper, felt something ugly snarl in the back of his mind. 'Don't you worry,' he said. 'I'll make sure I get in touch with him very, very soon.'

CHAPTER 11

As Connor had suspected, the Cash Converters store around the corner from the CastleCourt shopping centre in central Belfast was still open and had just what he needed. With the money he had taken from the drug-dealers, Connor bought himself a laptop – nothing too flash, just an HP model with enough memory to save and store documents and internet accessibility. The rest of the money – a quick count showed he had collected six grand and change – he could use as running cash over the next few days.

He snorted at the thought – running cash. But who, and what, was he running from?

He approached the safe-house cautiously, looking for anything out of place – a car that didn't belong, a curtain held open just a second too long in a window – but saw nothing. Satisfied, he let himself in, felt the knot of tension between his shoulders ease slightly as he slid the deadbolts on the front door. He made his way to the kitchen, grabbed a bottle of water and some painkillers from the medical kit, then headed to the living room. He swallowed the painkillers, wincing as he touched the bruise on his left temple, then booted the laptop and paired it to one of the burner phones to get online.

He looked at the blank internet search engine, tried to go through what he knew, find a place to start looking for answers. Danny's funeral. It all seemed to stem from that. Why were leading former paramilitaries, Republican and Loyalist, there? Why were they willing to put aside their religious prejudices and attend a Church of Ireland service? What was their connection to a psychology lecturer working in London? And why were they so desperate to get to Connor? He sighed, then pulled the watch and prayer book Danny's mother had given him from his pockets. The watch was still ticking faithfully, telling the precise time. A vintage Omega, it was probably rare, maybe even valuable, but worth killing for? Hardly. The prayer book was the same, filled with a selection of hymns and passages from the Bible. It was handsome, with a leather binding and gold leaf on the edges of the pages, which were yellowing with age. But there was nothing to indicate it was valuable or worth killing for.

Frustrated, Connor put aside the book and the watch. He closed his eyes, considered. If Simon was looking into the former paramilitaries who had attended the funeral, Connor would look into Danny. He opened his eyes, typed 'Daniel Gillespie', then paused. The name was almost laughably generic, and he could imagine the number of results it would glean. Leaned forward, and typed 'Doctor Daniel Gillespie, City University, London', then hit return. Sure enough, the search engine spat back the link to a webpage on the City website, which listed the academic staff. Danny was third down, described as a lecturer in psychology. Connor clicked the link and was taken to a page with Danny's headshot at the top. The sight of him as an older, professional man gave Connor a start. Gone was the young man he had known at university, always with a smile and eyes that glittered with mischievous good humour, replaced by a more worn version. His hair was neatly cut and peppered with grey, his once-angular face now softened and cushioned with a few additional pounds, most noticeably around his neck. His eyes, though they might still have glittered, were framed by a pair of thick spectacles.

Connor felt the same as he had at university, almost twenty years ago. He worked hard at the gym to keep himself in shape. But what would someone who had not seen him in years think if they saw him today? Would they see the same man, or an older, more battered version of who he had once been, ground down, blunted by life and the slow progress of years?

He shook off the thought, read the small biography that sat below Danny's picture.

Dr Gillespie is a clinical psychologist, specialising in the assessment and treatment of trauma-related conditions.

After studying at Queen's University, Belfast, Dr Gillespie helped to develop specialist trauma services within the NHS. With a focus on working with veterans, domestic-abuse survivors and those affected by violence, Dr Gillespie continues to consult in both the public and private sectors.

Below this there was a list of universities Danny had been employed by and some of his published books and papers. Connor scanned the list, paused when he came to a title about three-quarters of the way down: *Trauma Impact Prevention – Addressing the Legacy of the Troubles in Northern Ireland.*

Connor clicked on the link, found himself taken to another page, this time on the Queen's University website. It was the home page for a study Danny had led that explored the treatments of those who had been affected by the violence of the Troubles. Scanning the page, Connor found that the study had been wound up in April, just months before Danny had stepped into the road and been run over in Dunmurry.

Connor felt something itch in the back of his mind. Was this it? Had Danny found something as part of the study? But if he had, what could have been worth killing him for? He knew that the quest for justice for the victims of the Troubles was far from over, and he remembered a story a while ago when a judge in Belfast had ruled that the then-Tory UK government's plan to give immunity to most of the perpetrators of violence during the Troubles was in breach of human-rights laws, but what part did Danny's work play in that? And why would it lure senior paramilitaries from both sides to his funeral?

Frustrated, Connor opened a new window. It was like trying to put together a jigsaw without a picture of what the complete puzzle looked like. The bottom line was he needed information, more than he was able to get for himself, and more than was available to Simon's police contacts. He debated, churned the idea over in his mind, looked at it from all angles. Made a decision, then grabbed another burner phone. Powered it up, dialled the number. Waited.

'Sentinel Securities, Robbie speaking. How can I help?' Connor smiled at the confusion in Robbie's voice. Working in intelligence-gathering at Sentinel, the private security firm in which Connor was a partner, Robbie rarely took phone calls from the outside world. Especially from anonymous mobile numbers he didn't know. But that was part of Robbie's skill, one of the reasons Connor had called him. Robbie had a knack for finding out the things people really wanted to keep hidden. The phone Connor had called him on would be tracked before the call had ended.

'Robbie, it's Connor. Sorry for the call out of the blue. How you doing?'

'Boss?' Robbie said, the confusion in his voice increasing as he lowered his tone to a whisper. 'How are *you* doing is the real question? Your mobile went dark yesterday, and your laptop is showing there's been no activity in three days. I know you're away on a personal visit, but I still—'

'Sorry, Robbie.' Connor cut him off. The last thing he needed was one of his stream-of-consciousness rants. 'Time is short. Run into a wee problem here. Simon's helping me, but I wondered if you could do me a favour.'

'Name it,' Robbie said, his voice cool, clipped, like that of a waiter taking an order from a regular customer he had never quite warmed to.

'Need you to do a little digging, see if some names intersect.' He glanced at the watch and prayer book sitting on the table. 'Also, I'm going to send you a couple of images. Can you see if you can get me some details on the items, any significance they may have?'

'Not a problem,' Robbie said, and Connor could swear he heard knuckles crack at the other end of the line. 'Fire them over and I'll get to work. I take it this isn't official Sentinel business?'

'How well you know me,' Connor said. 'Now, you got a pen? Here are the names.'

CHAPTER 12

After leaving Ida, Simon took his time examining Connor's car. He worked slowly, methodically, checking the wheel arches and under the vehicle, anywhere that an explosive device or booby-trap could have been planted. He focused on the task, used it to calm the raging black fury he felt.

Someone had visited a confused, vulnerable old woman and turned her into a messenger to get to Connor. In doing so, they had crossed a red line in Simon's mind, a red line that he would fashion into a noose and use to garrotte them when he found them.

And he would find them.

Satisfied that the car was safe, he unlocked it and got in. The dash-mounted screen flared to life, first showing the Audi logo then settling on the satnav map showing his current location. Question was, where should he go next?

He tried to think logically, evaluate what he knew. When Connor had called him, giving him the names of Bobby McCandish, Colm O'Brien and Brendan Walsh to check out, Simon had done as he had asked. He had contacted an old friend in the PSNI, DCI Darren Michelson, and asked him to run their names and current locations. Being former paramilitaries – McCandish and O'Brien with the IRA and Walsh with the UVF– they would have been on record. But once the names had been run, all hell had broken loose, with someone very keen to grab Connor and retrieve something from him.

And since Simon trusted Michelson to be discreet, especially after some of the less-than-legal searches they had conducted together during his time as a police officer in Belfast, the men's files were flagged. Darren had run the names and somewhere an alarm bell had started to ring. An alarm bell that had brought trouble to Ida Fraser's door.

Despite himself, Simon smiled. While someone using Ida to get to Connor was grotesque, it gave Simon something to go on. Whoever was after Connor, whoever had delivered that note to the old lady, was on the ground, in Stirling or the surrounding area. Which meant they were within Simon's grasp. All he had to do was find them.

He considered heading back into the home, asking Aileen, the manager, if she remembered anyone else visiting Ida, or even if there was CCTV footage he could view. Realised it was a pointless exercise. Aileen might have tipped him off about Ida's deteriorating mental condition, but that was more for Ida's benefit than his. Aileen wouldn't tell him anything – which, of course, didn't mean he was helpless.

Whoever was looking for Connor had obviously profiled him. They knew about his gran, which meant they knew about the other people he cared for. Discounting himself, Simon could think of only one other person who could be used as leverage against Connor. Estranged or not, Simon knew Connor would set the world ablaze if one hair on Jen MacKenzie's head was injured.

He grabbed his phone, about to dial her number, planning to use Ida as an excuse for the call. Then he considered. Scrolled instead to another number, hit dial.

'The fuck you want?' Paulie growled, by way of a greeting. From the background noise, it sounded as if he was driving. He could imagine Paulie, wedged into the Mercedes that always looked like it had just rolled out of a showroom, one hand clamped on the steering wheel, the other holding the phone to his ear. Paulie had once confided in Simon that he hated hands-free phone systems – 'Ah can bloody well drive one-handed, and I dinnae want every bastard hearing my business,' he had said.

'Ah, Paulie, lovely to hear your voice. What about ye?' Simon said.

Paulie sighed, irritation making his voice harsh. And something else, something that trembled down the phone, something that set Simon's teeth on edge.

'Look, this really isn't a good time,' Paulie said, a horn blaring in the background.

'Sorry, I'll keep it brief,' Simon said. 'Connor's stepped in something in Belfast. Someone's looking for him, and they just tried to get a message to him through Ida, his gran.'

'Fuck.' Paulie sighed. 'I shouldae known this would be his fucking fault somehow.'

'His fault?' Simon asked, sitting up in his seat, the world jumping into sharp focus as the adrenaline started to kick in. 'What?'

'I'm on the road up tae Aberdeen,' Paulie said, 'driving Jen up there for, ah, a business meeting. She's passed out in the back, took a painkiller and dropped off, just outside Perth, heading for the Tay Bridge. Thing is, I'm pretty sure I'm being followed, have been since we left the yard in Stirling.'

Simon cursed under his breath. 'How sure are you?'

'Pretty bloody sure,' Paulie snapped, as though the question was an insult to his observational skills. It probably was. Paulie might have looked like a generic bouncer, all gut and gristle and scar tissue, but Simon had come to understand that a sharp, predatory intelligence lay behind those deep-set eyes. He was, in his own way, every bit the professional Simon was.

'Late-'twenty-three plate, BMW saloon. Black. Two occupants from what I can tell. Staying two cars back, but with me at every junction and every turn. I thought they were just coppers following us to see what we were up to – you know how much your pal Ford loves us – but if what you're saying about Fraser is right . . .'

Simon set his jaw, started the engine on the Audi. Played with the controls until he found a drive mode called 'sports dynamic'. Instantly, the quiet purr of the engine became harsh, coarse, a full V8 burble as the steering and suspension tightened and the engine reformatted for optimal performance. He looked at the satnav, calculated. 'You need to stop for fuel and something to eat in Dundee,' he said. 'There's a Tesco just over the bridge, café and petrol station.

Stay there, I'll call you when I arrive. We can maybe put a move on these bastards.'

'I don't need you charging to my rescue,' Paulie said, voice cold. 'I can handle these wankers.'

'No doubt,' Simon said. 'But while you do, who's going to look out for Jen? These folk aren't pissing around, Paulie. Connor had to put two of them down, permanently, yesterday.'

'Shit,' Paulie hissed. 'I'll stall as long as I can. How long will it take you to get there? An hour? I'll be there in thirty minutes.'

'I'll make it forty,' Simon said. 'Call you when I'm close.'

He killed the call, slipped the Audi into drive. Felt the car fishtail on the gravel as he left the car park, then hammered the accelerator when he got onto tarmac.

Whoever was following Paulie had answers. Answers Simon wanted very badly. And if that cost Connor a speeding ticket, so be it.

Least he could do for a pal.

CHAPTER 13

After making his research requests, Robbie had guided Connor to a series of websites that, he assured him, would mask his internet activity, and still give him access to his work email at Sentinel. Connor had raised his concerns over that – after all, whoever was after him must know of his job at Sentinel, and it wouldn't be hard to monitor his emails. Robbie hadn't quite laughed down the phone at Connor, but the incredulity was so soaked into his voice he might as well have guffawed and got it over with.

'Trust me, boss,' he had said. 'These servers are as secure as they come. You're golden. And if anyone did manage to hack us, I'd know about it as soon as it happened. I'd have an IP address and a physical location for them in under two minutes. Believe me, you're safe. I'll see what I can dig up, ping you a package.'

So it was that, just over two hours after he had called him, Connor was sitting in the small living room of the house on Glencairn Street, reading an email from Robbie as he absently rubbed at the swelling on his left temple. The ache had settled in with the stain of bruising, almost like toothache. He considered getting some more painkillers, decided against it.

> Boss, attached are the files I could pull together on Bobby McCandish, Colm O'Brien and Brendan Walsh. All three men have served time for paramilitary offences – McCandish and O'Brien for kidnapping, GBH and

attempted murder for the Republicans, Walsh for extortion and attempted murder for the Loyalists. They were all released as part of the Good Friday Agreement, seem to have kept their noses clean since then, though they're on police watch lists as senior paramilitaries. No obvious links to Dr Daniel James Gillespie, but I've still to take a proper look at his academic career. It might throw something up.

Connor sighed, sat back from the laptop and picked up the bottle of water beside it. No connection between Danny and the men he had seen at his funeral. So why had they been there? He leaned forward, opened the files on the men Robbie had attached. Found nothing unexpected, the usual patchwork of violence and threats, all cloaked in some grand crusade to either defend the British way of life in Northern Ireland or overthrow the oppressive boot that the British state had placed firmly on the Province's throat. However you cut it, they were, ultimately, violent men. Men who had killed. And, as Connor knew, once that line had been crossed, it was very easy to cross it again.

He was skimming through the file on McCandish, reading of an incident when he had blown a man's knees through the back of his legs over an unpaid debt, when his email chirped again. He flipped into the inbox, saw a fresh email from Robbie, again with attachments.

'Items you sent over', the subject line read. Connor double-clicked, opened the email.

Boss, – Robbie began. Connor hated the term, but Robbie seemed to find it more comfortable than using Connor's name – Had a bit more luck with the pictures of those items you sent over. The book is a standard breviary, used for prayer at prescribed times of the day. Nearest I can tell from the publisher, year and pictures you sent over, it's a standard Catholic one. Is there a stamp with the church name on it?

Second item is much more interesting. It's an Omega, model number CK2444. That model was made in 1944 for soldiers who were part of the D-Day landings. The north-pointing arrow on the face denotes it as military property. It's known as one of the 'Dirty Dozen' as Omega was one of twelve manufacturers who made watches for British soldiers during the Second World War. Your friend had good taste, it's a real collectors' item. If you look on the back of the watch, the serial number to confirm this should be there.

Connor picked up the watch, studied it. Military? What would Danny Gillespie be doing with a watch from the Second World War? He flipped it in his hand, studied the strap. On a whim, he unpicked the strap from the lugs then pulled it away, leaving only the watch. Frowned at what he saw.

There was another, larger, north-pointing arrow on the centre of the case. On the left side, snaking around to follow the contour of the watch, there was an engraving. Connor glanced back to Robbie's email, read the model number, CK2444. The numbers on the engraving didn't match up: C325 071887.

Connor ran a thumb across the engraving, eyes drawn back to the arrow. Something was nagging him about the watch, some vague alarm bell ringing in the back of his mind, telling him it was important. But why? It was just a watch, a way to mark time, to . . .

He remembered Robbie's email. *The book is a standard breviary, used for prayer at prescribed times of the day.* Was that it? Was the watch meant to be used with the prayer book? He picked the book up, flicked through it. It was only 112 pages long, so that ruled out 325 being a page reference. What about the other numbers?

Connor flicked through the book, but it was useless. If the watch was some kind of code, he still needed a key to understand it. But how . . .

A ping. Connor saw another email from Robbie. He had to give him credit: he was a hell of an investigator. This email was marked simply 'Context'.

Connor clicked on it, read:

Did a little further digging, think this might be the connection to the watch, boss. Have a look at the surviving family list at the bottom of the piece. I'll keep digging, R

Connor swallowed, felt his throat suddenly dry. Knew what the file would be, wasn't sure he wanted to read it. Sure enough, it was a clipping from the *Belfast Telegraph*, or more accurately, the obituaries section.

Gillespie, Dr Daniel James. Suddenly at the Royal Victoria Hospital on 26 April 2024 after a road traffic accident. A trailblazing clinical psychologist, Dr Gillespie dedicated his life to helping those affected by trauma to heal more than their physical wounds and go on to live fulfilling lives. A student of Queen's University Belfast, Dr Gillespie moved to London to continue his work with the NHS and private sector. He is survived by his mother, Mary, and his father, Colonel Alasdair Gillespie (retired). Service will be at Milltown Anglican Church, County Armagh, 2 p.m., 8 February 2025. Family flowers only, please. Donations to MIND, the mental health charity.

Connor let out a long breath he hadn't realised he was holding. The obituary was cold, almost clinical, but it got the job done. He thought back to the funeral, to Danny's mother, Mary, and the tall, ramrod-straight man who had been by her side. The man who, Connor now understood, had been standing to attention to stop himself collapsing under the weight of his grief. Connor had never met Danny's father, and Danny had never mentioned what he did when they were at university. Then again, why would he? When they were studying, the Troubles were a freshly treated wound, the scabs and scar tissue still fragile. Mentioning that your father had been in the British Army would have been asking for trouble in certain bars. But what did it mean?

Connor sighed with frustration. There was something here, he could feel it. Something he was missing. The links were there. He just wasn't seeing them. Danny's work on the trauma created by the Troubles, a link to the military, three paramilitaries turning up at his funeral. And then the items Danny's mother insisted Connor have: a vintage watch and an old prayer book. It was enough to put a target on Connor's back, but why? And how . . .?

He was interrupted by the chirping of his laptop. Not an email this time, but a voice call. He frowned, Robbie looking for a bit of credit, no doubt.

He sighed. Hit answer. 'Robbie, just got your emails. Good work. Not sure where it gets me, but . . .'

'Forget that,' Robbie said, his tone more serious than Connor could ever remember hearing it before. 'Boss, I've found something else. I was looking into Dr Gillespie's work, trying to find connections to those paramilitaries you had me run down. And I found it, right there in the files.' He whispered, 'Jesus,' more to himself than to Connor.

'Found what?' Connor asked.

'Well, that's just the point,' Robbie said.

'What?' Confusion needled the bruise on Connor's temple. 'What are you—'

'The case studies,' Robbie said, impatience sharpening his tone. 'For his paper, Dr Gillespie interviewed people affected by the Troubles. A series of case studies about victims and how they were treated afterwards. Six or seven of them. As you'd expect in his final report, there are footnotes with links to the initial reports on the incidents that happened. Bombings, kidnappings and the like. Not just news reports from the time, but declassified official reports from police and military. That's where the problem is. It's good work, I almost missed it, but someone got sloppy with the source code on one edit, and I managed to track it.'

'Track what?' Connor asked. 'Robbie, what the hell are you talking about?'

Connor heard Robbie take a deep breath, as though he was trying to centre himself. When he spoke, he was calm. 'The official reports on the paramilitary attacks, boss. The declassified ones. The events, whether it be a car bomb, a punishment beating, a parent or partner being kidnapped or beaten. They've all been changed. I don't just mean redacted to protect the anonymity of victims, I mean edited. Every incident that was logged by Dr Gillespie between May 1986 and March 1991 has been changed.'

'How?' Connor asked, something cold sliding through his thoughts. 'And why?'

'Why I can't do,' Robbie said. 'But I know the how. When you make a change, or an edit, to a document it's logged in the metadata. That's the document's properties, the details about its name, format, but also when it's been changed. You can't see it unless you go looking for it. It's standard practice for these online document changes to be tracked. And when I checked it, there's been a whole list of edits done on this document. So whoever edited these files knows the story they want to tell, but they don't know how online files are monitored for changes. So this is somebody non-technical.

'Danny Gillespie would have known about metadata. Whoever changed these files did not. Basically, boss, someone has been rewriting the last five years of history in Dr Gillespie's work.'

CHAPTER 14

Paulie had always liked the Tay Bridge. Unlike others across Central Scotland, like the Forth Bridge, with its almost lattice-like red beams and Meccano-style construction, or the new Queensferry Crossing, which seemed more sculpted than built, the Tay Bridge was a brutally plain tongue of double-lane concrete that snaked from Fife, over the Tay and into Dundee. And that was fine with Paulie. He liked things that were functional, that did only the job they were asked to do. Whether it was a bridge, a car or a gun, for Paulie the simpler the better.

He drove over the bridge and turned left, pushing through an amber light and heading for the petrol station Simon had mentioned. He knew the place, had stopped there many times before. Problem was, the tank on the Merc was still three-quarters full, so filling up wasn't going to provide much of a distraction or a time-killer until Simon arrived. He was just passing the new V&A museum, a futuristic blunt-faced building that looked as if giant wooden slats had been stacked at angles to create a curve, when he heard Jen stirring in the back. Cursed silently under his breath. With her injuries after the hit-and-run, losing her dad and facing up to the reality of what type of man he had really been, the last thing she needed was more suffering. And yet here he was, about to drive her into danger.

Chalk up another topic of conversation with a certain Connor Fraser when all this was over.

'Where are we?' she mumbled, breath sharp and shallow as she sat up in the back seat. It had been almost four years since she had been run over, and in that time she had worked hard at her rehabilitation and physiotherapy, but Paulie knew that her back still bothered her, that walking long distances was a problem.

'Dundee,' he said, with a brightness he didn't feel. He looked in the rear-view mirror, past Jen. There it was, three cars back. The BMW that had been tailing them since Stirling.

'Dundee?' Jen said, running a hand through her hair and straightening in her seat. 'Why are we stopping in Dundee, Paulie?'

'Need to get petrol,' he said. 'Plus I thought you might want to get out of the car for a bit, stretch your legs, get a cup of tea.'

Jen gave a noncommittal grunt. 'Not like you to let the car get low on gas on a long trip,' she said, more to herself than Paulie.

He felt a small pang of shame. So much for that excuse. She knew him, and his habits, all too well.

Paulie drove past the Tesco Express to the petrol station. The car park at the shop would give whoever was tailing him too many places to hide in plain sight. They could pose as just another shopper popping in for a few things. But the forecourt of a petrol station was much more exposed, and functional.

Which suited Paulie just fine.

The petrol station itself was quiet, just another grafted onto a large supermarket. Three rows of pumps and a small shop at the end. Luckily, the station was quiet, the shop dark and abandoned, as Paulie pulled up beside an empty pump.

He killed the engine, glanced in his rear-view mirror again. Saw Jen giving him a cool, even gaze, eyes hard and unblinking, just like her father's. Made a calculation. If whoever was following them was, as Simon had said, after Jen, he wanted to keep her close to him. But if they followed him into the petrol station, and Simon arrived, did he want her near that? Or did he want her somewhere public, safe? Like, for example, a coffee stand at a busy supermarket? He glanced into the rear-view one more time, then looked out of the windscreen. No BMW, yet. So he had time. A little.

'Look, the shop isn't too far, and it looks like they've got a Costa.

Why don't you head in and get us a couple of coffees? I'll fill up, then join you.'

Jen let the silence draw out. Took a breath before she spoke. 'What's going on, Paulie?' she asked.

'What? Not sure what you mean, Jen. I need some petrol and a coffee. Not as young as I used to be, and the A90 up to Aberdeen isn't a fun drive at the best of times. Just thought we could speed things up, get fuelled up and back on the road. But if you want to sit there while I fill up, fine by me.'

He reached for the door handle, made a show of getting out of the car. Heard the back door open, the plastic rattle of Jen's crutch clattering on to the tarmac a moment later.

'I'm not a child, Paulie,' she said, as she settled her grip on the crutch. 'It's not like you to stop once you're on the road, and you hate drinking in your car. If there's something going on, I want to know what it is, right?'

'Sure,' Paulie said, giving a smile that felt too big and too false. 'But there's nothing wrong, Jen. Honest. Just feeling my age a bit.'

She snorted, held his gaze for a moment longer than was comfortable, then turned away. Took a couple of steps, stopped, looked back over her shoulder. 'Americano, right?' she said.

Paulie blinked, took a moment to realise what she meant. 'Ah, yeah, please,' he said. 'And get me a muffin as well, will you?' He patted his belly, feigning hunger. 'And you're right about drinking in the car. Grab us a table. Five minutes and I'll be in.'

Jen shook her head, turned and headed for the supermarket. Paulie watched her go, eyes on the car park for any sign of the BMW. If anyone made a move on her, he could get there in time.

At least, that was what he told himself.

He had just opened the petrol cap on the car when his mobile buzzed in his pocket. He took it out, felt something halfway between relief and irritation when he saw Simon's name on the display.

'Where the fuck are—' Paulie started.

'Inbound. Be at the petrol station in less than a minute,' Simon said. He was all business now, a copper on duty. 'I've got the BMW in my sights, one car in front of me. Two occupants. Can't really tell, but they look big.'

Paulie nodded, glanced up the road, saw Jen's blonde hair disappear into the supermarket. One problem solved.

'Got Jen safe for the moment,' he said. 'So we take these fuckers out here, before they get the chance to move on her.'

'What do you have in mind?' Simon asked, voice edged with a cold excitement.

'They're going to drive past, see me in the petrol station. Two options, either they drive into the forecourt and front up to me here, or they park in the supermarket car park and wait, see what I do.'

'They'll take the former,' Simon said. 'Whoever tried to take Connor out in Belfast, they did it in broad daylight, no care for risk. If they want Jen, and think she's in the car, they'll come straight at you.'

Paulie felt a smile play across his lips as he picked up the petrol pump and jammed it into the car. 'That's fine with me. Let them park up, then box them in with your motor best you can. Can't stop them leaving, but we can sure as fuck slow them down.'

'Copy that,' Simon said, then killed the call.

Paulie pocketed his mobile, rooted around in his pocket for the other item he kept there, closed his fingers on it. Felt a thrill of adrenaline shriek through his veins as the BMW appeared a moment later; sleek, aggressive, predatory. Took a breath of the cooling afternoon air, watched as the driver hesitated for an instant, then nosed the car into the forecourt, taking the pump diagonally across and down from Paulie. A moment's pause, and then a man emerged from the driver's side of the car. He wasn't broad, but he was tall, at least six foot five, Paulie guessed, with the type of build you normally associated with marathon runners. He wore a suit that was clearly tailored, shirt neck open to show the first hints of a tattoo that crawled across the top of his chest, like a noose hanging around his neck. His face was plain, almost forgettable, apart from the silvering scar that ran from under his chin to his left cheek, cleaving a path through his short, dark beard.

He smiled as he stepped towards Paulie, keeping eye contact. It was an old trick, one Paulie had used many times before. Distract with eye contact, let your partner sneak up on the target unnoticed. Problem was, Paulie *had* noticed, seen the passenger emerge from the car at the same time as the driver looped round the back to come at Paulie from the other side.

Paulie didn't return the smile, just kept pumping petrol. Eased his grip to slow the flow of the pump to a trickle. Didn't want it clicking out too early.

'Mr King, isn't it?' the man called, his voice clipped in the way only an upbringing in the Borders can achieve. 'May we have a word with you, please?'

Paulie shrugged. So, they knew his name, were making no pretence of ignorance. Confident or cocky? It was too early to tell.

The man flicked his eyes to his partner as he closed the distance on Paulie, his partner mirroring his approach from the opposite side of the car. Measured, controlled steps, taking in every part of Paulie as he moved, like a predator stalking prey.

'We'd like to talk to you and Ms MacKenzie about a very pressing matter,' the driver said, the cold, empty smile reasserting itself on his face as he spoke. *Killer's smile*, Paulie thought suddenly. *Seen a few over the years.*

He was about to respond when he heard the growl of another engine and the squeal of tyres on tarmac. Smiled as he saw Connor Fraser's Audi pull into the forecourt, angled in close behind the BMW.

The two men froze, whirling as Simon got out of the car. ''Bout ye?' he said, looking over to Paulie. 'Fancy seeing you here. And with friends too.'

The tall man turned to face Simon. 'Mr McCartney, isn't it? Good to see you. We were planning on speaking to you . . .'

He never got the time to finish the sentence. Paulie pulled the pump free, squeezed it as hard as he could, stepped forward and doused the man with petrol. He staggered back, coughing and spluttering, clawing for his eyes. His partner darted forward, around the car, poised to spring. Stopped dead when he saw what Paulie was holding in his free hand, which he had just pulled from his pocket.

'I wouldn't, son,' he said, as he flicked the top off his heavy silver lighter. 'Unless you want your pal to end up as a crispy briquette, I'd stand the fuck down.'

Indecision mixed with hatred on the man's face, turning it into something cruel and ugly. The impotent defiance of the expression made Paulie want to laugh.

'Right,' Paulie said, stepping around the car slowly to rehang the petrol pump. 'Here's how it's going to work. My friend there,' he gestured to Simon with his chin, 'is going to pat you down, make sure you're not carrying anything naughty. Then he's going to take your car keys and, before the police arrive and accuse me of spilling petrol, we're going to drive to somewhere nice and quiet. Then you can tell us all about why you want Connor Fraser.'

Paulie felt something flip in his stomach as the man on the ground smiled and shook his head, as though he was at a dinner party and had just been told a joke it would be rude not to laugh at. 'Fine,' he said. 'We'll play your game, for now. But the longer you piss around, the worse things will be for Mr Fraser.'

Paulie opened his mouth, was cut off by a shrill cry. He looked round, saw Jen limping towards them as fast as she could. 'Paulie!' she shouted, eyes flitting between him and Simon. 'What the hell . . .?'

The man on the ground stood slowly, smile intensifying. 'Busted,' he whispered.

CHAPTER 15

After the call with Robbie, Connor studied Danny Gillespie's watch and prayer book again. Despite the information Robbie had given him, that declassified reports from the Troubles had been altered, the items refused to give up whatever secrets they held.

Abandoning the watch and prayer book in frustration, Connor considered his options. For some reason, declassified reports and documents related to paramilitary activities during the Troubles had been edited. Had Danny discovered this? Had that got him killed? Or was there something else, something Connor was missing? And why would the reports have been edited in the first place? After the end of the Troubles and the Good Friday Agreement, measures had been taken to release paramilitaries early from prison, and the UK government had passed a law giving amnesty to soldiers and paramilitaries who participated in an independent commission to review Troubles-related deaths and injuries. So why doctor the reports? And what was the link between Danny Gillespie's work and the three former paramilitaries Connor had seen at his funeral?

The funeral . . .

Connor glanced back to the watch and the prayer book. His mouth dropped open as the realisation hit him.

'Always were a clever little shite, weren't you, Danny?' he whispered.

It was obvious. So obvious he should have seen it sooner. Probably would have, if he hadn't spent the last forty-eight hours running for his life. Danny had known that those three men, Bobby McCandish and Colm O'Brien from the IRA and Brendan Walsh from the UVF, would be at the funeral. He had wanted them there. They were as much a message to Connor as the watch and prayer book Danny's mother had insisted Connor should have.

But while Connor didn't understand the message yet, he got the theme loud and clear. Danny Gillespie's voice echoed from beyond the grave with one simple command: Avenge me.

Connor glanced at the watch again, saw the arrow on the face that denoted its military heritage. Thought back to the funeral, to the man he now knew was Danny's father. The man who had stood to attention throughout, refusing to let whatever private grief he was feeling bleed into his public façade.

Colonel Alasdair Gillespie.

Connor knew nothing about Gillespie, and the information in the obituary Robbie had found had said only that he was retired. What had he done in the military? Where had he served? Could he have been in Northern Ireland during the Troubles? If so, how would he have felt knowing that three paramilitaries were at his son's funeral?

'Hold on,' Connor muttered, a thought forming in his mind, like a slow-moving ship emerging from fog. 'It couldn't . . .'

He grabbed the laptop, opened the file Robbie had sent containing Danny's obituary. Skimmed it again. It was impersonal, businesslike, almost brusque. He read one line again: *He is survived by his mother, Mary, and his father, Colonel Alasdair Gillespie (retired). Service will be at Milltown Anglican Church, County Armagh, 2 p.m., 8 February 2024.*

It wasn't an obituary. This was no tribute to a cherished son from a devastated family. Where was the colour, the idiosyncrasies that told you who Danny was? They were nowhere, because they weren't needed, weren't essential to the message: that Colonel Alasdair Gillespie (retired) would be at Milltown Anglican Church at 2 p.m. on 8 February. Which Bobby McCandish, Colm O'Brien and Brendan Walsh had obviously received, loud and clear.

CHAPTER 16

He almost didn't make it in time. The laugh came from nowhere, rumbling up his chest and into his throat almost before he could bite it back. He gave a strangled cough, raised one hand to cover his mouth, the other to wave to Paulie and Jen that he was okay.

Paulie's head darted up, eyes narrowing. Jen merely turned to Simon, the fury in her gaze undimmed, then back to Paulie, who seemed to shrink again under her glare.

After she had found them at the petrol station, a plan had been quickly formulated. Paulie had bundled Jen's would-be kidnappers into the front of their car, getting into the back seat and training his gun on them. It was a double threat: the promise of a bullet in the back of the head for the first person who had a bright idea, and any shot would probably ignite the petrol fumes from the man Paulie had hosed down. It worked, and they made a strange motorcade. Simon in the Audi, Jen in Paulie's Mercedes, both following Paulie, who was in the back of the thugs' car, directing like the taxi passenger from hell. He led them a mile or so up the road, turning into the car park of what looked like an old-style football pavilion, a squat, white-walled building with tiles that had long since given up any pretence of being red. Beyond the pavilion, a large, open park stretched down to the banks of the Tay, the famed silvery waters winking between trees, almost in defiance of the sullen sky above.

They waited a moment, then Paulie, grunting, extricated himself from the back of their attackers' car, his face calm.

'Don't worry about the Chuckle Brothers there,' Paulie said, as he threw a thumb over his shoulder, back towards the car. 'I zip-tied both of them to the steering wheel and took the keys. They'd need to be fuckin' Houdini to get loose from that.'

'Would either of you like to tell me what is going on?' Jen said. Paulie's expression collapsed. His eyes darted to Simon, part confusion, part pleading. 'I just saw you threaten to turn someone into a fireball, Paulie, and you, Simon, what the hell are you doing here, and in Connor's bloody car?'

Simon sighed. He had wanted to avoid this, keep Jen away from what was going on. Not because he thought she couldn't handle it – previous experience had shown she was more than capable of handling herself – but more because her involvement would trigger a chain reaction that would lead to an inevitable conclusion: she would call Connor, and a whole world of shit would be unleashed.

He filled her in as quickly as he could, keeping the details sketchy about how much trouble Connor was in. He told her about the use of Connor's gran as a pawn in whatever game was being played, the message in the newspaper, and his concern that Jen would be targeted next, a suspicion confirmed when he called Paulie, who told him he and Jen were being followed.

Jen turned to Paulie, her presence seeming to fill the deserted car park as she leaned heavily on her crutch.

'You knew we were being followed?' she whispered. 'You knew we were being fucking followed and you lied to me? Sent me to get sodding coffee like your bloody secretary? Why? So you could keep me safe? Wrap me up in cotton wool and—'

'Jen, I . . .' Paulie said. 'I was just . . .'

Simon took a step back, leaned against Connor's car. Felt the laughter bubble up in him – Paulie, a man who had calmly blown off a man's head in front of him, a man whose love of violence was telegraphed to the world in the deadness of his gaze, brought low by a five-foot-six woman with a crutch.

He let them speak, tuning out the conversation, trying to think of the next move. The chain reaction had begun. Connor would be called, Jen would insist on it. But how to keep Connor safe, make sure he didn't do anything rash when he heard that Jen and his gran had been threatened?

Jen yanked him from his thoughts. 'I'll deal with that shite later. Right now,' she jerked her thumb at the car with the two men bound inside, 'we've got more immediate problems. Let's see what they've got to say for themselves.'

Paulie's smile flickered again, and Simon could almost smell the relief radiating from him. He wasn't equipped to handle Jen's fury, didn't have the emotional awareness or bandwidth to deal with it. It didn't compute, like the cost-of-living crisis to an over-entitled, over-titled man who lived in a palace at the public's expense. But two men who had tried to kidnap her and possibly hurt him in the process? That was as natural to Paulie as breathing.

He pulled his gun with one hand, a long, wicked knife appearing like a punchline in the other. He lumbered to the car, dragged first the passenger then the driver out of the passenger door. Took a step back, gun trained between them.

'On yer knees, now,' he said, his voice as rough as the tarmac they stood on.

The men glanced at each other, the tall one with the beard and the scar nodding slightly. *So he's the boss*, Simon thought, as they knelt.

'Right, fellas,' he said, clapping his hands together as he approached them. 'Couple of questions. What do you want with Connor Fraser, and whose fat fingers do I break for daring to try to use his grandmother and Jen here as a way to get to him?'

The man with the beard smiled, dropped his head. Beside him, his partner, a man so plain that it seemed his features had been selected by committee, shook his head, as though the bearded man had psychically transmitted a joke to him.

'I say something funny?' Simon asked, drawing his own gun and clacking the slide to make his point.

'Not really,' the man with the beard said. 'It's just funny that you're fumbling around in the dark with not the first clue about what is going on, Mr McCartney. Wonder how that's going to sit with your new boss. DCI Malcolm Ford, isn't it? Doesn't suffer fools, we've heard. And you're acting like a prime arsehole right now.'

Simon blinked, took a beat. So they had background on him. So what? His name had been in the papers a few times, and as one of the most senior officers in Scotland, Detective Chief Inspector Malcolm Ford wasn't a hard man to find. And yet . . .

'So enlighten me,' Simon said. 'What is this all about? Why do you want Connor Fraser so badly? Is it anything to do with Bobby McCandish, Colm O'Brien or Brendan Walsh by any chance?'

Something cold and predatory flashed across the bearded man's eyes, then hardened into contempt. When he spoke his voice was as grey as the sky overhead. 'Call Mr Ford,' he said softly. 'Tell him you have two men in custody. Tell him you have two Box 500s held at gunpoint. We can confirm via codeword. After that, cut us the fuck loose. Then we can have a chat about your friend, Fraser.'

Jen stepped forward, searching Simon's face for answers. 'What the hell is he talking about?' she asked. 'Box 500s? Simon, what the . . .'

Simon gulped, heard his throat click. He tried to look at Jen, but couldn't make his eyes leave the men in front of him. 'Box 500 is code for a government officer,' he said, after a moment. 'It's a reference to the PO box for MI5 headquarters during the Second World War.'

'Officers?' Jen said, eyes growing wide. 'You mean . . .?'

Simon finally tore his gaze from the men. 'Yeah,' he said. 'He's saying they're secret service, running an op, and Ford knows about it.' He felt a wave of unreality wash over him, almost as if someone had reached into his brain and given it a squeeze. 'Jesus, Jen. What has Connor got himself caught up in?'

CHAPTER 17

He was one of those men who wore a uniform even when he wasn't in one. Connor watched Alasdair Gillespie walk into the Botanic Gardens, not far from the university, as though he was on a parade ground. Shoulders back, head high, iron-grey hair immaculately swept off his forehead, he approached the bulbous cast-iron dome of the Palm House as though it was a soldier awaiting inspection. He paused outside, casting his gaze across the benches that lined the path to the glass house, a faint impatience digging a furrow into his brow and causing his mouth to curl in a sneer.

Connor smiled from his position behind a nearby tree. Not a man who was used to being kept waiting.

After making his discovery about the obituary, Connor had had Robbie run a background check on Colonel Alasdair Gillespie. Wasn't surprised when the information came back less than a minute after the request was made, with a note from Robbie:

> Wondered when you were going to ask for this. Backgrounded him to see if I could find a link to paramilitaries at funeral. Nothing yet. Will keep you posted. R

The attached file detailed a distinguished, if uneventful, military career. Gillespie had joined the army at eighteen, presumably as a way of getting out of Leith, where he was born, and served with the Royal Scots Dragoon Guards. He had been with the unit when it carried out a tour of duty in Northern Ireland in 1980. During that tour, Gillespie met Mary Bannon, and the two had married two years later. Transferring to the 2nd Battalion, The Rifles, he was based at Thiepval Barracks in Lisburn. He worked his way up to the rank of colonel, retiring three years ago. Robbie couldn't find any information that linked his tour in Belfast with any paramilitary-related incidents, but that was no surprise to Connor.

Satisfied that Gillespie was alone, and not being followed, Connor left the shelter of the tree he was standing behind and approached him. It had been a risk calling Gillespie to arrange this meeting, but a calculated one. If Gillespie was involved with the attempt to grab Connor off the street, this was the best way of finding out. Of course, Connor could have doorstepped him at home, but that ran the risk of dragging Danny's mum, Mary, into whatever was going on. And that was a line Connor did not want to cross.

'Colonel Gillespie?' he said, as he approached. Gillespie turned slightly, facing Connor and meeting his eye. There was a horrible moment of familiarity for Connor, as the ghost of Danny Gillespie expressed itself in the curve of his father's jaw and the shape of his eyes. But then Gillespie spoke, and the illusion evaporated like rain on hot tarmac.

'Mr Fraser,' he said, eyes darting to the bruise on Connor's temple. 'You were a friend of Danny, I believe. I saw you at the funeral.'

'Yes, sir,' Connor said. 'Thanks for agreeing to meet me.'

Gillespie raised a dismissive hand, as though swatting away a fly. 'Not at all. Least I could do for a friend of Danny. Though I'm sorry to say I don't remember him ever mentioning, you. Not that we were particularly close . . .'

His voice drifted off, and Connor saw something soften in his gaze. Guilt. The sorrow-tinged guilt of a father who had never really got to know his child as the person they were rather than the fantasy he'd hoped for. Jen had lost their child when she was only a couple of months pregnant, but Connor felt the same guilt, and the mourning for the child he would never know.

‘Sir,’ he said, forcing his mind back to the present, ‘I wanted to ask a couple of questions if you don’t mind. There were a couple of faces I saw at the funeral, people who didn’t, ah . . .’ he fumbled for the best way to put it ‘. . . didn’t really fit. Do the names Bobby McCandish, Colm O’Brien or Brendan Walsh mean anything to you?’

Whatever had softened in Gillespie’s eyes at the thought of his son sharpened again. ‘No,’ he said slowly, ‘I’m not sure those names are familiar to me. Friends of Danny, you say?’

‘Friends,’ Connor said, ‘or colleagues. Tell me, how much did you know about Danny’s work with sufferers of trauma caused in the Troubles?’

Gillespie teased non-existent lint from his jacket sleeve. ‘Not a lot, Mr Fraser,’ he said, the guilt creeping back into his tone. ‘As I said, I didn’t know Danny very well. When he decided to study psychology rather than following me into the military, well, it created, ah, problems. We were civil, of course, for Mary, and he never missed Christmas or a birthday, but we just, well, you know, drifted apart.’

Connor nodded. He knew all right. It was like listening to a version of his own history with his father, a man who had never forgiven Connor for not following the path he had dreamed of for him. ‘You said Danny didn’t mention me,’ he observed, ‘but your wife insisted that I be given two items at the funeral – a watch and a prayer book. The watch seems to be an antique, but the prayer book is generic. Any idea why Danny would be so insistent that I be given them?’

‘No,’ Gillespie said, the sudden interest in his voice matching the glint in his eyes. ‘I gave Danny a watch for his eighteenth birthday, a vintage Omega, military edition. A fine watch. Family heirloom. If it’s not too much of an imposition, I’d like to see it again. Perhaps you would be open to me buying it from you. I’m sure you’ll agree, it would be more appropriate for it to be with family rather than a friend.’

Family, Connor thought. *But you just said your son was a stranger to you.* And there was something else that bothered Connor, the crassness with which Gillespie had offered to buy back a family heirloom, judging that Connor was more motivated by self-interest than any sense of loss over Danny’s death.

'Sorry,' Connor said, with an apologetic shrug of his shoulders. 'I didn't think to bring it with me, left it at home.'

'Ah,' Gillespie said. 'And where would home be at the moment, Mr Fraser? Perhaps I could call round at some time, pick the watch up. Maybe have a look at this prayer book as well, see if I can spot anything special about it.'

Connor nodded, the first churning of unease stirring in his guts. He resisted the urge to look over his shoulder, make sure no one was sneaking up on him.

'That would be great, but I'm staying with a friend who works shifts, wouldn't want to disturb them more than I already am. Look, I've got a couple of calls to make, some old friends to see before I head back over the water to Stirling. How about I give you a call? We can arrange a catch-up before I go. Maybe raise a jar to Danny while we're at it.'

It was the most fleeting of moments, but Connor caught it. A flash of disappointment darted over Gillespie's features, chilled by something Connor could have sworn was panic.

No, he thought. That's not right. Not panic.

Desperation.

'Of course,' he said, after a moment. 'You have my number, give me a call. And do be careful, Mr Fraser.' He paused, a blade of a smile passing across his face, distorting it into something sadistic, cruel, as he raised a finger to point at Connor's temple. 'It looks like you've already been in the wars. Belfast is a fine city, but it can still be a dangerous one if you take a wrong turn.'

'Oh, don't worry about me,' Connor said, surprised by the sudden, cool fury that rippled across the back of his neck, 'I know my way around Belfast fairly well. And if trouble comes looking for me, I'll make sure I'm ready.'

CHAPTER 18

The tension seemed to ooze out of the phone, wrap itself around Simon as he listened.

'Yes,' DCI Malcolm Ford said, voice so tight Simon was afraid it would snap like a violin string, 'I can confirm that we have two government operatives working in the area at the moment. They contacted me yesterday, said they needed to speak to your pal Fraser as a matter of urgency. Knew I was a . . .' he lowered his voice as though imparting a guilty secret '. . . friend of his.'

Simon pinched the bridge of his nose with his free hand, closed his eyes tight as he tried to rein in the onslaught of ideas that threatened to overwhelm him.

'I take it they've made contact with you, and this call is to verify they're legitimate?' Ford said. Simon felt the laughter bubble up in him, and opened his eyes to see the two men still on their knees in front of them, Paulie padding back and forth, a predator waiting to be told he could pounce.

'Contact?' Simon said. 'Yeah, you could say that. They give any indication what they wanted to talk to Connor about?'

Ford made a noise that should have been a laugh but came out like a snarl. 'They were, how can I say, less than chatty? Told me only that it was a matter of national security, and Fraser had blundered into something that could cause the government some extreme embarrassment. They then took great pains to remind me of the

Official Secrets Act, which, in case you've forgotten, applies to you as well.'

'Foremost in my mind, sir,' Simon said, teeth gritted.

'Look, McCartney, I don't know what Fraser is involved in. Truth is, I don't much care. But I do not want it turning my patch into a firing range, is that clear? Tell them what you know, help them in any way you can, and get this squared away before we're all neck-deep in shite, clear?'

'Crystal,' Simon said.

'Get me an update as soon as you can,' Ford said, then ended the call.

Simon looked at the phone, pocketed it. In front of him, the two men knelt, each wearing the type of arrogant I-know-something-you-don't smile that made your knuckles itch to hit it.

'Well?' the bearded man said. 'I take it your boss vouched for us.'

'Unfortunately he did,' Simon said, nodding to Paulie. He saw a flash of disappointment on Paulie's face. Then he produced his knife and cut the men's hands free of the fresh zip-ties he had bound them with while Simon was calling Ford.

'So, you got names?' Simon said, as he watched the men rise to their feet.

'Why?' the man with the anonymous face asked, as he made a show of rubbing at his wrists. 'You want to swap phone numbers, maybe send us Christmas cards?'

'No,' Simon said, the arrogance in the man's voice striking a chord with his anger, making it quiver in his chest, 'but I'd like to know the names of the arseholes who thought using an old woman was a fair tactic to get to my friend. I don't care what the fuck you think he's stumbled on, but using civilians isn't on.'

'Fuckin' right,' Paulie rumbled, menace in his voice.

'See, that's where we've got a problem,' the bearded man said. 'We haven't made contact with any old woman. We contacted DCI Ford to see if he could illuminate us as to Mr Fraser's whereabouts. We were following Ms MacKenzie here,' he nodded towards Jen, who was sitting in the front seat of Paulie's car, passenger door open, watching proceedings as she occasionally drummed her crutch on the tarmac, 'hoping she might lead us to Mr Fraser. After all, he's gone dark in Belfast, so it's possible he might have made his way back to Scotland.'

Simon ignored that remark, focused on the only fact that interested him. It had sent a shiver of dread worming through his guts.

'Hold on. You're saying it wasn't you two who left a threatening note with Ida Fraser, telling Connor to get in touch with a mobile number?'

'No,' the bearded man said, in a tone that wouldn't have been out of place in a classroom as the teacher tried to explain long division to a group of three-year-olds. 'That wasn't us. We don't operate that way. But it tells us that your friend has definitely stumbled into something nasty. You said there was a mobile number. Care to tell us what it is? We might be able to track it.'

Simon shook his head. 'Maybe,' he said. 'But, first, a little quid pro quo. You've been sent to find Connor because of something he found in Belfast. Something, I'm guessing, to do with the three paramilitaries who were at the funeral of his friend, Danny Gillespie. What do you think that is? And were you responsible for the grab squad that tried to ambush him yesterday after cloning my phone?'

The two men exchanged a quick, sharp glance. 'No,' the bearded one said, 'that wasn't us either. But it means this is more serious that we thought, and it might confirm something. What can you tell us about the men who tried to grab him?'

'We'll get to that,' Simon said. 'But, first, a couple of matters. Put a protective detail on Ida Fraser at Montrose House, Bannockburn. If you didn't leave that message, someone else did, which means she's still in danger.'

'Agreed,' the bearded man said, nodding to his partner, who turned to Paulie and gestured a gimme motion to him. Paulie handed him his mobile phone, and the man walked off.

Simon opened his mouth, about to speak, when Jen beat him to it. 'Look,' she said, 'this is all very fascinating, but as far as I can see, everyone here wants to talk to Connor. Simon, I'm betting you can arrange that. So could you do that, please, so I can get moving. Not to be heartless, but I still have to get to Aberdeen.'

The bearded man turned to her, a smile on his lips. 'I'm sorry,

Ms MacKenzie, but that won't be happening. If you don't know where Mr Fraser is, you're still connected to him, which means you're staying with us for the duration.'

Jen lowered her head, shook it. When she looked up again, the coldness in her smile shocked Simon. It was, in that instant, as if she had been possessed by the spirit of her father.

'I've got more at stake here than the rest of you combined,' she said, placing the words with the calculation of a chess master making a move on the board. 'You're talking about Connor Fraser. I want him home. Safe. But I also have a business to save, and to do that, I need . . .' she paused, seemed to edit herself '. . . I need to get to Aberdeen for a meeting. If there's something I can do to help Connor, I will, but in the meantime, I will not sit meekly by like a good little girl while the menfolk do all the big stuff. I've done nothing wrong so you have no grounds to hold me. If you try to detain me, I will scream blue murder, and then I will phone his girlfriend.' She jutted her jaw at Simon.

The bearded man blinked. 'Girlfriend? What?'

'Donna,' Simon said, feeling a smile break across his lips. He could have kissed Jen for thinking of it. 'Donna Blake. You might have seen her. Reporter for Sky News. Loves a good story, does our Donna. And this is one hell of a story. So unless you want it splashed everywhere, and unless you want Donna asking some embarrassing questions of your bosses in Whitehall, you'd better start at the beginning. And the beginning is here – what do you think Connor is involved in?'

CHAPTER 19

Leaving Alasdair Gillespie in the Botanic Gardens, Connor went walking. He knew he was taking a risk – whoever had tried to grab him on the Falls Road was no doubt still after him, and being out in the open was a gamble – but he needed to think.

And, if he was being honest with himself, if someone gave him an excuse to get into a fight, that was fine. Being on the run, being hunted, was like a string being slowly tightened inside him, minute by minute, hour by hour. He could almost feel it, the rising tension, the need to strike back, reassert control. But the only way to do that was to figure out what was going on.

He walked without direction, on instinct, heading back into the city centre, hoping the crowds would make him more anonymous – just another tourist or shopper. As he walked, he thought of Alasdair Gillespie's reaction when Connor had mentioned the watch and the prayer book. The flicker of panicked desperation when Connor had lied and told him he didn't have them with him, the clumsy way he had tried to get Connor's address out of him. And his reaction to the names of the three paramilitaries at the funeral: Bobby McCandish, Colm O'Brien and Brendan Walsh. It was only a flicker, but Connor knew a lie when he heard one.

And Alasdair Gillespie had lied to Connor that he didn't know those men. Connor was convinced of it.

He pulled the watch from his pocket, studied it again. Saw nothing new, just an antique watch with military branding. But it meant something: Gillespie's reaction had told him as much. It was a message for Connor from Danny. And if Danny was trying to leave him a message, he would have left him with a way to understand it. He was struck by a sudden thought. If Danny had left Connor the watch and the prayer book, he had known his life was in danger, had known he had blundered into something serious. Which meant there was a good chance Danny's death had been no accident.

But why had he come home? The version of events his mother had given Connor was that Danny had come home to Dunmurry from London to visit friends and family. But was there more to it than that? Was he working on something, or chasing up a lead he had found in his work on trauma inflicted on those who had lived through the Troubles – work that, according to Robbie, had included official documents that had been edited?

He pulled out his phone, pinged Robbie a message. A moment later, the phone rang.

'You wanted me to call?' Robbie said, by way of a hello.

'Yeah,' Connor said, slowing as he turned a corner, the huge dome of Belfast City Hall looming up in front of him. 'This line secure?'

'I'm bouncing the call around the UK and a wee bit of Europe for good measure so, yeah, it's secure. Speaking of that, who is it you think is after you?'

Connor considered this. The men who had tried to jump him on the Falls Road had been calm, detached, professional. The way in which one had parried Connor's attack into a means to stun him had told him that much. That they were using military-issue weapons and had managed easily to clone a car number plate, keeping the attack out of the news and police reports, told him they were resourced as well.

'Could be official, government or some affiliated agency. And given what I'm poking around in over here, it would make sense if there's something that might embarrass the government in Danny's work. You had any luck identifying what's been edited yet?'

'Not really,' Robbie replied. 'As I said, it's good work. I only noticed the problem as someone got sloppy on one document and I noticed the changes in the metadata. Every official document and Danny's case studies from 1986 to 1991 have been given an airbrush, but it's so subtle it's hard to pin down. I'm cross-referencing the witness statements with the news reports of bombings and the like at the time, but some of this stuff reached back to the sixties and seventies, and not all of that is online. I'm tapped into the National Archives and a few other sources as well, but it's taking time.'

'Okay,' Connor said, trying to keep the disappointment out of his voice. 'In the meantime, I need another favour.'

'You amaze me, boss,' Robbie said.

Connor grinned. 'Aye, that's me. A constant surprise. Look, when Danny died, he was apparently on a family visit home, got hit by a car when he stumbled out onto the road. I want to know if there was more to the trip. Can you access his work diary, see if he had anything in there for meetings or something? He might have been here doing work on his trauma study.'

'Makes sense,' Robbie said, his voice taking on the distracted tone that told Connor he was already focusing on the task, working out how he would hack into Danny's work email to access the relevant information. 'Give me twenty minutes. Can't imagine London University has overly sophisticated encryption.'

'Thanks, Robbie, I owe you.'

'Yes, you do, boss. Remember that when it comes to bonus time, will you?'

'Cross my heart. Speak to you in twenty,' he said, then ended the call.

Connor skirted the perimeter of City Hall, stopping at a set of double doors that led into a bar and restaurant called Hellcat Maggie's. When he was a student, the place had been a style bar called the Apartment, a venue that traded on sophisticated cocktails and the floor-to-ceiling windows that framed the Baroque splendour of City Hall. It had been there, while he was waiting for his former fiancée Karen MacKay, that Connor had decided to become a policeman. It wasn't a road-to-Damascus moment, or a revelation of his life's calling, just a simple coincidence. He had watched as, on the street below, two police officers had manhandled a young man to the ground. Had seen the terror in the kid's eyes, the pleading. Had seen the policemen enjoying their power over him, little more than school bullies with badges, guns and stab vests. And in that moment Connor had known he would join the police. Not to arrest terrified kids, but to stop the bullies who hid behind uniforms and enjoyed the power just a little too much.

Connor didn't regret the decision, but he regretted the impact it had had on his life, driving a wedge between him and Karen that had ultimately split them up, Connor moving back to Scotland, first to Edinburgh and then to Stirling. Where, he wondered, was Karen now? Was she married? Had she had the kids she so desperately wanted?

He felt the familiar twist of hollow regret in his stomach at the thought. He had always assumed he would be a father at some point, had known Karen's desire mirrored his own. When they had separated, the desire had left him, a road not travelled, an ambition unfulfilled. But when Jen fell pregnant, which Connor had learned only after she had lost the baby, he had felt that dream splinter inside him for a second time. He mourned the child he had never known, felt their absence in the quiet moments before bed or when he was pushing himself too hard in the gym. What would they have been like? Boy or girl? Would they have taken after Connor with his too-thin nose and piercing jade-green eyes, or would they have inherited Jen's blonde hair, perfect skin and the blue eyes that never failed to draw Connor into them?

The melancholy the thought evoked drove him into the bar, and the sudden desire for a drink to drown his demons. He wanted to get home. Get back to Jen. Do whatever it took to heal the schism that had formed between them when her father had died. He loved her, needed her to know that with the certainty he did.

He got to the bar, ordered a pint of Guinness. Had just paid when his phone chirped. He pulled it out, smiling. Typical Robbie. Say twenty minutes, get the job done in ten. But it wasn't Robbie's number that was calling him. It was another. One he had memorised long ago.

'Simon,' he said, 'how you going? I'm making some progress with Robbie's help. Should be able to—'

'Connor,' Simon said, his voice low, atonal, as though he was reading someone their rights instead of talking to his friend, 'I can hear noise in the background. You in a bar or something?'

Connor felt guilt scald him briefly, as though his father had just found him stealing a swig from the malt whisky when he was fifteen. 'Aye,' he said, pushing away the pint. 'Just revisiting old haunts, waiting for Robbie to call me back.'

'Get yourself somewhere private, and call me.'

'What's going on?'

'A world of shit,' Simon said. 'Get yourself squared away, then call me. But make it quick, I'll need to board in about half an hour.'

'Board?' Connor said. 'You mean—'

'Yeah,' Simon said. 'I'm at the airport now, waiting for the flight to Belfast City. Should be with you in a couple of hours.'

CHAPTER 20

Before calling Connor, Simon had phoned Donna. They had planned to have dinner that night, and Simon was loath to cancel it, especially with the engagement ring weighing as heavily in his pocket as it did in his mind. He wasn't sure he would have proposed that specific night, but he knew it was coming, as inexorable as the setting of the sun and the rising of the moon.

'You're going where?' she had asked, when he told her.

'Belfast. Look, I'm sorry, but something's come up. Connor needs my help.'

'Oh, aye,' Donna said, her tone sharp. Simon could almost see her in his mind's eye, leaning forward at her desk, tucking a stray strand of hair behind her ear. *Tell me more*, the gesture said. 'And what manner of crap has Connor stepped into this time?'

Simon had bitten back the urge to laugh. *If only you knew*. It was a story big enough to lead the news cycle for days, maybe even weeks. And if Donna got a whiff of what was going on, of the story the two MI5 officers had told Simon, she would make sure she was in front of the camera for every report. He thought briefly of Jen, wondered if she would reach out to Donna, despite the warnings of the bearded agent, who had reluctantly admitted his name was Spires.

Standing there in that car park in Dundee, Paulie looming behind them like an approaching storm front, Spires had told them that Connor's deceased friend, Danny Gillespie, had been on government watch lists for years due to his work on the Troubles. As he was delving into sensitive areas, including the treatment of prisoners and alleged acts of murder by British forces, his work was being closely monitored, and his associates, both during his work and afterwards, were a matter of close scrutiny.

So when Danny died, and three paramilitaries plus a former PSNI officer called Connor Fraser turned up at his funeral, it was of some interest. There was a belief, Spires said, that Danny had stumbled on some information that could embarrass governments on both sides of the Irish Sea and, potentially, rock the foundations of the Good Friday Agreement. Simon had pushed Spires on this, trying to get an answer on what that could be. To his credit, Spires was refreshingly blunt in his answer: 'I can't and won't tell you that. But we have good reason to believe that your friend Fraser is now in possession of it.'

'So that's why you tried to scoop him up in Belfast?' Simon had asked, thinking back to that first call from Connor. 'You cloned my phone and lured him into a trap, so your men could scoop him up, and get him to hand over whatever you think he has.'

'That wasn't us, Mr McCartney,' he had said, his eyes as cold and impersonal as his voice. 'I've checked and I can assure you that no agents were tasked to blackball Mr Fraser. Neither were any agents authorised or engaged in the use of Mr Fraser's grandmother to blackmail him into handing himself in. I assume you understand what that means?'

'It means he's caught in the middle,' Simon had said. 'It means you guys want what Connor has, but you're not the only interested parties. So, who do you think is after him? Paramilitaries who want whatever he has for, what, blackmail? Political extortion?'

Spires had flashed a you-know-better-than-to-ask smile that was about as legitimate as Simon suspected his name was. 'You know I can't tell you that, but whoever they are, they're organised, professional and determined. Your friend is in trouble, and the sooner he turns himself in to us, the better.'

Simon had looked at Jen, her face a plea aimed straight at his heart.

'I'll go to Belfast, get him to come in,' Simon said. 'But, in return, I want some assurances. The guard on Ida Fraser, you keep that in place until this is over, twenty-four hours a day, seven days a week. You keep an eye on Jen here,' he saw the warning in her eyes, course corrected, 'as soon as she gets back from her business trip to Aberdeen. Agreed?'

Spires had made a show of considering Simon's deal, then gave up the pretence and accepted. So Simon had headed home, grabbed what he needed, then phoned Donna.

'You'd better make this up to me,' she had told him, and the engagement ring flashed across his mind again.

'Promise I will. Love you,' he had said.

'Love you too. Be safe,' Donna said, then ended the call.

He looked at the dark, empty face of the phone. Be safe? It was a nice idea, but whatever he was stepping into, Simon knew it would not be safe. For him or Connor.

He was still considering that when the phone leaped into life again: Connor's burner number.

Simon took a deep breath. Looked across the departure lounge of the airport. All those people engaged in busy nonsense, shopping and eating and living, their only worry being the amount of sun cream they had with them and whether the kids would stay quiet on the flight. Normal, domestic, peaceful lives. He wondered if he and Donna would ever have one. He wanted it, but was it possible for a man like him? A man whose best friend was Connor Fraser, who seemed to have an almost supernatural talent for attracting trouble.

He let out the breath. Fantasy was for other people. Hit answer on the phone and took his friend's call.

CHAPTER 21

Donna Blake didn't like secrets. She had been one when she had carried out an affair with Mark who had scuttled back to his wife as soon as she had told him she was pregnant, leaving her with a son to raise on her own. She had seen secrets destroy lives, reputations, marriages. And she had seen, in the case of Andrew's father, how secrets could kill.

So, the question she had was simple – what was Simon not telling her?

He had told her that Connor was in Belfast to attend the funeral of an old university friend. How had that suddenly evolved into a dash to the airport and a flight to Belfast because 'Connor needs my help'? She felt the sting of anger and self-admonishment. She was a reporter: it was her job to ask questions, get answers. Instead, when he had told her he was leaving and wouldn't see her that night, she had reacted like a spurned teenager, gone along with it and forgotten who she was.

But it was, Donna knew, exactly because of who she was that she had reacted in that way.

She hadn't been looking to fall in love. After her fling with Mark Sneddon had crashed and burned, she had moved from Glasgow to Stirling and started again. She had bought the flat she now sat in, got a reporting job at a local radio station and started teaching journalism at Stirling University part time. When a decapitated body was found in Stirling, Donna had pounced on the story, used it to get her current job as a Scotland reporter for Sky News. She had settled into a routine, raising her son with the help of her parents, and slowly building a career. She was content to be a single mum, didn't need or want anyone else to complicate the picture she had painted for herself.

And then she had met Simon McCartney.

It had been casual at first, the odd drink, dinner. The usual. But, over time, their relationship had grown and changed. She couldn't remember the first time he'd told her he loved her, couldn't remember when she'd first said it to him. But there'd been no awkward silence when it was said, no feeling of jumping off a cliff. Just an acceptance that that was the way things were with them. She was comfortable with Simon, at ease with him in a way she had never experienced before. From his constant bad jokes to his easygoing manner with Andrew to enthusiasm and dedication in the bedroom, everything about her relationship with Simon just . . . worked. And in an effort not to cause problems, not to upset what they had, she had gone quiet the moment he had said he was going to Belfast.

Self-loathing bled into her recriminations. She had promised she would not change herself for anyone, at work or in her personal life, but that was exactly what she had done.

She stood up from the couch, headed for the small box room at the back of the flat that acted as her home office. With Andrew at her parents', as she had expected to be out with Simon, she had the afternoon and the rest of the night to herself. She would pour herself a glass of red, then crack open the laptop.

And she would not stop until she had found out exactly what Connor Fraser had just dragged Simon into.

CHAPTER 22

After calling Simon, Connor fell into a stupefied daze, as though his friend had reached out of the phone and hammered a left hook into his jaw. He supposed, in a way, he had.

The revelation, via Ford, that government agents were interested in whatever Danny Gillespie had made sure Connor got if he died was bad enough. That the information, whatever it was, had put third parties on Connor's track, third parties that he had seen could be lethally efficient and had no qualms about using potentially deadly force, was almost too much for him to process – like a Neanderthal trying to comprehend particle physics.

He suppressed the urge to go back to the pub, make the Guinness his starter and move on to the main course of whichever whisky he could find. But he needed to think – and to do so, he had to get moving.

He put the City Hall to his back and got walking. Nowhere specific, just moving his legs, as though momentum would power his cognitive processes. He didn't want to get too far from the city centre – Simon had said he was flying into Belfast City, which meant a taxi into the centre of town. The easiest drop-off point was the Europa Hotel in front of the bus station. Known as the most bombed hotel in the world during the Troubles, the Europa had been a preferred target for paramilitaries because of its status as a local landmark, and a symbol of investment in Northern Ireland. The message was clear:

you do business here, you support the British state, the enemy, you're a target.

After Simon's call, Connor could sympathise.

He thought back to the men who had tried to grab him behind the pub on the Falls Road. The way they had moved, and the weapons they'd carried, had put the suspicion into Connor's mind that they were either government or plain-clothes police. But, if what Simon said was true, no official agency had sanctioned an operation to blackball Connor and take him off the street. So who were they? Former soldiers or police officers who had gone private, taking a more militaristic route with their skills after service than Connor had? And if that was the case, who had sent them? Hiring professionals hardly seemed like Bobby McCandish, Colm O'Brien or Brendan Walsh's style. No, they would just order a few foot soldiers to grab their guns and balaclavas and hit the streets. So who?

He pulled the watch from his pocket, looked at it. Squeezed it hard between his fingers, as if he could wring out the secrets it held with enough pressure. But it yielded nothing, just patiently ticked, seconds accruing into minutes, transmuting into hours, marking days, which were ticked off on the date dial on the watch face.

Dates.

The thought hit Connor with an almost physical force. He stopped abruptly, heard a muttered curse as the person walking behind him had to take a sudden sidestep to stop themselves colliding with his back. He muttered an apology and stood into the side of the pavement, tight up against the wall of a shuttered office.

He slipped the strap from the watch, studied the back. Specifically, the serial number that didn't match the one Robbie had found: C325 071887. Ignored the first four characters, concentrated on the last six digits – 071887. What was it Robbie had said? The watch was made for soldiers in the D-Day landings. Some of those soldiers would have been American. And Americans wrote dates differently from the British, the month coming first, not the day. Connor looked at the numbers again: 07 18 87 didn't make sense, but if you read it in the American format, with the first four digits turned round, you got 18 07 87, 18 July 1987. Connor stared at the back of the watch. It was a stretch, but he felt instinctively he was on to something. But even if he was, what did it mean? And what was 'C325'?

He pocketed the watch and set off, then stopped. He had, unthinkingly, walked back into the city, to the entrance to the CastleCourt shopping centre. Looking up, he could see the Cash Converters where he had bought the laptop. Had that really only been a couple of days ago? It felt like a lifetime.

He got moving again; his plan was to stake out the Europa from the Crown Bar across the road, a favourite with tourists and locals alike, thanks to its ornate Victorian-tiled walls and floors, private snug booths and gas lighting that still worked. He would hide in plain sight, see if he could track down anything about the date he had found on the back of the watch. If, that was, there was anything to find. But before he could get into his stride, his phone buzzed in his pocket. He fished it out, cursed under his breath. With everything Simon had told him, he had forgotten the assignment he had given Robbie to check into Danny's movements when he'd been back in Belfast before he died.

'Robbie,' he said, as he answered the call, 'thanks for getting back to me. Any luck?'

'Aye, you could say that,' Robbie replied, his tone filled with the almost childish enthusiasm Connor knew meant he had found something juicy. 'Didn't take long to get into his work diary. Encryption was fairly standard. Would have expected better from a university holding a lot of personal information, to be honest, but—'

'Robbie,' Connor said, his voice a warning. The last thing he needed was one of Robbie's tangential rants.

'Sorry, boss,' Robbie said, his voice deflating a little with disappointment, like a child denied the chance to show the class his new toy. 'Anyway, I got into his work diary. Nothing there for the period he was in Belfast preceding his death.'

'But I thought you said—' Connor started.

'I did, boss,' Robbie said, pride reinflating his tone. 'See, his diary was synced to his phone, which was linked to his iCloud account. Wasn't a big leap to get into that and his personal diary. And there it was, a week before he died, a meeting at an address just off the Falls

Road with an A. Fielding. Couple of other things, a time for the meeting, and something else, not sure what it means yet, but I'll have a wee dig around while I'm looking at his other files.'

'What was it?' Connor asked.

'I think it's a reference or something,' Robbie said. 'C325. Not sure what it refers to yet, but I'll do my best to find out, boss. Promise.'

CHAPTER 23

The wave of relief Connor felt when he saw Simon emerge from a taxi outside the Europa Hotel was only counterbalanced by the sudden stab of guilt in his gut. His friend's head was on a swivel, shoulders tensed, face set. He moved with the fluid grace of a ballerina, stepping around people as he took in every angle a possible assailant could attack from.

So much for a happy homecoming.

Connor watched as he crossed the street, heading for the Crown Bar. He stepped out from the small alleyway beside the bar that he had been watching from, slipped in behind Simon.

'I wouldn't go in there,' he said, leaning in close, 'I hear they let some right dodgy bastards in.'

Simon whirled, his whole body tensing and, in the second before recognition bled into his eyes, Connor felt the chill of the void staring back at him. This was the Simon he had seen on a few occasions. The cold, detached professional who would not blink at inflicting serious harm on anyone who got in his way.

'Connor!' he said, throwing his arms around him. 'Jesus Christ, man, you near gave me a heart attack.'

'Sorry,' Connor said, returning the hug, relief overwhelming guilt. 'Couldn't help myself. Thanks for coming, Simon. I appreciate it.'

Simon pushed Connor to arm's length, studied him, eyes falling on the bruise to his left temple. 'Sure it's not a bother,' he said. 'After all,' he nodded to Connor's temple, 'look what happens when I leave you out in the big bad world all alone.'

'Aye,' Connor said, rubbing the injury and stirring the ache back to life, 'it's been a hell of a few days.'

'Well, a crowded bar with a clear line of sight to the entrance sounds like just the place to tell me all about it,' Simon said. ''Mon away in and we can catch up. First pint's on you.'

They entered the pub, made their way through the throng to the bar. It was a huge, altar-like construction, with ornate cream porcelain tiles offset by a massive slab of red granite that served as the bar top. Connor flagged down a barman who was all tattoos and smiles, and ordered two pints of Guinness.

'Jesus,' Simon said, as Connor produced a wad of notes to pay, 'do I even want to know where that came from?'

'Nah,' Connor said, with a smile. 'You really don't. Besides, it's like you said. You leave me to fend for myself, and look what happens.'

They took their drinks to a table that stood outside the dark wooden panelling of one of the snugs that lined the wall of the bar. Without speaking, Simon dragged his stool round to the side of the table facing the door.

'So,' he said, as he sat down, 'official business first. The agents back in Stirling who were following me think I'm here to bring you home to their loving embrace. To hell with that. That aside, this is an interesting wee jam you've got us into, isn't it?'

Connor smiled at that. *Us*. Typical Simon. There was no question in his mind. His friend was in trouble. That made it his trouble. And he would do whatever it took to keep Connor safe. What, he wondered, had he done to deserve such a friend? And how could he ever repay that loyalty?

'Aye, well, it just got more interesting,' Connor said, taking out Danny's watch and passing it to Simon. 'Danny's mother gave this to me at the funeral. I'm not sure, but I think it's a message. Something linked to a date back in 1987. And a reference to a meeting Danny had here just off the Falls not long before he died.'

'That's a hell of a leap,' Simon said, turning the watch over in his hand. 'You got anything to back it up?'

'Well,' Connor said, 'I didn't until I spoke to Robbie a wee while ago and . . .'

It was so brief Connor almost dismissed it. But something flashed across Simon's face at the mention of Robbie's name, as though Connor had just reminded him of something important he had forgotten.

'What?' he asked. 'Simon, what is it?'

Simon handed the watch back and reached for his pint. 'Ack, nothing. Just something I forgot to ask Robbie to do.'

The knot of ice that was forming in Connor's gut seemed to lurch. Simon wouldn't look into his eyes, as if doing so would unlock some terrible dark admission.

'Simon, don't bullshit me, especially not now, in the midst of all this. What is it? What's wrong?'

Simon took a deep draw from his glass, then set it aside. He clenched his mouth tightly shut, the muscles in his jaw bulging, eyes darting. It was like watching a computer working in real time, calculating possible scenarios and outcomes of what he was about to say.

'First,' he said, after a moment, 'the situation is in hand, okay? She's safe. The suits that were following Paulie and me have put a guard on her, and Ford has confirmed it's in effect, and he's got eyes on her as well, okay?'

'She?' Connor said, voice flat. 'Jen? What's wrong with Jen? Is she—'

Simon held up a hand, then fished in his pocket with the free one. 'It's not Jen,' he said, the words etching pain into his eyes as he spoke, ageing him. 'It's your gran. Jen got a call from the home, telling her Ida had had a wee turn. They couldn't get you as you'd dumped your phone, and Jen was listed as a next-of-kin contact. I went to see your gran. She's fine, just got her memory a little more scrambled than normal. But when I visited her, I found this.' He handed Connor the folded sheet of newspaper he had pulled out of his pocket. Simon hesitated, as though unsure if he should say more. Then he spoke, voice soft. 'It rattled her a little, Connor. Might have been what made her memory slip.'

Connor took it with numb hands, unfolded it. It was a page from

The Times, the crossword section his gran loved. Seeing her spidery writing in some of the clue boxes made his heart twist. But what made it worse was the message scrawled in an altogether more aggressive hand in the blank section below the main puzzle:

> We can get to your gran, Mr Fraser. We can get to anyone. We know what you have. We want it back. Do it, or things will get very ugly.
> You have 12 hours.

Instinctively, Connor glanced at his own watch. He opened his mouth to speak, found no words were available. Scenarios flashed through his mind. Getting into a taxi. Now. Straight to the airport. Next flight home. Get to Stirling. Then find the bastards who had delivered this obscenity to his gran and rip them apart with his bare hands.

'I, ah, I was going to get Robbie to run that phone number,' Simon pointed to the numbers below the message, 'but then things kicked off a bit. Trust me, Connor, she's safe. Ford's on the case, and Paulie is going to look in on her, as well as keeping an eye on Jen. Whoever these fuckers are, they're never getting near Ida again.'

Connor looked back at the newspaper, still unable to speak beyond the ball of revolted outrage that had formed in his throat. 'Who . . .' He coughed, as though he was choking on something. In a way, he was. 'Who the hell are these people? And what could they want with this bloody watch?'

'No idea,' Simon said. 'But from what you said, we've got a place to look. You said Robbie found details of a meeting your friend had here, something linked to whatever that number is on the watch. So why don't we try that as a starting point? I don't know about you, but I'm tired of only having questions. How about we start getting some answers?'

CHAPTER 24

Jen collapsed onto her couch, letting her crutch clatter to the floor. She stared up at the ceiling, forced herself to breathe through the pain in her back and hips as the physiotherapist had taught her. Felt the anger swell to meet the pain, the fury at being left in this state by a driver who'd had a place to be and hadn't minded if she was in his way. There was a sudden moment of vertigo, a fragmentary impression of being hit by an immense force, then the world pinwheeling around her until . . .

She forced the memory back. What was done was done. Self-pity wasn't going to make it better. 'Play the cards you're dealt,' her father had always told her. The problem was, although she knew which cards she held, Jen had no idea what game she was playing.

After the incident in Dundee, and the revelation that Connor had, once again, invited chaos into his life, Jen had had Paulie drive the rest of the way to Aberdeen. He knew enough to keep quiet, only starting to talk when they were just outside the city. He explained that he had arranged a meeting with an Angela Barr, the owner of three hotels across Aberdeen. They were a front to launder the money Angela and her husband, Iain, made from his side of their business empire: bringing drugs into Aberdeen, and Scotland, through the port and the crane-hire company Iain ran from there. Paulie had explained it was through the Barrs that Jen's father, Duncan, had forged his connections and the business dealings that kept MacKenzie Haulage afloat.

The set-up was simple: the Barrs would bring in the drugs, Iain's cranes unloading ships docked at the harbour and, helpfully, missing some items from the manifests. These would be stored in a warehouse at the port. A warehouse that, conveniently, Duncan MacKenzie had rented from the Barrs and used to load his trucks with goods delivered to the port that he would then transport across the country via MacKenzie Haulage. The business had been discreet, methodical and, until Duncan died, extremely lucrative. But when her father had died, killed, mutilated and dumped in the loch at Stirling University, the Barrs had decided to move their business elsewhere.

Jen's job was to get them to move it back.

Paulie had driven them to the prearranged meeting location, a small townhouse hotel set in manicured grounds on the outskirts of the city. On arrival, they were shown to an anonymous-looking conference room, and Jen was hit with the sudden, fleeting impression that she was walking into a job interview. In a way, she supposed she was. It was just that this one might claim a bit of her soul in the process.

Sitting behind a large table, a bag worth four figures sitting on one side of her and a carafe of coffee on the other, Angela Barr looked every inch the polished hotelier, from the tailored charcoal grey business suit to the subtle make-up that accentuated the aquiline elegance of her features and downplayed the delicate web of crow's feet around her grey-green eyes. They had flicked to Paulie as he entered the room, something that could almost pass for a smile crossing her lips.

'Paulie,' she said, her accent soft, gentle, as well manicured as her hands. 'Good to see you again. How you keeping, these days?'

To Jen's shock, Paulie had sounded almost bashful as he spoke. 'Aye, no' bad, Angela. Just trying to do my best for Jen here now that Duncan is gone. Which is why we're here . . .'

The smile flicked into life again, then died as Angela held up a hand and turned her gaze to Jen. It was like being pinned by a spotlight.

'Paulie never was one for small-talk,' she said, folding her hands in front of her. 'But he is a good man. Loyal. Discreet. Efficient. Which is why you're here. What can I do for you?'

Jen had felt a sudden wave of uncertainty. How had it come to this?

How had she gone from being a personal trainer with a child on the way to sitting in a room with a drug-trafficker, about to beg for her help to save her murdered father's business? And just why was she trying so hard to save that business anyway? To honour his legacy? Or to maintain the lie that he'd been a respectable businessman, an employer in Stirling who had built an empire for his family and brought jobs to those who needed them?

'Please, I'm Jen,' she said. Something in Angela's eyes told her the offer of a handshake would not be appreciated. 'I'm, ah . . . I'm here because you had certain business arrangements with my dad, and I'd like to see what we could do about re-establishing some of those contracts.'

Angela's eyes moved slowly to Paulie. She stared at him, then gave the slightest nod. Jen wondered what Paulie had done behind her back. Given the nod? Broken out the semaphore flags? Drawn his gun? Whatever it was, it worked.

Angela sighed, as though the meeting was boring her. 'I assume,' she said, pouring a coffee and sliding it across the table to Jen, 'you mean the items your father distributed to us from Aberdeen docks. I'm afraid there's not much I can do about that. The contracts have been reassigned. This business cannot operate in a vacuum, and we needed to move on quickly.'

Move on, Jen thought, a flare of contempt for Angela's callous indifference igniting in her chest. *Try moving on when it's your father who's been killed.* 'That's why I'm here,' she said, her voice as dark and bitter as the coffee in front of her. 'You see, I want to move on with my life as well. And part of that moving on is to ensure the future of my dad's company. A company I watched him build over decades. I understand that your working relationship with him was lucrative and, well, discreet. All I'm saying is that our, ah, networks are still fully in place, and we could start moving your products tomorrow, if needed. You know us, know the company. You said yourself, Paulie is loyal. I'm asking for some of that loyalty now. Give us a chance to prove we're the same MacKenzie Haulage you worked with before. One run. One distribution. Paulie will oversee all of it. If you're satisfied, we can talk about a more long-term arrangement.'

Angela had studied Jen for a moment. It was like being observed by a shark.

'Paulie,' she said, her gaze not moving, 'what do you say about all of this?'

Jen heard Paulie shuffling behind her, then taking a position on her left-hand side. Out of the corner of her eye, she saw him lean forward, his shovel-like scarred hands falling on the desk, reducing it to a plaything in a doll's house.

'I think,' he said, no bashful coyness in his voice now, 'that this is the daughter of Duncan MacKenzie. You know, the Duncan MacKenzie who floated you and Iain the cash you needed to start up back in the day. The Duncan MacKenzie who sent me up here for a couple of weeks in 2014 when the Drylaw boys were looking to muscle in on your business. The Duncan MacKenzie who kept the Minto business . . .'

Angela's eyes widened as her cheeks coloured. For a moment, Jen saw the woman behind the confident façade, the woman who wore her designer suit and perfect make-up like armour.

And that woman was terrified of what Paulie might say next, what secrets he could reveal.

'All right, that's enough,' she said. 'I get the point.' She glowered at Paulie, the only sound in the room Paulie's bull-like breathing at Jen's side. Then her gaze snapped back to Jen. 'Okay,' she said, lifting her own coffee cup. Jen briefly wondered if she was going to throw it at her. 'Paulie makes a good point. Loyalty counts for something, no matter what our politicians and the newspapers might try to tell us. One run, Ms MacKenzie. We'll liaise with Paulie, just like we used to. If it goes well, we'll talk.'

'Thank you,' Jen said, the words somehow bitter in her mouth. She rose, leaned on the table, swallowed the flare of agony from her back, determined Angela Barr would not see it. Offered her hand, which Angela took in a surprisingly tender shake. Left without another word.

Outside the conference room, she had leaned on her crutch, her hips adding to the chorus of pain from her back, turning it into a hellish symphony.

'You okay?' Paulie asked, stepping towards her. 'We can get a room, here or elsewhere. Rest up, head back tomorrow.'

'No,' she had said, using the pain to focus her resolve. 'I want to get home. There's still all this crap with Connor to deal with, remember?'

The small-talk on the drive home had exhausted itself quickly, and they fell into silence, Jen lost in her own thoughts. About Connor, the danger he was in. She had pushed him away because of the violence his work as a security consultant brought into his life, moved back to her own flat instead of into the mobility-adapted house they had bought together. Did what she had just done with Angela Barr make that decision hypocritical? She had agreed to assist with drug-trafficking. And although her side of the business was more a matter of logistics than street dealing, they both led to the same place: a pill, powder or needle feeding an addiction that could turn on you at any moment, destroy your life before ultimately taking it.

Paulie had dropped her off at the flat, promised he would be keeping an eye to make sure she was safe. She was too tired to argue, just trudged up the stairs and collapsed onto the couch.

And now, sitting there, she wondered what she should do next. She thought back to that car park in Dundee. What had Simon said to the two agents? *Donna Blake. You might have seen her. Reporter for Sky News.*

She turned the idea over in her head. Considered. 'Why not?' she asked the silence of the room, then reached for her phone.

CHAPTER 25

The address Robbie had provided for Connor was on Iveagh Drive, just off the Falls Road. It was, Connor thought, not that different from the safe-house he was in, a narrow street lined with red-brick terraced homes, black wrought-iron fences topping the low walls they huddled behind. Cars were bumped on pavements like anti-tank fortifications on the beach. You can walk these streets, the cars said, but don't think we're going to make it easy for you.

They approached cautiously, though the danger was minimal. An electoral roll check had shown that the sole occupant of the property was an Arthur James Fielding, born in 1944. Unless Arthur answered the door with a sawn-off shotgun, Connor thought he and Simon could take him.

He walked up the path to the front door, Simon standing guard at the gate. Rang the doorbell, waited. Heard the shuffling of feet, saw a shadow form and grow bigger through the cross-hatched rippled glass that made up the top half of the door.

A chain rattled clear, a lock clunked, and the door swung open to reveal a broad-shouldered man who appeared to be listing to the left, leaning on a heavy wooden cane. His heavily lined face and waxy, liver-spotted skin told Connor that his eighty-one years on the planet had been more a war of attrition than a life well lived, but his eyes told a different story. Magnified by thick glasses, they were a pale, almost translucent blue that glinted with mischief, like those of a boy who had been told a risqué joke.

'Yes, son,' he said. 'Can I help ye?'

'Mr Fielding?' Connor said. 'I'm Connor Fraser. I was a friend of Dr Daniel Gillespie. I was wondering if my friend and I could talk to you for a wee minute?'

Fielding's eyes raked Connor, as if his face was a map and he was looking for a memorable landmark. Then he smiled, showing small teeth so white and uniform that they had to be dentures. 'Oh, aye,' he said. 'Dr Gillespie. Nice lad. I read about what happened to him in the papers. Terrible thing. Come on away in. I'll make us a cup of tea.'

Connor turned, nodded to Simon, who came up the path facing the road. They were led down a small, narrow hallway into a living room that was groaning under the weight of heavy oak furniture and a large TV bolted about a heavy stone fireplace. The mantelpiece above the fire was lined with pictures of a young couple in a variety of locations: a beach, a pub, a forest somewhere, standing outside a shop, loaves of bread in their hands. In each picture, Connor could see Arthur Fielding's twinkling blue eyes staring back at him, undiminished by the passage of years.

'Maureen,' Fielding said, as though reading Connor's thoughts. 'Met her when I was nineteen at the dancing. Never looked anywhere else.' There was something in his voice that was at once more profound and more fleeting than pride. 'Cancer took her three years ago. Bastarding thing. But at least I have these,' he gestured at the hearth, cane in hand, like a punctuation mark, 'to remember her by. Now, take a seat, I'll get that tea.'

Connor opened his mouth, closed it. Refusing a host's tea in Northern Ireland was about as socially acceptable as taking a dump on their carpet.

Fielding disappeared and returned a few minutes later with a tray holding a teapot, three mugs and a plate crammed with biscuits.

'Here,' Simon said. 'Let me give you a wee hand with that.'

Fielding smiled. 'It's fine, son. My leg's been no good to me for almost forty years now. I'm used to getting about.' With surprising grace, he laid the tray on a coffee-table in front of the fireplace, plonked himself down in a chair and gestured for Connor and Simon to sit on a couch running along the back wall of the room.

Fielding busied himself pouring the tea, then snatched a biscuit and sat back in his chair. 'Now then,' he said, 'you wanted to talk to me about Dr Gillespie. Nice lad. Terrible shame about what happened to him.'

The casual repetition of 'nice lad' sent a chill through Connor, his mind throwing up images of his gran. Was she all right? Was she aware of where and who she was? Or had the dementia claimed her again, dragged her into the labyrinth of her past, turning the present into a smeared blur of half-remembered conversations? He needed to finish this, get home to her. And Jen.

'Mr Fielding,' he started, dragging his thoughts back to the moment, 'I understand Danny wanted to speak to you about something that happened during the Troubles. Could you maybe tell us what that was?'

Fielding's face slackened, the mischief in his eyes dulling, as though a massive shadow had fallen over them. Then he coughed, sipped his tea, and seemed to draw himself into his chair, take comfort in it.

'Aye,' he said. 'I remember that. Nice lad. Not nice what he wanted to talk about, though.'

'And what was that, sir?' Simon encouraged, the calm in his voice a counterpoint to the raging impatience Connor felt.

'Oh, that's easy, son. He wanted to talk to me about the worst day of my life.'

Connor exchanged a glance with Simon, who shrugged. Turned back to Fielding, saw the mischief had returned to his eyes, rekindled by his delivery of a melodramatic cliffhanger. He had a captive audience now, and he knew it.

'I was a baker,' he said simply, raising his cane and gesturing towards the fireplace, the picture of him and his wife holding loaves. 'Family business. Served this area for nigh-on a century, the business passed down from my grandfather to my da to me. Problem was, I inherited the business in the 1980s, and that wasn't a good time to be in business in Northern Ireland.'

'What happened?' Simon asked, before Connor could speak.

'You'll be too young to remember, but the eighties were a bad time in the Troubles,' Fielding said, settling back into his chair. 'The IRA was running a bombing campaign, both here and over the water. Car bombs were popular, along with attacks on RUC bases around the Province. They needed vehicles, you see, and my wee baker's van was just the dab.'

'They stole it from you?' Connor asked.

Fielding gave a chuckle. 'Not at first,' he said. 'I was in the pub one night, approached by a fella and asked to donate my van "to the cause". Well, I'll admit I was tempted, I'm no fan of those flag-waving, God Save the King arsehole Brits, but I said no. Needed the van for my business. He was polite, bought me another pint, told me to stay well.' Fielding took a shaky breath, closed his eyes, tilted his head up to the ceiling, then looked back to Connor and Simon, eyes dead, empty things.

'Two days later, they turned up at my door. Kicked it in. Tied up Maureen, threatened to rape her and worse if I didn't hand over the keys. So I did, no argument.' He shook his head, as though he was a punter in a bookie's who had just watched the favourite in the four-twenty come in last, taking his life savings with it. 'Bastards still blew my left knee out with a shotgun. Said I was lucky it was only the one knee, not a full six-pack, knees, elbows, ankles. A lesson, they said, in loyalty to the cause and the country, and an example of their mercy as patriots.'

'So they used the van for, what, a car bombing?' Connor asked. 'Did you ever find out which one?'

'Oh, it was worse than that, son, much worse,' Fielding said, looking into his cup as though it was a portal to the past. 'You ever hear of the Carryduff massacre?'

Connor shook his head, looked at Simon, who mirrored his action.

'Told you you'd be too young,' Fielding said, a sad smile touching his lips. 'The twentieth of July, 1987. Three members of the IRA launched a mortar attack on the RUC police station in Carryduff. It's a wee place, on the southern outskirts of the city. It was one of the worst attacks of the Troubles. Seven dead, forty-three injured, some of them losing legs and arms, others horribly burned. I was just a baker, for

Christ's sake, and they used my wee van to do that. Bastards.' There were tears in his eyes now. Connor couldn't tell if they were from regret or anger.

'Hold on,' Simon said. 'You said this happened on the twentieth of July?' He looked at Connor. 'But the file Gillespie had was marked for the eighteenth. So how does that fit?'

'The eighteenth?' Fielding cut in. 'That was the day they stole the van. The Saturday morning. First thing. Takes time to mount mortars into a Ford Transit, son. They needed the weekend to get it ready.'

'Aye, fair play,' Simon said, chastened.

Connor smiled, leaned forward. 'Mr Fielding, do the names Bobby McCandish, Colm O'Brien or Brendan Walsh mean anything to you?'

It was as though a switch had been flicked. The humour in Fielding's eyes was gone, drowned by cold hatred. Connor could see a killer in those eyes. Worse, he could see the hunger, the need, to kill that his words had aroused in Arthur Fielding. It was as if Connor had unchained a door in the basement of Fielding's soul, and let the demons he had locked away down there pour out. And those demons were hungry.

'McCandish and O'Brien,' he said, his voice as dead as his eyes. 'Oh, I fucking knew them all right. They were the bastards that broke into the house that night. I mean, they wore hoods, didn't they, but the arrogant bastards were always in the pub up the road. Knew it was them the moment they opened their mouths. It was . . .' Connor saw a single tear escape the barricade of Fielding's glasses and slip down his cheek '. . . it was O'Brien who threatened to rape Maureen. Tied her up, put his hand up her skirt, made me watch. Said she . . .' He closed his eyes, head shaking as he tried to banish the memory.

'I'm sorry,' Connor said, feeling bad at stirring up such anguish in an old man.

Fielding gave a twitch of a smile, took off his glasses and swiped at his eyes with a hand that wasn't quite steady. 'Not your fault, son,' he said. 'My bad luck to live in a war zone. What was that other name? Walsh? Brian Walsh?'

'Brendan,' Connor corrected gently.

Fielding made a show of searching his thoughts. 'Nah, can't say I know that name, sorry,' he said, after a moment.

'No problem,' Connor said. 'One last question, then we'll get out of your hair. When you met Danny, what was his interest in what happened to you?'

Fielding's eyes seemed to soften again. 'Dr Gillespie? Ah, nice lad. He wanted to talk to me about the effect of what had happened, you know, up here.' He raised a finger, tapped his temple quickly. 'What I thought would help other people who had been through a traumatic event, whether I'd ever got any counselling.' He gave a short laugh, a mix of humour and regret. 'I told him that the only counselling we had around here was at the bottom of a bottle. We keep our mouths shut and keep going. What other choice do we have?'

Connor felt a shiver of disappointment. More pieces of the puzzle, still no clue as to what the picture he was trying to develop looked like. 'Well, thanks for your time,' he said, making to stand up. 'We'll get out of your—'

'Time,' Fielding muttered. 'Aye, time. That was the one odd thing Dr Gillespie did say.'

'What was that?' Connor said, as a thrill of electricity arced through him.

'Time. He asked if the army or RUC had been back in touch after they took our statements, made sure we weren't part of the bombings, that sort of thing. What did he call it? Pastoral care, that was it. I told him about one visit I got, about three weeks after everything. Some colonel or something, wasn't sure of the rank, but he had one of those uniforms that was designed to impress, you know?'

'Yeah,' Connor said. 'I don't suppose you remember his name?'

'No. Like I told Dr Gillespie, he never gave a name. Only thing I really remember about him was he was tall, dark hair, moustache that looked like he'd been born with it. Had a tic as well. Was looking at his watch every two minutes, like I was wasting his time when it was him that had knocked on my door. Really nice watch it was, too. Looked old. Black face, gold numbers on it. One of those fancy straps. Aye, Dr Gillespie was very, very interested to hear about that watch. Couldn't see why at the time. I mean, it was a nice piece but, at the end of the day, a watch is just a watch, isn't it?'

CHAPTER 26

It wasn't a call Donna had expected but, thinking about it, it was one she should have made. After deciding to find out what the hell was going on in Belfast, she had disappeared down a virtual rabbit hole and found . . . nothing. She had the obituary for Connor's friend, a Dr Daniel Gillespie, and it hadn't taken long to locate his CV and biography on the City University website. But there was nothing in the cuts or news sites Donna could see from Belfast that would justify Simon dropping everything and jumping on the first plane to Northern Ireland.

But then Jen MacKenzie had called, and everything had changed. She had suggested meeting at her flat for a bottle of wine and a catch-up. It had been a routine for them since Donna and Simon had got together, and had drifted over the border between current affairs and historical fact when Jen's relationship with Connor had hit a rough patch. Donna wanted to help, could see that Jen and Connor loved each other, but she knew it wasn't her place and, ultimately, there was nothing she could do. The intensity and sudden violence that had thrown her and Simon together after one of Connor's cases had driven a wedge between Connor and Jen. Only they could decide if they could overcome it.

Half an hour after she had called, Donna was outside Jen's building on the outskirts of Stirling. As she climbed the stairs to Jen's floor, she thought about the house less than ten minutes from the flat that had once been Connor's and was now Simon's. It was a large, sprawling property, a grand old sandstone and granite villa that Connor had bought and spent months adapting to make it as accessible for Jen as possible. But instead of Jen moving in, it had lain mostly empty. From what Simon had told her, Connor barely stayed there, as if the ghosts of possibility that haunted the freshly decorated and renovated rooms were too much for him to bear.

The door to Jen's flat was ajar when Donna reached it. She knocked, calling as she did.

'Come on in,' Jen said, and Donna could hear the tapping of her crutch on the laminate hallway floor as she walked towards the door.

Donna stepped inside, and Jen's face lit up with the familiar, infectious smile. But there was weariness in it now, a fading of its vitality, like a marquee sign with some missing light bulbs.

'Donna,' she said, closing the distance between them and giving her a hug that told Donna she had lost weight. 'It's been too long! Come on in. As promised, dinner is on me. I've got the best takeaway menus in Stirling waiting on the coffee-table.'

Donna smiled at the joke, shrugged off her jacket, then held up the bag she was carrying. 'Red or red?' she asked.

'Red it is. I'll get the glasses. See you in the living room.'

As promised, the coffee-table was awash with takeaway menus. On a side table next to the sofa, she spotted a picture – Jen and Connor before the car crash, in the gym Jen used to work at. They were smiling into the camera, glistening with health and a thin sheen of sweat. Donna wondered what the people in the picture would think of the people they had become. Would they recognise themselves? Or would they scoff, unable to believe life could be so random and cruel to two people whose future had looked so bright and certain?

'So,' Jen said, as she walked into the room, two glasses hanging by their stems from her left hand, the other on her crutch. 'How you doing? I bet Andrew's getting big now.'

'Yeah,' Donna said, smiling. 'Too big. Can't keep him in clothes or out of trouble. At least my folks have him tonight.'

Jen set the glasses on the coffee-table then folded herself into the couch, a flash of pain tightening her features.

Donna poured the wine and slid a glass over to Jen. 'Cheers,' she said, raising hers and clinking it with Jen's.

They drank. Donna noticed Jen looking at her over the lip of her glass, uncertainty in her eyes. It was as though she had planned this moment but, now it was here, she was unsure if or how she should proceed. First rule of interviewing, Donna thought, open the door for them.

'So,' she said, 'how are things with the business? Last time we spoke, you said you were trying to get back some of your dad's old contracts. If it would help, I can speak to some folk in the local press, get a profile piece on the company. Local employer, new era with daughter taking over family business, that sort of thing.'

Jen flashed a smile that was more polite than genuine. 'Thanks,' she said. 'Might take you up on that. Look, Donna . . .' she took another mouthful of wine, delaying the moment '. . . I actually wanted to talk to you about something. Something that happened today. It's about Connor. I think he's in trouble, and I need your help to figure out how bad it is, and what, if anything, I can do to help him.'

Donna thought again of Simon. Felt a sudden, burning fury with Connor Fraser for dragging Simon into whatever trouble he had found. 'I'll do what I can,' she said. 'What happened?'

Jen told her. About the men who had followed her to Dundee, about Simon and Paulie grabbing them, the story they had told about Connor and something that could be embarrassing to the government. 'They tried to keep me with them, some sort of custody,' she said. 'I threatened to go to you and get the story on TV.' She looked around the room. 'Guess that was my plan the whole time. But what do you think, Donna? Is there anyone you can call to find out if this is true, if Connor's in trouble? I know we're having a bad time at the moment but I still . . .' Her voice trailed off and she shrugged, as though frustrated that the rest of the sentence wouldn't form.

'I know,' Donna said, mind racing. It was like her internal dialogue was an old vinyl record that was pitted with scratches. She couldn't keep to one line of thought: her mind constantly jumped from concern for Simon to the ramifications of a story about government embarrassment in Northern Ireland and back to Simon. She forced herself to think, reason out what Jen had just told her. Came up with one conclusion. And a question. She ran the idea through her mind one last time, nodded. Decision made. Only the logistics remained.

'I know a few people we can talk to,' she said. 'But before all that, I've got one question.'

'Go on,' Jen said, leaning forward.

'Do you have a valid passport?' Donna asked.

CHAPTER 27

After leaving Arthur Fielding, Connor and Simon headed back onto the Falls Road. They didn't speak, and Simon could see by the set of Connor's jaw and the furrow of his brow that talking would be a waste of time.

He wasn't surprised by their destination: the Old Dog pub, where two men had tried to grab Connor. It was typical of the area – Victorian frontage, bay window jutting out into the street, as if challenging anyone to find fault with the bilingual sign that proclaimed the Old Dog in both English and Gaelic, and the Irish tricolour waving from a flagpole.

For a moment, Simon thought Connor was going to walk into the pub, but at the last minute he veered off, heading down the alleyway beside it. Simon followed, watching Connor's shoulders hunch, as though he was expecting a blow. Maybe he had already taken one, he thought. Memory could strike at any time.

Connor got to a bottle skip at the end of the alleyway, turned. Looked around, then hunkered down, studying the ground.

'He fell here,' Connor said, not looking up. 'I crushed his windpipe. Poor bastard's lips went blue before he hit the deck. And then,' Connor looked up, a shimmer in his eyes as he raised his hand, pointed down the alleyway, 'his partner came out the car. Drew his gun. I fired and . . .' He shook his head, unwilling to complete the sentence. Two men dead in less than two minutes.

Simon had never taken a life. He had come close, left men standing in the no man's land between life and death, but he had never crossed the line. He wondered whether he could if and when the time came, whether his natural instinct for self-preservation would be enough to drive him to commit the original sin. And what, he wondered, would that do to him? Could he learn to live with it, incorporate it into his life, just another fact about himself, like his love of coffee with sugar and aversion to peaty malt whisky? Or would it mutate inside him, grow and fester, like a tumour, until it destroyed the man he had been, replacing him with someone colder, less feeling? To kill was the ultimate test of character. The question was, what character did it leave in its wake?

'Connor,' he said, taking a step forward, 'they didn't leave you with a choice. They came for you, two professionals. They took their shot, you won. That's the way it goes.'

'But who?' Connor asked, his voice raw with anguish and frustration. 'Who were they? And what the hell does everyone want with this bloody watch? I mean, a serial number with the date of Arthur Fielding's van being stolen on the back of it isn't enough, is it?'

Simon took the offered watch. Studied it. Saw nothing unusual. 'I don't know, big lad,' he said. 'All I know is the agent back in Scotland told me your pal Gillespie was working on something sensitive, something that could embarrass the government and, potentially, set back the peace process here. So, either he was lying, and the men who came after you were government agents with orders to blackball you, or they were hired by someone else to grab you. Either way, you've got a target on your back until we figure this out.'

Connor stood up, gazing down the alleyway. Simon could tell he wasn't really seeing what was in front of him. Was instead looking down another alleyway, the one in his mind that led to his next decision.

'You still got that piece of paper they left for my gran?' Connor asked.

'Yeah,' Simon said warily, unease prickling his skin.

'Give it here,' Connor said.

'What you thinking, Connor?' Simon asked, not sure he wanted to hear the answer.

'I'm thinking that I'm tired of being on the defensive, going on the run,' he said. 'Whoever is after me knows why, what this is all about. They've threatened my gran, dragged you into this shit along with me. So, enough. No more running. They want me, they can come and get me. And when they do, I'll beat the answers out of them.'

'Now hold on a minute,' Simon said. 'We don't know who we're dealing with here. You call that number,' he gestured to the piece of paper Connor now held, 'Christ alone knows what's going to come a-calling.'

Connor looked down at the paper, then at Simon, something like indecision clouding his jade-green eyes for the briefest moment. 'Look, Simon,' he said, 'I know you didn't sign up for this. I appreciate you coming here to help, but if you want to walk away, I'd understand. You've got a good thing going with Donna, the flat's shaping up nicely. Hell, you've got Tom to think of as well, so if you want to walk away, I'd understand.'

Simon smiled at the reference to Tom, the stray cat that had come as a free extra when he had bought Connor's garden flat from him. It had been a simple plan. Move to Stirling, take over the flat when Connor moved into his new home with Jen. Put down some roots, find the courage to ask Donna to marry him. Build a life. But what would that life be worth if he abandoned his friend when he needed him most?

'Nah,' he said. 'Yer grand. Besides, Tom wouldn't take kindly to me wimping out on you. You know what that cat's like. She has standards.'

Connor held his gaze, as though trying telepathically to impress his gratitude on his friend. Then he drew his phone from his pocket, dialled the number that had been left with his gran.

Simon watched as Connor waited, then straightened. He locked eyes with Simon, then drew the phone from his ear, pressed the speaker key and held it up.

'Mr Fraser,' said a voice that would have been at home telling you the time sponsored by Accurist. 'I see you got my message. I'm glad you had the sense to call. Finally.'

'Aye,' Connor said, his voice a hard, dead thing that seemed to grow wings as it ricocheted off the walls of the alley. 'I got your message all right. Using defenceless old women to do your dirty work, is that how you get your kicks? Some man. I'm looking forward to meeting you and discussing that.'

The voice at the other end of the phone gave a bark of laughter, and something in the flattened bass told Simon that whoever they were talking to was using a voice distorter.

'I apologise for my methods, Mr Fraser,' he said, 'but this is a most, ah, pressing matter. I take it you have the watch and the prayer book in your possession.'

'Aye,' Connor said, his face impassive. 'And if you don't want me to head down to the harbour and throw it into the Lagan, you'll listen very carefully.'

'Mr Fraser, I hardly think you're in a position to—'

'You don't need to talk, you need to listen,' Connor said, 'so shut the fuck up and answer me a question. Was it you who sent those goons after me on the Falls the other day?'

Static on the line, a long, drawn-out silence that seemed to quiver with tension.

'Yes,' the voice said. 'They were my men.'

'Something else to thank you for,' Connor said. 'There's a coffee shop at the front of the Victoria Square centre in town. Used to be called Ground and Around. Be there in one hour. Bring any more of your goons and I'll make a very public scene, which I'm assuming you don't want. And,' he glanced at Simon, 'if you piss around, I'll also make sure that a third party destroys the watch and the prayer book by the time you've finished spooning the foam off your latte.'

'One hour,' the voice said, 'is impossible. I have arrangements to make, and I'm not, well, in the immediate area. I will make arrangements and call you back. No tricks, I assure you.'

Connor grimaced, no doubt having the same thought as Simon. They had played their card, and whoever was at the other end of the line was trying to dictate the rules of the game.

'Fine,' Connor said. 'You can get me on this number. Do not piss me around. I haven't heard from you in an hour's time, the watch and the book go bye-bye.'

He ended the call before the man at the other end of the line could reply.

'Well, that stirred things up,' Simon said. 'Now what?'

'We wait,' Connor said. 'See what happens. Interesting, though, wasn't it?'

'The not-in-the-immediate-area crack, you mean?' Simon asked. 'Makes sense if whoever that was in Stirling left the message at your gran's. And it shows he's well financed, if he can pull a team together here while—'

Simon was cut off by the chirping of his own phone. He pulled it out, gave the display a glance and was pleasantly surprised and confused.

He hit answer, lifted the phone to his ear. 'Donna,' he said, 'everything okay?'

'No, it is bloody not,' Donna said, the sounds of traffic in the background. 'I've just booked a flight for Belfast tomorrow. I'll send you the details. Find a place to meet me. And bring that arsehole Connor Fraser with you. I've got a few questions for the both of you.'

CHAPTER 28

Jen sat in her father's study in his Cambusbarron home, unable to shake the feeling that she was the one haunting the room, not her father. Sitting there, barricaded behind the slab of polished mahogany that served as his desk, the leather of his throne-like chair hissing softly as she tried to get her back comfortable, Jen felt as though he was still alive, about to walk through the door at any minute. From the books that lined the walls to the framed industry awards and scattering of family pictures, the spirit of Duncan MacKenzie seemed to seep from the walls, the whole place a shrine to the man and the sheer force of will he had used to build his empire.

Beside that, beside a lifetime of accomplishments frozen in the amber of the study, Jen felt like a shadow, a sketch to her father's oil painting.

She uttered a soft curse. She had time for self-pity and self-doubt later. Right now, she had a job to do. And while part of her, the part that loved Connor and wanted nothing more than for him to be home, screamed to be in Belfast, another part, the part her father had nourished and encouraged to face the world head on, told her that business came first.

She wondered how the Barrs would take the news. After all, they had based their decision to try working with Jen on the fact that Paulie would be handling the logistics, Jen being an unknown quantity they did not yet trust – like a rogue contaminant in a batch of their drugs.

But now Paulie was heading for Belfast with Donna Blake at Jen's insistence, leaving her alone to handle the deal and prove she could be trusted as a cog in the Barrs' drug-trafficking empire.

There were, she concluded, only two answers. The Barrs would accept the deal, or they would call the whole thing off. But, looking at the sheets of paper in front of her on the desk, printouts daubed with her father's handwriting, Jen had a feeling they would opt for the former course of action.

For Angela and Iain Barr's sake, she hoped they did.

She picked up the receiver of the phone on her father's desk, dialled the number. Didn't have to wait long for Angela Barr to answer, her voice clipped and precise.

'Ms MacKenzie?' she said. 'I must admit, you gave me a start. For a moment there, when I saw the number flash up on my screen, I thought your father was reaching out from beyond the grave.'

Jen bit back her anger, refusing to rise to Barr's barbed taunt. But she filed it away. For future reference. 'Sorry to disappoint,' she said, keeping her tone neutral. 'I won't take up much of your time. Just a quick courtesy call to tell you that something's come up this end. Paulie is indisposed so I'll be handling the, ah, transaction we discussed.'

A moment of silence down the line, Barr's calculations echoing in it. When she spoke, her voice was a toxic mix of amusement, boredom and disdain. 'I'm afraid that's not the arrangement we made, Ms MacKenzie,' she said. 'We agreed to a trial of your services purely on the understanding that you would be leaning on Paulie's expertise, which we have come to know and rely on over the years. Working with you, an untested individual, is unacceptable. Our clients demand the best. We would be remiss in letting an amateur, forgive me, handle their business on our behalf.'

Jen laid a hand on the papers in front of her. Heard her dad whisper in her mind: *No more games. Show this bitch who's in charge here.*

'You don't seem to understand, Mrs Barr,' Jen said, emphasising the title as Barr had hers. 'I'm letting you know about the change as a professional courtesy. I could just as easily have let the shipment go with me supervising, and not telling you a thing. But I don't work like that, you see, as I'm not an amateur.'

'Ms MacKenzie, I hardly think—'

'I take after my dad,' Jen said, cutting her off. 'See, he wasn't an amateur either. When it came to business, he was a total professional. Exact and fastidious. Right down to the books he kept on the contracts he fulfilled.'

'I hardly see how that is relevant,' Barr said slowly, her tone telling Jen she knew exactly how relevant Jen's veiled threat was.

'Well, it's simple really,' Jen said. 'Dad kept a record of everything. Sizes of shipments, delivery networks, division of profits between, ah, network affiliates. It's all there. All commercially confidential, of course, but all very, very interesting. I'd hate to think what would happen if your competitors got hold of these trading routes and third-party handlers, but they could undercut your business quite easily. Don't worry, though. I'm not going to let that happen.'

'No?' Barr said, her voice the sound of ice being dropped into a crystal tumbler.

'No,' Jen said. 'I'm handling the transaction now, not Paulie. So you liaise through me. I'll make sure everything is kept confidential, and when the delivery is complete, we can talk a more permanent business arrangement. Agreed?'

'Agreed,' Barr said, with a voice as vibrant as rain-soaked concrete.

'Good,' Jen said. 'I'll be in touch.'

A moment of silence, then the sound of a drink being swallowed. Savoured.

'I apologise,' Barr said. 'I misjudged you, Jennifer. You may be new to this game, but you're no amateur. Your father would be proud.'

The call ended before Jen could reply. She let out a deep breath, hung up the phone. Sat back in her father's chair and looked around the room. Would he be proud? Or would he be dismayed that, despite all he had done to shield her from his world and the less legal aspects of his business, she had jumped straight in behind him?

'Like father, like daughter,' she whispered, wondering why the thought left a sour taste in her mouth.

CHAPTER 29

Donna's flight arrived at Belfast City just after 11 a.m., and she texted Simon to tell him she was on her way into town in a taxi. After a brief discussion, Connor and Simon opted for a snug back at the Crown bar opposite the Europa Hotel, reasoning that whoever was after them was unlikely to try anything before their meeting with the mystery caller who had left his number with Connor's gran.

The small booth was crowded, the space seeming to contract around them. Part of the reason was Paulie, who sat across from Connor, Simon and Donna on the bench seat that ran along the back of the booth. Connor felt a rush of unreality whenever he looked across the table. He associated Paulie with Stirling, the louring threat of violence and the almost pathological desire to keep Jen safe from the world in general, and Connor in particular. Yet here Paulie was, sitting in one of the most famous bars in Belfast, all rumpled suit, boulder-like shoulders and flat, dead eyes trained on the door of the snug. It was like seeing an orchid blooming on a waste dump.

It didn't take Connor long to lay out what had happened since Danny Gillespie's funeral – the attempt to abduct him on the Falls Road, the revelation that Danny's work on profiling those who had suffered trauma during the Troubles was being monitored by government agencies, meeting with Arthur Fielding, his recollection of the Carryduff massacre and the part Bobby McCandish and Colm O'Brien had played in the attack.

'And all we've got to go on, what everyone is looking for,' Connor said, as he finished his story, 'is this watch and a simple prayer book that Danny's mother gave to me at the funeral.'

Connor laid the items on the table in front of them. As he did, he noticed Simon relax a little, no doubt glad the focus was off their recent adventures and his part in them. When they had met Paulie and Donna at the taxi rank outside the Europa, Donna had given Simon a glare of such unbridled fury that Connor thought the paintwork on any vehicle in the surrounding area would surely blister as the metal beneath started to buckle. She had relented after a moment and wrapped him in a hug, which Simon seemed to melt into. But there was obvious tension between them, which Connor could understand. He had called, and his friend Simon, the man Donna loved, had charged off to face the danger with him, no questions asked. Connor felt a strange mix of gratitude and guilt. He knew Donna had not had an easy time romantically since her former partner had been murdered, and the last thing he wanted to do was drive a wedge between her and Simon.

Donna picked up the watch, turned it in her hand. Placed it back on the table, then picked up the prayer book and began leafing through it. Connor leaned forward to retrieve the watch, and was intercepted by Paulie's paw-like hand engulfing it.

'Aye,' he rumbled, after studying it. It looked as fragile as cut glass in his hand. 'Nice piece. Old Omega, one of the Dirty Dozen watches they gave out for the D-Day landings. Very nice. Rare.' He flipped the watch over, unthreading the straps from the pins holding it. Looked up, smiled at the dumbfounded look Connor could feel plastered over his face.

'I like watches,' he said simply, pulling back the sleeve of his shirt to reveal a thick silver band and a Rolex diver's watch. 'They're like a good car, precisely engineered to do one job, and do it right. And,' his smile widened, and Connor felt a shiver of unease, 'in a tight spot, a heavy watch makes for a hell of a knuckle-duster.'

Connor took a gulp of his coffee. The simple, earnest way in which Paulie had spoken had threatened to make him laugh. Whether from humour or nerves, he wasn't sure.

'Anything stand out about that one?' Simon asked. 'A lot of people seem keen to get their hands on it.'

Paulie turned his attention back to the watch, which he had flipped over. 'Well, this is interesting,' he said.

'What?' Connor asked, unable to stop himself leaning forward as he spoke.

'Well, first, the serial number engraved on the back doesn't match with this model of watch. And, second,' he held the watch up, pointed at the large arrow in the centre of the back, 'this arrow shouldn't be here. It's not standard on the back of this model watch. It's from a later model. So this isn't the original backing for this watch.'

'You mean it's been replaced?' Donna asked, before Connor could speak. 'You think that's important?'

Paulie shrugged his shoulders in a way that made Connor think of shirts ripping in the old *Incredible Hulk* TV series he had watched as a child. 'No way of telling,' he said. 'Won't know that until we get it off, have a look at it properly. I wonder if old man Simpson is still working.'

'Simpson?' Connor asked.

'Huh?' Paulie said impatiently, as though roused from a thought. 'John-Paul Simpson. Watchsmith here in Belfast. Did a bit of business with him back here in the day. He knows his stuff. He'll be able to get the back off the watch, see what's what.'

Connor nodded, running a calculation. If there was something about the watch, this was the best shot they had at finding out what it was. But did they have enough time to investigate before their mystery caller arrived in town and requested the meeting?

'How long will it take?' Connor asked.

'Couple of hours,' Paulie said, as he threaded the strap back onto the watch then pocketed it. As he did, Connor saw a flash of challenge in his eyes. *Take it back if you think you can*, the look said.

'Okay,' Connor said. 'Can you call us if you find anything?'

'Well, I'm hardly going to keep it to my bloody self, am I?' Paulie said, his voice hard with irritation. 'I'm only here as Jen asked me to keep an eye on Ms Blake and make sure you don't get your arse in a sling. I want this done, pronto, so I can get home and make sure Jen's okay with . . .' he coughed '. . . the business.'

Connor felt a question rise in his throat, swallowed it. What Jen was doing with her father's business was her concern. He was just glad that, joke or not, Paulie had implied she still cared what happened to him. The thought kindled a melancholic hope in his chest that they could work things out. But to do that, he had to get himself out of whatever shit he had been dropped in.

'And while Paulie's doing that,' Donna said, 'I'm going to take a closer look at Bobby McCandish, Colm O'Brien and the Carryduff massacre. With that being the last interview your pal Gillespie conducted before he died, makes sense it's a factor in all of this.'

'Hold on a minute,' Simon started. 'Don't you think that's a bit—'

'No, Simon,' Donna said, voice hardening as she turned to him. 'I don't. Why do you think I'm here? To act as cheerleader for you and that big lunk there?' She threw a thumb at Connor. 'Sorry, but no. I'm a reporter in case you've forgotten, and all of this, the doctored Troubles reports, the attempt to snatch Connor, the government officials warning you're involved in something sensitive, is news. So I'm going to do my job, find out what the story is, then report it.'

'That's you telt,' Paulie rumbled, his voice lightened by a mix of humour and admiration.

'I guess it is at that,' Simon said. 'But, please,' he turned to Donna, the humour slipping from his face, 'be careful, okay? We've got stuff to do when we get home.'

Connor suddenly felt as though he was intruding on a very private moment. He started to rise, froze when his phone began chirping. Sat back down, pulled it out. It was a text message. Simple. Blunt. To the point.

> Be at the café you mentioned yesterday within the hour. Bring the watch and prayer book. No tricks.

'What?' Simon asked him, his face stone.

'Game on,' Connor said, sliding the phone to him.

'Aye,' Simon said, as he read the message. 'But it's a poker match now.'

'You mean as Paulie will have the watch we're supposed to be giving him?' Connor asked.

Simon gave a cold, hard grin. 'Well, we were never going to do that anyway,' he said, eyes sliding to Paulie, then back to Connor. 'Whoever this bastard is, the watch and the prayer book are important. They're our cards to play, and we'll play them whenever we choose. But I want to look this fucker in the eyes for what he's done, have a nice wee chat. And if that means fronting him out, so much the better.'

'Simon.' Donna's voice cut into the moment, like a pin pricking a balloon. She was staring at him evenly, face unreadable.

Simon opened his mouth to speak, was silenced by Donna raising a hand.

'I know you're going to say you have to do this,' she said. 'It's your job, just like mine. But please,' her eyes darted to Connor and Paulie, 'be careful. Like you said, we've things to do back home. Together.'

Simon's grin returned, this time warm. 'Aye,' he said, and Connor could have sworn his friend's cheeks reddened. 'That we do. Let's get this dealt with and all go home.'

'Okay by me,' Paulie said. 'Belfast is fine to visit, but it all gets a little stale after a while. Gimme Stirling any day.'

Connor blinked, then did the only thing he could. He raised his mug to toast Paulie, and let loose the laugh that was clawing its way up his throat.

CHAPTER 30

Connor had assumed he would know who he was meeting the moment he saw them, his instincts homing in on a fellow predator and a potential threat the moment he set eyes on them. But, as it turned out, spotting the person he was there to meet was a far more basic process. He knew the face sitting at the café table outside the Victoria Square shopping centre. And, as with Paulie, he was hit by another wave of unreality. The last time he had seen that face was in Stirling, in relation to the case that had got Jen's father, Duncan MacKenzie, murdered.

'Is that who I think it is?' Simon whispered into Connor's ear, the surprise in his tone resonating with Connor's.

'Yeah,' Connor said, taking in the skin browned by LA sun, the long, elegant fingers wrapped around the coffee cup, the sleek dark hair. 'Amanda Lyons. Or Gillian Flint, depending on what she decides to tell you.'

'Whatever her name is, she's trouble,' Simon said. 'What the hell is our favourite secretary-slash-terrorist-hunter doing mixed up in all of this?'

'No idea,' Connor said, his mind racing. Flint, or whatever her name was, had posed as Amanda Lyons, the assistant to a US TV journalist who was looking into his father's suspicious death in Stirling. What hadn't been known was that Lyons was using the presenter, Jonathan Rodriguez, as part of an elaborate plot to flush out a former IRA sympathiser. Which, given the link to Republican and Loyalist paramilitaries, made this exactly the type of case that would interest her.

But the question that had reared its head the last time they had met remained. Who was she, really? And who was she working for?

Connor shook himself from his thoughts. 'Well, standing here isn't going to get us anywhere,' he said. 'Think I'll go and ask her. You sweep the perimeter, message me if there are any problems.'

'Copy that,' Simon said, drifting away and dissolving into the crowd of shoppers and pedestrians.

Connor approached Flint slowly, eyes darting over other tables. Not that he was really expecting to see anything: whoever they were dealing with were professionals, unlikely to be polishing knives while sipping lattes and leering at Connor with predatory eyes.

'Ms Flint,' Connor said, opting for the name she had given him after their last encounter in Stirling. 'Fancy meeting you here.'

She looked up at him, a smile that started and ended at her cheeks breaking across her face. 'Connor Fraser,' she said, gesturing for him to take a seat. 'I knew we'd see each other again. How've you been?'

'About how you'd expect after two men tried to snatch me at gunpoint and someone used my grandmother as a method of getting to me,' Connor said, feeling the first cold flickers of anger spark like a lighter in his gut. 'Was that your idea, or the work of the guy I was meant to be meeting here? You know, the one I'm guessing you're working for.'

Flint cocked her head, gave Connor a glare as hard as her name. 'No,' she said flatly. 'That was nothing to do with me. I told them involving your family only complicates the situation and, I dare say, makes you less sympathetic to our cause.'

'"Our cause"?' Connor said. 'And just what is that, exactly?'

Flint took a sip of her coffee, then set it aside, her eyes lingering on the cup as though her next words were written there. 'Look, Connor,' she said. 'There are things I cannot tell you. But, believe me, you've stumbled into something very sensitive, something people on both sides of the Atlantic have a vested interest in making sure does not enter the public domain.'

Connor leaned forward, close enough to get a whiff of her coffee. 'Let me guess. Whatever it is, it's linked with Danny Gillespie, the Carryduff massacre, and three paramilitaries.'

Flint reached for her coffee, another smile pinching her lips. 'Very good, Connor,' she said. 'Like I told you before, you'd do very well in the States working with me.'

'Yeah, working for whom?' Connor asked. 'Near as I can make out, there's two groups working here, the official intelligence services, and some freelance privateers who have been asked to make all this go away. They sent the team who tried to grab me on the Falls Road, and they're led by whoever is pulling your strings. So who is that, Gillian, or whatever your name is, and how much are they paying you to be here to win me over?'

A flash of something uglier than anger sparked in Flint's eyes, then receded. She studied him for a moment, as though trying to make a decision. When she spoke, her voice was low, flat, the twang of her accent almost completely gone. 'Okay, you're right,' she said. 'I'm freelancing on this. Former terrorists and US involvement in some of the, ah, grubbier aspects of the Troubles is something of a specialism for me. My employer, let's call him Mr Green, has been tasked with getting back the items you have. When he looked into your past, my name came up, so here I am. But, Connor,' it was her turn to lean forward now, her eyes locking on to his, 'these people are not amateurs. They will get what they want. For your sake, I hope sanity has prevailed. Give me the watch and the prayer book, then get out of Belfast. Go home. See your family. Try to patch things up with that girlfriend of yours.'

Connor ignored the stab of guilt he felt at the references to his gran and Jen, fought to keep his expression casual. 'Wish I could help,' he said. 'But your boss made a mistake.'

'What was that?' Flint asked.

'He didn't ask me nicely,' Connor said, feeling his earlier anger start to glow in his chest, fanned by memories from the last few days. 'So, whoever he is, government, freelance, whatever, he can go fuck himself. Don't worry about delivering that message though, I'll do it myself.'

'And how,' Flint said, a sneer curling her lip, 'do you think you're going to manage that?'

Connor stood up, took in his surroundings. Normal people going about normal lives. How many of them had been forced to kill? How many had put their friends in mortal danger? He lived an abnormal life. No wonder Jen was repulsed by it. 'Simple,' he said. 'You've given me everything I need. You've confirmed that the watch and the prayer book are keys to some embarrassing information that governments in London and Washington don't want disclosed. You've also told me that someone close to this is worried, personally worried, about this information coming to light. That's the person who hired you and your boss to try to get to me. Got to say, they have a point. Takes governments forever to get anything done. You didn't blink when I mentioned Carryduff, which means you were briefed on it. So all I have to do is find whoever hired your employer. And when I do, I'll make sure they tell me everything I want to know. And then, Gillian,' Connor leaned forward, knuckles on the table, 'I will speak to him directly about using those I love to get to me. So thanks for the chat. It's been informative.'

Flint gave a minute jerk, as though controlling the instinct to flee. 'Connor,' she said, 'please. You have no idea what you're involved in.'

'No,' Connor admitted, 'you're right. I don't – not yet. But I'll find out. And when I do, I'll make sure a friend of mine, the one who spends a lot of time on TV, gets to know all about it. I'll even give her your name, for what it's worth. So find another identity, Gillian, because this one is about to be burned to the ground.'

CHAPTER 31

It hadn't taken long to track down John-Paul Simpson, who was still working out of the same anonymous-looking shop in Smithfield Market that Paulie had first visited almost three decades ago. For a man who worked with time he seemed immune to it, the face that looked up to greet Paulie almost unchanged by the years – small eyes magnified to cartoonish size by thick glasses, a large, bulbous nose riddled with a network of burst blood vessels: scar tissue from a lifetime of brandy and cigars. Something between terror and curiosity flashed across his face when Paulie entered the shop. No real surprise – the last time they had met, Paulie was wiping blood from his knuckles as he handed over his Rolex for Simpson to repair after it was damaged in a fight.

He still wore the watch. It never missed a second.

It didn't take Paulie long to put Simpson at ease and explain what he needed. Took even less time for Simpson to pluck the watch from Paulie's grasp and examine it.

Now, less than twenty minutes after walking into Simpson's shop, Paulie was back on the street, his wallet a hundred pounds lighter and his head crammed with questions.

What did Simpson's discovery mean? How much trouble was Fraser in, and how much of it could blow back on Jen? He looked at the object in his hand, thought about dropping it down the drain and jumping into a taxi for the airport. But he could not, would not do that, for two reasons. First, he had made a promise to Jen. Second, whoever was after Fraser, they had targeted his grandmother to try to get to him. And for Paulie, that crossed a line. He had killed, threatened and maimed in his life to get what he wanted, but he prided himself on never targeting a civilian. After all, he had standards. And when someone violated those standards, Paulie felt it was his duty to remind the transgressor that, even in a game as bloody and violent as this, there were rules. His rules.

He pulled out his phone, found Donna Blake's number and hit dial. He had agreed that he would meet her after he had seen Simpson, make sure she wasn't getting any trouble from the three former paramilitaries Fraser had seen at his friend's funeral.

'Paulie,' she said, by way of hello after a couple of rings. 'How did you get on? Anything interesting?'

'Could say that,' Paulie said, glancing down at the object he held in his free hand. 'Where are you now?'

'At the BBC office on Ormeau Avenue. Pulled in a favour from a pal to get a look at their cuts, see who we're dealing with.'

'Anything interesting?' Paulie said, a hint of humour in his voice as he mimicked Donna's earlier tone. The truth was he liked her – the determination to get what she wanted, the willingness to push aside fear and her own safety to get it. The drive reminded him of Jen, and the comparison pleased and worried him.

'Could say that,' Donna replied, her voice mischievous. 'I'll be done in about ten minutes. Why don't I meet you back at the Crown? I've got a line on one of the men, Colm O'Brien, and the Crown is on the way.'

'Fair enough,' Paulie said. 'I'll see you there in . . .' he glanced at his watch '. . . twenty-five minutes?'

'See you then,' Donna said, and killed the call.

Paulie pocketed his phone, got walking again, was interrupted a minute later by its buzz. He sighed, reached for it. Felt a pang of panic when he saw Jen's contact details on the screen.

'Jen,' he said, tone neutral. 'What's up?'

'Paulie, I . . .' Her breath hitched, and Paulie could hear tears in the raw raggedness of the sound.

'Jen, what's wrong? Has something gone wrong with the—' he caught himself, remembered he was on an unsecured line '—with the Aberdeen deal?'

'What?' Confusion in Jen's voice now. 'Oh, no. No. Nothing like that. I, ah, I need you to get a message to Connor. He needs to come home. Now.'

CHAPTER 32

The roar of the engines as the plane hurtled down the runway filled the cabin, drowning out the world as human ingenuity screamed its defiance at gravity. The plane's nose jerked up, those sitting at the front suddenly looking as though they were on a roller-coaster making a steep climb. Connor closed his eyes, let the cacophony wash through him, resonating with the silent scream that filled his mind.

He had known what was wrong the moment Paulie had approached him. There was something in the man's eyes, an awkward, apologetic sympathy that telegraphed the news to him before Paulie had even told him he had to phone Jen. But he had taken the offered phone and dialled the number, even as he felt concrete fill his lungs and a balloon beginning to inflate in his head.

'C-Connor,' she had said, with the hesitancy of someone who had rehearsed their lines but was now unable to deliver them, 'I'm so sorry. I, ah, I just got a call from your gran's home. They tried to get you, but your number's ringing out. It seems, ah, it seems . . .'

Connor closed his eyes, felt something hot and molten at the back of them. Forced his lungs to fill and deflate, fill and deflate.

'Did she suffer?' he asked.

'No,' Jen said, the hard finality of the word plunging a fresh shard of grief into Connor's heart. 'They went to her room to check on her. Found her in her bed. They think it was a massive stroke or a brain aneurysm. She wouldn't have known what was happening, they said.'

Connor forced his eyes open, looked for the first time at a world that was now without his gran. A world that would never again know her kindness, her grace or her determination to provide the love and care for Connor that his father never could. A world grown colder, harder.

Uglier.

He realised Jen had stopped talking, that a question was hanging on the line between them.

'Sorry, what?' he said.

'I asked if you can get back tonight,' she said. 'The home said there were things that only you could deal with. They need you here.'

Ah, but do you? Connor almost said. He caught himself, tried to think through the kaleidoscope of memories tumbling through his mind, each one tugging at him like a child desperate for attention.

'I'll get the next flight,' Connor said. Then, after a moment, he added, 'Thanks, Jen. I, ah, I know this can't have been easy for you.'

'She was a nice woman,' Jen said, her voice a contradiction of tears and a steely determination not to shed them. 'She thought the world of you, Connor. And I know you did your best to make sure she was comfortable in that home. She was proud of you.'

He opened his mouth, found no words, swallowed, then tried again. 'She thought the world of you too,' he said, voice hoarse. 'She loved you, Jen. Just like . . .' He trailed off, the words at once too small and too large for him to say.

'Let me speak to Paulie,' she said, voice sharp now, the tears overwhelming the steel.

Connor passed the phone to Paulie, and felt numbness steal through him. His gran was dead. Another person he loved, gone. Was it him? Was he cursed? Or did he just draw pain and death towards him, like some foetid magnet?

Paulie ended the call, turned back to Connor, his face a mask of carefully constructed ambivalence. 'Jen wants me to fly back with you,' he said, as he pocketed the phone. 'That works for me, got business in Stirling anyway.'

'Can you do me a favour?' Connor said. 'Call Simon, tell him what's going on? I've got a couple of things to tidy up at the place he arranged for me, then I'll head to the airport. We can meet there, get the next flight back.'

Paulie nodded. 'No problem,' he said, in a tone anyone who didn't know him would have mistaken for gentle.

Connor turned and walked away. What happened next was a series of snapshots in his memory. A walk through the city. The safe-house on Glencairn Street. A taxi to the airport. It was as though life had become an ocean and he was treading water, afraid to dive below the surface and face what waited for him there.

He wasn't surprised to see Donna and Simon when he arrived. Simon grabbed him in a bear hug, whispered, 'I'm so sorry, big lad,' into his ear. But it was Donna who almost broke him. It was the smallest gesture: a kiss on the cheek, a squeeze of his arm, a sympathetic smile. The choreography of condolence. Something about the normality of it made Connor's grief scream for release. Tears or violence, the method didn't matter, only the venting of it.

'We're going to stay here, chase down those paramilitaries you saw at the funeral,' Donna said, her eyes meeting Simon's. He nodded agreement.

'We'll follow you back as soon as we find anything,' he said. 'Probably be tomorrow. In the meantime, you take care. Remember, these folk are still after you.'

Cold fury sparked in Connor's chest. 'These folk'. A casual term for men who had threatened his life, tried to get at him through his gran. Had that been a trigger for the stroke that killed her? The stress of knowing someone was looking for him? Or was that just his way of avoiding the guilt and loss he felt, by transmuting it into rage and throwing it at those who had targeted Ida?

He didn't know for sure, but if it kept him upright and moving, that was all that mattered.

'They won't be after me for long,' he had said, more to himself than Simon. 'I'm done running. They want me, they can come and fucking get me.'

And now his stomach lurched as the plane soared into the sky, taking him to a place that was now home in name only. Jen's words came back to him: *She wouldn't have known what was happening.* He hoped that was true, knew in his heart he would never believe it. His grandmother, the third parent, the one who had actually understood him, had died. Alone. Why? Because Connor had wandered off into whatever he was involved in, and was playing a game of deadly cat and mouse.

He turned to Paulie, suddenly eager to be out of his own head and away from the recriminations and memories and guilt.

'You find out anything about the watch?' he asked.

Paulie blinked at him, as though he was talking in a thick accent he couldn't quite follow. Then understanding swelled in his eyes, and he nodded. 'Aye,' he said, reaching into his pocket. 'Didn't take old man Simpson long to get the back off it. Like I thought, it wasn't an original part. It was specially designed, had a wee bracket on the back to hold this.' He opened his hand, a magician revealing the card you had picked earlier.

Connor took the item Paulie held out. Inspected it. 'A mini SIM card?' he asked.

Paulie shook his head. 'That's what I thought at first, too,' he said. 'But Simpson put me right. Told me that's a micro USB drive. You put it into a pen-drive adapter, then plug it into a computer and away you go. Question is, what's on it?'

Connor studied the small sliver of plastic in his hand. 'Haven't a clue,' he said, 'but I know a man who can help us with that. And he won't be too far from the airport when we land.'

CHAPTER 33

Death was too close for comfort.

The thought came to Jen as she ended the call with Paulie. Sitting in the almost monastic silence of her father's study, it was hard to argue against the thought. Less than two years after the death of her own father, another person in her life had been taken.

It surprised Jen how much the death of Connor's grandmother had affected her. She had only met Ida Fraser a handful of times – as the dementia had encroached on her mind, visits from people she hadn't known well became fraught, tense interludes poisoned by the potential that Ida would either confuse Jen with someone else, or become upset that she couldn't remember who she was. But there had been days when the dementia had receded and the real Ida Fraser had peeped out, like the sun emerging from behind a bank of dark cloud. And on those days, Jen had met a kind, warm woman who doted on her grandson as much as he did her. A woman who was convinced that Connor had 'found the one' in Jen and the two of them were destined to be together.

She picked up her phone and scrolled through the pictures, finding one taken at the care home about a month before her father had died. The three of them, Connor, Ida and Jen, were sitting on a bench in the gardens at the care home, smiling into the camera, Connor's body twisted awkwardly as he held out the camera for the selfie. She felt a pang of bitter melancholy as she looked at the picture. She had been happy then. The house that Connor had bought in Stirling was almost complete, the adaptations to accommodate her mobility issues being finalised. They had visited Ida that day with pictures of the house, and a promise of a visit as soon as they moved in. But then, a month later, Jen's father had been found floating in Airthrey Loch at the university, and her world had fallen apart.

Intellectually, she knew she shouldn't blame Connor for her father's death. He hadn't put in motion the events that had led to Duncan MacKenzie's brutal murder. Indeed, he had done as Jen asked – well, demanded – and investigated the case, tracking down the killer before Paulie took final, brutal revenge with a single shot to the head. But there was a resentment that had driven a wedge between her and Connor. She was crippled and her father was dead, yet Connor Fraser sailed on, like some indestructible battleship, while the storm of life battered those around him.

But sitting there, looking at the picture of the three of them, Jen felt for the first time the hollowness of her resentment – and the lie around it. The truth was, she was using her anger at Connor as a shield from her own grief. She felt the same urge now – to blame Connor for Ida's lonely death because he was off investigating another case. But the smile that radiated from Ida's face on the phone made a mockery of that temptation. Connor would, she knew, torture himself for not being in Stirling and at Ida's side when she had died. Her adding to that guilt would be a form of cruelty Ida would never have understood, let alone condoned.

She locked the phone, felt tears threaten that were part grief, part anger. Looked around the room that would always be her father's. Remembered something Ida had told her the day they took the picture.

'Connor can be a stubborn bugger, love,' she had said, one warm, brittle hand resting on Jen's, 'but he's got a good heart. That belongs to you now, I can see it. So give him a little time to figure it out. You're meant to be together. Trust me, I know.'

She smiled, remembering the calm, measured certainty in Ida's voice. If death was close, it was also an antidote to pretence. The truth was Jen loved Connor. She wanted him home, wanted them together in the home they had designed, living the life they wanted.

And to do that, they needed to be honest. With each other and themselves. And, in that honesty, Jen found herself lost. She had started on a path to save her father's business, stepped into the shadowed side of his life that he had fought all his days to protect her from. And she had compounded that by what? Blackmailing one of the biggest drug-smugglers in the UK and threatening to expose them if they didn't play by her rules? Was that who she wanted to be? Was that the woman Ida Fraser would want for her grandson?

She stood, cursing as a lance of pain flashed up her back. The study suddenly felt too stuffy, too weighed down with the ghosts of her father and Ida. She needed to get out of the house, go somewhere to think.

And there was only one place to truly do that.

Home. Or, at least, the home that almost was.

CHAPTER 34

It hadn't taken Donna long to track down Colm O'Brien – his name blossomed, like rust on a dumped car, the moment she had put it into the cuts library at the BBC. A prominent member of the IRA during the Troubles, O'Brien had been arrested and jailed for terror-related offences in 1988, a year after the Carryduff massacre. Sent to the notorious Maze prison on the outskirts of Lisburn, he was released in April 1998 as part of the Good Friday Agreement that brought an end to the Troubles. According to the reports and interviews Donna had found, O'Brien had used his time in prison to transform himself: he had immersed himself in books, mainly history and social politics, renounced armed struggle (publicly at least), and stepped out of the Maze a changed man with a clear purpose – to stop youngsters making the mistakes he had.

'I wasn't given a choice when I was a lad,' he had told an interviewer from the *Guardian* in 2002. 'Violence and hatred of the "British oppressors" was as much a part of my diet growing up as my ma's beef stew and my da's rants about that bitch Thatcher. It was like an apprenticeship in violence, and when you came of age, you were given a gun and a hit list. It was only when I was in prison that I had time to think about that, that I could reflect on what had happened to me. So I educated myself. And I realised there is another path. You just have to open kids' eyes to it.'

To do this, O'Brien had started a construction firm in the Short

Strand area in the east of Belfast. He won a series of contracts with the city council to build and redevelop housing, making a key part of his business the insistence of taking on and training school leavers to ensure they had a trade.

'It's simple,' he told the interviewer. 'You give these kids a way to make an honest living, a way to learn self-respect and discipline without ever having to pick up a gun or run with the gangs, and you're giving them a fighting chance at a better life. I didn't get that, but I'm damned sure these kids will.'

In the years that followed, O'Brien had rehabilitated himself from violent paramilitary to pillar of the community. He was feted by politicians from all sides, and had won several community activism and humanitarian awards. At the last St Patrick's Day, he had appeared in New York, the guest of a young politician with her eyes on Washington and the Senate.

All of which, Donna thought, went some way to explaining the building she and Simon were standing in front of. It was a neat, two-storey office block sitting just off Mountpottinger Road, red brick seeming to glow in the dying evening light. A large sign bolted to the top, like a front-page headline, proclaimed it was 'O'Brien Construction', while a sub-deck below carried the slogan 'Building tomorrow today'.

'Catchy,' Simon said, as he followed Donna's gaze. 'So, how exactly did you blag us an interview with Mr O'Brien?'

Donna turned, gave Simon a look of mock shock. 'Blag?' she said. 'I'll have you know I'm a respected journalist. I don't blag. I called, told his PA I was a reporter with Sky News, and wanted to talk to him about the challenges facing construction in Belfast in light of ongoing border issues and regulatory challenges due to Brexit.'

Simon's face twitched into the boyish smile Donna had grown to love. 'Right,' he said. 'Sorry, my mistake. You didn't blag him. You outright bullshitted him. And how are you, Donna Blake, face of Sky, going to explain away that you've not got a cameraman with you, just me?'

'Easy,' Donna said, a smile playing across her lips. 'This is a pre-interview to get the facts and his side of the story. Pretty common when we're doing a big investigative piece. And you,' she pointed at his chest, 'are my junior researcher.'

'Ah,' Simon said. 'So I'm your note-taker.'

'And so much more,' Donna said, and strode off towards the office.

Telling the receptionist, a slight, narrow-shouldered teenager, hair gleaming with gel, who they were was like proclaiming the arrival of a higher being. His eyes went wide, and he lunged for the phone in front of him.

'Yes, that's the reporter and her, ah,' his eyes darted to Simon, then back to Donna, 'her colleague. Yes. Okay. Thanks.'

He hung up, turned his attention back to Donna. Almost won the battle to keep his eyes on hers rather than her chest. 'Mr O'Brien's assistant, Ms Baxter, will be down in a moment,' he said.

Donna gave him a smile of thanks, which seemed to ignite a furnace in the teenager's cheeks. She barely had time to sit down in a chair opposite the desk when a woman emerged from a door at the end of a hall. She was tall, elegantly outfitted in a grey business suit, dark hair shot through with iron grey. Donna could see an echo of the boy at reception in her chin and the slightness of her build. Her suspicion was confirmed when the woman glanced briefly at the boy. She knew from experience that only a mother could assess their child's situation and pass judgement so quickly.

'Ms Blake,' she said, offering her hand. 'A pleasure to meet you. I'm Yvonne Baxter, Mr O'Brien's executive assistant.'

Donna took the hand, the grip cool and firm. 'Thanks for seeing us at such short notice. This,' she half turned, gestured to Simon, 'is Simon McCartney, my research assistant on this story.'

Baxter gave Simon a twitch of a smile, then dismissed him and turned her attention back to Donna. 'We were pleased to hear from you,' she said, leading them towards the door she had emerged from. 'The Brexit issue is a key concern of Mr O'Brien's, and he's keen to help Sky report on the issue accurately.'

Donna caught the pointed look Simon gave her, ignored it. *Bullshitter*, she heard him whisper in her mind.

Baxter led them up a flight of stairs, and into a large room dominated by a huge circular conference table. At its head, standing as they entered, was Colm O'Brien. Donna knew from his bio that O'Brien was sixty-eight, but she would have taken him for a man twenty years younger. He wasn't tall, but his stance was stiff and erect, his shoulders broad and powerful, his stomach still flat. His dark hair was swept back from a wide, almost brutish forehead, and his skin glowed with the kind of health and vitality that regular holidays in the sun gave you.

'Ms Blake,' he said, approaching and offering his hand, 'a pleasure to meet you. I'm Colm O'Brien.'

'Mr O'Brien, thank you for seeing us,' she said, taking his hand. His grip was warm where Baxter's had been cool, and Donna could feel the restraint in the shake, knew he could have snapped her fingers with a single squeeze.

O'Brien nodded to Baxter, then gestured to the conference table. 'Won't you and your colleague . . .'

'Simon McCartney,' Simon said, in reply to the question O'Brien had left hanging.

'Quite,' he said. 'Won't you and Mr McCartney take a seat? Can I offer you something to drink? Tea? Coffee?'

'No, thank you,' Donna said, as she sat, Simon sliding into the chair beside her and producing a notepad and pen from his jacket.

O'Brien nodded, and Baxter retreated from the room. 'So,' he said, 'I believe you wanted to talk about my business and the Brexit problem. I'd be delighted. Where would you like to start?'

'Well . . .' Donna said, taking a moment to get comfortable. She needed to control this interview, get O'Brien to open up. Best to take it slow. 'Obviously, I've read your biography, the journey from the Falls Road, the Troubles and your time in the Maze, but I wondered if you could tell us a little more of your personal story. What was it that finally made you turn your back on violence as a way to achieve change, and focus on giving people like yourself a better future?'

O'Brien settled back in his chair, sinking into the role he was playing as he sank into the leather. Donna could tell this was familiar territory for him, his reactions honed by years of interviews. And in that gesture, she saw the lie of him. He was no different from a politician bleating out the soundbite of the day about 'the right thing to do'. This was a practised performance for him, a way to craft the narrative, let people see only what he wanted them to see.

Time to change that.

'I came to understand that violence is ultimately self-defeating,' he said. 'Martin Luther King said that violence begets violence, and in, ah, in prison, I saw the truth of that. I was put in prison for committing acts of violence for a cause I believed in. But what did those acts actually achieve? Mass imprisonments, deaths on both sides, army crackdowns on civilians after an attack? It was pointless. The cycle had to be broken. So I broke it.'

'I see,' Donna said. 'And was there one act that highlighted to you how pointless the killing was? The Hyde Park bombing maybe? Omagh? Or perhaps the massacre at Carryduff?'

Something cold flashed across O'Brien's eyes as his face pinched and hardened. He leaned further back into his chair, as though trying to distance himself from Donna. 'No,' he said, after a moment, his voice as cold as his eyes. 'I mean, the attacks you refer to were heinous, but it was more a cumulative realisation that the road we were on would only lead to more blood.'

'I see,' Donna said. 'I mentioned Carryduff as I understand that was personal for you?'

O'Brien's gaze jumped past Donna to the door, then back to her. 'I'm not sure what you're driving at, Ms Blake, but I'm pretty sure it's nothing to do with the story you said you were here to talk about. So why don't we call it a day, and I can give your editor a call for a little chat about false representation and journalistic ethics?'

'Good idea,' Donna said, settling back into her seat. 'While you're at it, could you tell her the Gillespie story is going well, and I've got a solid link between his death, the Carryduff massacre, and your appearance at his funeral along with Bobby McCandish and Brendan Walsh?'

O'Brien's mouth twitched. Beneath his mahogany tan, Donna could have sworn she saw him blanch as his eyes darted between her, Simon and the door.

'What did you just say?' he said. 'I'm not sure what you're implying, Ms Blake, but . . .'

'I'm not implying anything,' Donna said, biting back the thrill she felt in her stomach. She had him. 'Fact, Danny Gillespie was investigating the psychological effects of trauma suffered by victims of the Troubles. Fact, the Carryduff massacre in 1987 was one of those incidents. Fact, a reliable source has named both you and Bobby McCandish as being involved in the Carryduff massacre, which your release under the Good Friday Agreement helpfully sweeps under the carpet. Fact, you, McCandish and another man, Brendan Walsh, were all seen at Mr Gillespie's funeral. So my question is why, Mr O'Brien? Why were you at Danny Gillespie's funeral? Why would you pay your respects to a man who was digging into a past you've worked so hard to distance yourself from? And how far would you go to keep that past quiet?'

O'Brien sagged in his chair, as though Donna's verbal onslaught had hit him like a flurry of body blows. He closed his eyes for a moment, then placed his hands on the table in front of him, as though it was an anchor and he was a ship caught in a storm. He took a deep, hitching breath, then fixed Donna with a dead gaze. In it, she saw the man capable of threatening to sexually assault a man's wife in front of him to bend him to his will. She hated him for it.

'I knew this day would come,' he said, and Donna could swear she heard relief in his voice. 'This is, how do you say it, off the record?'

Donna nodded, not trusting herself to talk, as though doing so would shatter the spell she had cast on O'Brien.

He nodded. 'Fine,' he said. 'Yes, I was at Danny's funeral, with Bobby and Brendan. You asked how far I would go to keep my past quiet, Ms Blake. I'm afraid you've got it the wrong way round. I don't care who knows what I did. I'm ashamed of it and it's all there for the world to see. But there's another story, other people involved. And I would go,' he gave a bitter laugh, 'have gone, to great lengths to see that story told. And I think,' he fixed her with that dead gaze again, 'that's what got Danny killed.'

CHAPTER 35

Paulie knew the taste of impending violence. He had experienced it countless times in his life: in pubs before the first punch was thrown, when he stepped into the hay-bale-surrounded ring in a barn before a bare-knuckle fight, before he had to break someone's knees or exact another toll from them for an indiscretion against his employer. It was a fizzing in the back of his mouth, as though he was sucking old copper pennies. It made his saliva thick, viscous, hard to swallow. And in those moments, Paulie also felt an electric arc of excitement, as though his entire body had been plugged into the mains to charge up for what came next.

Watching Connor Fraser pace around the room, Paulie wasn't sure what was coming next. Only that someone was going to suffer. Very, very badly.

When they landed they had headed for the long-stay car park at the airport. Connor's phone was clamped to his ear almost as soon as they got out of the terminal. He made two calls, one to the nursing home where his gran had died, the second to a more work-related contact. Then Paulie had watched as Connor swept the exterior of his car, which Simon had left there, before getting in. Their destination was no surprise to Paulie: the offices of Sentinel Securities, the company Connor was a partner in, at the Gyle Trade Park, a ten-minute drive from the airport.

When they arrived, Connor ushered Paulie into the building,

where a lift took them up to the top floor. Paulie could read desperate purpose in Connor's movements, as though concentrating on the case meant he didn't have to contemplate the horror of his gran's death. They stepped into a standard, if spacious, conference room: large circular table in the centre, huge TV mounted to the wall, a table with tea and coffee facilities tucked into an alcove to its left.

At one of the seats facing the TV sat a scruffy-haired man Paulie vaguely recognised. He smiled at Connor, the smile fading into confusion as he saw Paulie standing beside him.

'Robbie,' Connor said. 'Thanks for coming in. This is Paulie King. He's an, ah, associate of Jen's. He found the drive I told you about on the phone.'

Robbie nodded, stood. Ignored Paulie totally. 'Connor,' he said, clearing his throat, 'I, ah, I heard about your gran. I just wanted to say how sorry I am and—'

Connor held up a hand. Paulie saw it tremble slightly. 'Thank you,' he muttered. 'Really, thank you. But for now, we need to work. I need to work.'

Robbie nodded, turned to Paulie. 'Mr King,' he said, his tone cool and professional in the way that only someone who had worked for the police could truly master, 'it's a pleasure to meet you.' He extended a hand, and Paulie almost mistook it for a greeting. But then he saw doubt cloud Robbie's eyes again and understood. He shrugged, too tired to take offence, reached into his pocket and produced the micro drive he had found in the back of the watch. Robbie took it, and in that instant, it was as if Paulie ceased to exist for him.

'Interesting,' he said, turning the sliver of plastic in his fingers. 'Not seen one of these in a long time.'

'Can you read it?' Connor asked, and Paulie got another taste of copper at the back of his mouth.

'What?' Robbie looked up, as though stirred from his thoughts. 'Oh. Yes, yeah, no problem. Just need to fit it to this,' he picked up a small rectangular object that looked like an old USB finger drive, 'and we should be good to go.'

Connor nodded, no words needed, and Robbie got to work.

He sat down, inserted the micro drive into the USB, then inserted it into his laptop. Leaned forward, the light from the screen making his features over-pronounced, as though his face was a tracing someone had gone over too many times, then frowned.

'Hmm,' he said.

'What?' Connor asked, stepping forward.

'See for yourself,' Robbie said. There was the clatter of keys, then the wall-mounted screen flared to life. It mirrored what Robbie was seeing on his screen, a simple one-line message, with a flashing cursor below it.

'RO one two one nine four,' Connor read. 'What the hell does that mean?'

Robbie sat back in his chair, chewing at his bottom lip absently. 'Could be a file number,' he said, 'identifying the data that's on the disk. But it's not in a format I'm familiar with and . . .' He trailed off, lost in thought. Then his eyes snapped into focus, and he gave Connor and Paulie an almost childish smile. 'It's a password challenge,' he said.

'A what?' Paulie asked.

'A password challenge,' Robbie said, as though talking to a child. 'It's a security measure. The file is asking you for a password in response to RO one two one nine four.' His face darkened. 'Which probably means there's an autodelete on the file if we get it wrong.'

'RO one two one nine four,' Paulie repeated. 'Where do you start with that?'

'Context,' Robbie said. 'There must be some clue to look at where the answer might be. Where did you say this drive came from?'

'An old watch,' Paulie said. 'Omega. A model used in the Second World War.'

Robbie stared at the screen. 'RO one two one nine four,' he said, then started typing. 'Nothing coming up on the numbers that's watch-related,' he said after a moment. 'But one two one nine four is the service number of a Private Charles Howlette, who was awarded the 1914 star in—'

'It's not the watch,' Connor said, his voice little more than a whisper. Paulie could see embarrassment in his eyes, as though he had had the answer in front of him the whole time and hadn't been able to see it. He reached into his pocket, produced the prayer book he had been given along with the watch.

'When Danny's mother gave me the watch, she gave me this as well,' he said, laying the book on the table. 'Could this be it?'

Robbie leaned forward, took it. Rifled through the pages. Stopped, looked up at the screen then held the book up to Connor and Paulie. 'Passages from the Bible,' he said, tapping the book with one finger.

'So what's R zero one two one nine four?' Connor asked, as he silently cursed, for the first time in his life, his parents' atheism.

'This is the New Testament,' Robbie said. 'R could be Romans from the Epistle of St Paul. Or Revelation. Look at the names and numbers before each short passage. Chapter and verse. Literally.' He looked closer at the page. 'It's not R zero. It's Ro. Romans.'

'And one two one nine four?'

'Word number? Look, see before that short verse, where it says Romans 1?'

'Yeah, but there's not ninety-four words in the verse.' He flicked the pages forward. 'And there's no Romans one nine four.'

Connor nodded. Considered. Then understood. 'It's not Romans one. It's Romans twelve, verse nineteen. Then word number four.'

Robbie found the page. Started reading. 'Romans twelve, verse nineteen. Do not take revenge, my dear friends, but leave room for God's wrath, for it is written.'

'Fourth word,' Paulie said. 'Revenge.'

'Revenge,' Connor said. 'Pretty appropriate, given Danny seems to have made sure I got this drive and the prayer book to seek revenge on those who killed him.'

'Want me to try it, boss?' Robbie asked.

Connor said nothing, merely nodded. Paulie forced himself not to hold his breath as Robbie typed in the response, then hit enter. There was an awful moment of silence, then the screen dissolved into what looked like a file directory. It was marked C325.

'It's the unedited background research, Gillespie's trauma studies related to the Troubles,' Robbie said after a moment. 'And the unredacted official reports.'

'Case studies, reports and witness interviews,' Connor said. 'Why go to all this trouble to hide them? What could be in them that was so important he—'

'Ah, boss,' Robbie interrupted, eyes on the screen in front of him, something between horror and fascination etched onto his face. 'Think you'd better see this.'

'What?' Connor asked.

'When you were running dark in Belfast, I put a track on your emails, remember. Made sure you had secure access to our server so we could communicate. Well, I just had a ping. You got an email.'

'From whom?' Connor asked.

Robbie took a breath, let it out slowly. 'Danny Gillespie,' he said.

CHAPTER 36

After their meeting with O'Brien, Donna and Simon decided to stay in Belfast and checked into a small hotel close to the centre of town. Simon had suggested that, after what O'Brien had told them, the safe-house he had arranged for Connor might have been safer, but Donna was adamant.

'I'm not hiding,' she said. 'Besides, whoever we're dealing with has made it clear they want to stay in the background. If they've been following us, they know where we've been and who we've met. Which means they know I was at the BBC office earlier today. Do you really think they're going to take the risk of kidnapping or killing a national broadcast journalist and a serving police officer? Besides, thanks to his meeting earlier, the focus is on Connor right now. They know he's got the watch and whatever it holds, so he's their priority.'

Simon thought back to the blank desolation he had seen in Connor's face after he had been told his grandmother had died, the hard, coiled mass of muscle he had felt when he'd hugged his friend.

'God help them,' he said.

They checked into the hotel, showered, then strolled out into the early evening, Simon heading for a restaurant he knew in the Cathedral Quarter. They walked in silence for a time, both alone with their thoughts, each processing what O'Brien had told them.

According to him, he, Bobby McCandish and Brendan Walsh had

been contacted by Danny Gillespie as part of his work in trying to understand the lasting impact of the Troubles.

'He found me an easier audience than the other two,' O'Brien had said, with a humourless laugh. 'I learned my lesson from the Troubles, wanted to share it with others. McCandish and Walsh, well, they took more convincing.'

'And how did Danny do that?' Donna had asked.

O'Brien's face twisted into something halfway between a genuine smile and a sneer. 'Simple,' he said. 'He appealed to their self-interest – and offered them a chance at revenge.'

From what O'Brien had said, Danny's work interviewing survivors and victims of attacks in the Troubles had started routinely enough, but then a pattern began to emerge. In several of the interviews he conducted, the interviewees reported being visited by a tall, dark-haired man. His rank, title and name varied, from Colonel James to Pastor Farrell, but there were two consistent features: a dark, perfectly trimmed moustache and a nervous tic of checking a large, expensive watch every two minutes. The questions he asked, according to Gillespie, were always the same. Has anyone else contacted you about this? What was the codeword used for the attack? Did the men you saw or were attacked by hesitate or give any clues to their identities?

'Problem was,' O'Brien had told Donna and Simon, 'Danny couldn't find any official reports of after-incident visits to victims by the military. So, whoever that was, he was either playing dress-up or he was real black ops.'

'Okay,' Donna had said. 'It's an interesting anomaly. But why did Danny think it was so important? You get plenty of ghouls looking to rubber-neck at others' misery, so what made this different?'

'Because it kept happening,' O'Brien had replied. 'And it showed a pattern. The visits happened after a bigger attack or when someone was killed.' He looked down, voice growing small. 'Like Carryduff. And those same two questions – did the men hesitate, did they give themselves away? What does that sound like to you?'

'A performance review,' Simon said. 'That sounds a lot like a CO checking in on his troops' performance after an action.'

'Exactly,' O'Brien had said. 'But the problem was that it was happening on both sides. Unionist and Republican. Which, Danny thought, opened the door to another Stakeknife incident. And that was a whole different world of shit.'

'Stakeknife?' Donna had asked. 'What's—'

'A spy,' Simon had replied, taking the baton before O'Brien could get to it. 'He was a British double agent, worked for the army, infiltrated the IRA during the Troubles. Fed information on operations back to the military.'

'And Danny thought this visitor was another, what, double agent?' Donna had asked, incredulity in her voice. 'Someone playing both sides of the coin, making sure the killing went on. Why?'

'Business,' O'Brien had said, in a tone so matter-of-fact it made Simon want to hit him. 'You play both sides off against each other, and who benefits? The man in the middle? Keep the Troubles going and paras on both sides retain their strangleholds on Northern Ireland, the military has an excuse to keep boots on the ground and the politicians have an easy headline waiting the next time they need a distraction from the latest minister caught with his trousers around his ankles.'

'You can't believe that's true,' Donna had said.

O'Brien had shrugged. 'Didn't matter if I believed it or not. Danny did. He became obsessed by it, trying to track down whoever this was. Asked me, McCandish and Walsh to tap any contacts we still had, see if we could get a lead on the guy. Hell, he even asked his dad to check with his contacts, see if there was anything the military knew. As he said, "If either side was manipulating the Troubles, that was an act of psychological torture and manipulation on an unimaginable scale."'

'And that's why you were all at the funeral?' Simon had asked. 'To check in with his dad, see if he had found anything?'

O'Brien had nodded. 'Exactly. But no joy. He said he ran into a dead end. Not really a surprise. A tall man with dark hair, a moustache and a fetish for checking his watch? Not exactly *Crimewatch*'s e-fit of the week, is it? But he asked us to keep looking, for Danny's sake.'

'You think it's real, don't you?' Simon had asked, putting it together in his mind, thinking of the watch Danny's mum had given Connor.

'That someone was playing both sides. That Danny got close to it and that was why he was killed. He got too close to the truth?'

'Think about it,' O'Brien said. 'Like I said, it's business. The Brexit shite you blagged your way in here with is real. It's a threat to the Good Friday Agreement that ended the Troubles. If it was discovered that the Troubles had been manipulated for political or financial gain, can you imagine what that would do to the place?'

Simon remembered what Connor had told him Gillian Flint had said about embarrassing information that governments in London and Washington wanted to keep quiet. That, plus Gillespie's death, the missing files and the attempt to grab Connor, gave the story a horrible grounding in plausibility.

He blinked himself from his thoughts, realised Donna was talking to him as they walked.

'Sorry,' he said. 'Million miles away. What did you say?'

She gave him a smile that was both infuriated and affectionate. 'I said, do you think whatever is on that drive Paulie found is the key to all this, that Connor has found some answers?'

Simon considered. Normally, if Connor had made a discovery on a case, Simon would be the first to know. But with Ida's death, Simon knew Connor would have other priorities. He just hoped they wouldn't blind his friend to the very real danger he was in. 'I don't know,' he admitted. 'I hope so. Either way, Connor's got a hard time ahead of him. Sooner we get back and I can help him, the better.'

Donna's eyes hardened for a second, her mouth pinching into a thin line.

Simon gave her a smile. 'I know,' he said. 'This is dangerous. I'm sorry I'm dragging you into it, and I'm sorry I'm putting you in harm's way, especially after what happened to Mark.'

Donna flinched at the mention of her ex. 'It's not that,' she said. 'You're about as far from Mark as you could be. He could barely survive a paper cut, while you . . .' She shook her head. 'It's just this is the job, Simon, for both of us. You risk your neck for Connor. I put myself out on a limb to get to the big stories first. We both accept it's part of the job. But now that we're together, and what you said about having things to do when we get back to Stirling, I just . . .' She looked up as though what she was struggling to say had been written in the sky. 'I don't . . .' she took a breath, waved a hand into the space between them '. . . I just don't want this, whatever it is, to end because one of us gets careless or sloppy.'

Simon felt a blast of icy adrenaline sear through his veins. A tsunami of thoughts and fears crowded into his mind as the world seemed to contract around him, until all that was left was him and Donna, standing on a street in Belfast. His heart hammered in his ears, but he knew what happened next was as unavoidable as the sun rising or the tide coming in.

'I don't want it to end either,' he said, his voice sounding too loud in his ears. 'I love you, Donna. I want this to work. So let's tell Connor what we've found, get this sorted out. And then,' he looked her straight in the eye, 'we can get home and start working on what's next. For both of us. Together.'

CHAPTER 37

Connor sat in the Audi, his gran's care home looming in front of him like some Gothic gargoyle, its eyes the light spilling from the windows. Felt something between gratitude and irritation when the sound of a phone ringing filled the car, the dashboard display telling him Simon was calling.

He took one last glance out of the windscreen. Opted for cowardice, and the deferring of what he would face the moment he walked into the building where his grandmother had died.

'Simon,' he said, hearing a catch in his voice he hadn't expected, as though opening his mouth had uncorked the grief that was churning in his chest. 'What's up?'

It didn't take Simon long to recount his and Donna's conversation with O'Brien, and the revelation of the moustached man with a military bearing who cropped up in so many of his reports. Connor's view of the care home seemed to fade as Simon spoke, his mind dragging him away from the moment and into a labyrinthine maze of possibilities and scenarios. He understood what was happening now. Or, at least, he thought he was beginning to.

'It makes sense,' he said, after Simon had finished. 'The drive Paulie found in the watch holds all of Danny's interviews and background research, with the unedited official reports. I've got Robbie combing through the data now, but I think that's the key – that the identity of this guy, and what he was up to, is held somewhere in all of that.'

'Think Robbie will be able to find it?' Simon asked.

'I hope so,' Connor replied. 'But he's not working alone. Danny's giving him a little help.'

There was a moment of silence. Then Simon's voice, somewhere between bemusement and confusion: 'Come again,' he said. 'I thought Danny was dead.'

Connor smiled, looked up at the care home. If only the dead could be conjured so easily.

'In a manner of speaking,' he said, pulling his attention back to the call. 'When we opened the drive and got past the password protection, it triggered an automated email sent to me from Danny. The email is basically a validation of what we've found. Danny details how, in the course of his work, he became increasingly convinced that a third party was involved in several of the terror attacks, either targeting them, in the case of Carryduff, or letting the attacks happen despite having knowledge beforehand and giving the authorities the chance to stop them.'

'Like Stakeknife,' Simon said. 'And the claims that the RUC failed to investigate IRA murders in order to keep him entrenched with them. Christ, no wonder you got government heat on this.'

'Not just government,' he said. 'Remember, there's also Ms Flint and those private operators who tried to scoop me up in Belfast. Wouldn't surprise me if their employer has a moustache and a military bearing.'

'Jesus,' Simon whispered. 'Any hints in Danny's email about where to look?'

'Maybe,' Connor said. 'The email was dated the day after he visited Arthur Fielding, the guy whose van was snatched for the attack on the Carryduff police station. He mentioned that the case seemed to be the key, and he was hoping that Fielding's story might give him the answers he needed. He must have thought he was getting close, or thought he was being followed, because he said in the email that he was going to give the watch, the files and the prayer book to his mother to get them to me as insurance if something happened to him.'

'Hold on,' Simon said. 'If he was getting heat like that, why didn't he go to his dad for help? He's former military, and from what O'Brien told Donna and me, he knew what Danny was working on.'

'You said it yourself,' Connor replied. 'Former military. If Danny had told his dad how close he was to identifying a double agent, and he kicked that up the chain of command, what would they do? Remember what Flint said, about the government not wanting this to get into the public domain? The military would have shut Danny down faster than you could say "cover-up". And Danny wanted the truth to be told.'

Simon sighed. 'And it cost him his life,' he said.

'Aye,' Connor agreed. 'So, what's your plan?'

'First flight back in the morning,' Simon said. 'As Donna pointed out, the focus of all this is on you, so Stirling is the place to be. Besides, I can't trust you not to get yourself hurt when I'm not around to look after you.'

Connor smiled again, felt a pang of melancholy as he looked up at the care home. 'Not going to argue,' he said. 'Let me know when you're due in and I'll pick you up, seeing I boosted the Audi from the airport.'

'Don't worry about it,' Simon said. 'We'll find our own way. You just watch your back until I get there, okay? These people aren't messing about, Connor, and if what Danny suspected is true, they've got a vested interest in making sure you don't get to the answer that got him killed.'

'I'll watch my tail, promise,' Connor said, instinctively glancing into the rear-view mirror as he spoke.

There was a moment of silence. Then Simon spoke again, his tone gentler than before, echoing with the grief in Connor's chest. 'How you holding up?' he asked.

'I'm, ah, I'm okay,' Connor said. 'Dropped Paulie off at his place, just at the care home now.'

'Aw, man,' Simon said. 'I'm sorry, Connor. Just take it slow, do what you have to.'

'Aye,' Connor said. 'Thanks, Simon. I just want to know what happened. They said it would have been quick, but what brought it on? Did the stress of the message you found in her paper have something to do with it?'

'Connor, don't let that eat you up. When I saw her, she looked frail, man. Like the dementia had finally got into her foundations. But she was still your gran. Still looking out for you. You really think a scrawled message on a scrap of paper could put Ida Fraser off looking out for her boy?'

'No,' Connor said. 'Probably not. But if it speeded up the stroke, that's another thing I owe these bastards for.'

'We,' Simon corrected. 'We owe them, Connor. And we'll settle up with them soon. Promise. Just watch yourself until I get home.'

'Okay,' Connor ended the call. He sat in the silence for a moment, let it seep into him, quiet the churning of his guts. Then, taking a deep breath, he got out of the car and walked towards the care home, the rock in his chest growing heavier with every step.

CHAPTER 38

The last thing Paulie wanted was another phone call.

After being dropped at home by Fraser, all he wanted was to get in, get his shoes off and crack open a bottle of Laphroaig, which he would enjoy with a cigar.

But as he stepped into the hallway of the house, he noticed that the answering machine on the hall table was flashing. It was a rare occurrence for two reasons – one, hardly anyone used landlines these days, preferring instead the immediacy of the mobile. And, second, only a handful of people had Paulie's landline number. Which meant that, unless this was another sodding message about the 'minor accident' and the compensation he was due, the message was important.

He hit the play button, listened as Angela Barr's clipped tone filled the corridor.

'Paulie, it's Angela. I took that meeting with MacKenzie's daughter as a courtesy to you – old times' sake and all that. But she's taking liberties with the arrangement. I think you need to remind her that this is serious business, and the penalty clauses we use are not to be trifled with. Give me a call when you get this.'

Paulie rubbed his eyes, felt the first snarls of a tension headache. He had known opening the door to the Barrs for Jen had been a bad idea. And it was a move her father, Duncan, would never have approved of. He should have said no, but when he had seen Jen's insistence, and her naked need to keep her father's memory alive through his business, he had been powerless to deny her. But at what cost had that agreement come? And what had Jen done to displease Angela Barr so badly that she had felt the need to leave Paulie a message?

He sighed, walked further down the hallway, heading for the living room. He would pour himself a whisky, light a cigar, then call Jen, find out what she had done. He had meant to phone her the moment he'd got off the plane, but Fraser's almost manic desire to keep moving and find out what was on that drive hadn't left him a moment to think.

He reached out for the door of the living room, stepped inside. Froze when he saw the figure sitting on the couch, legs crossed at the knees, one of Paulie's crystal glasses in one hand, the bottle of Laphroaig sitting on the table in front of him.

'Ah, Mr King,' he said, voice as cold as his eyes, 'I hope you don't mind, I indulged myself while I was waiting for you. A lot of people don't like the peaty whiskies, say it's too strong for them, but I find it adequate. In moderation, of course.'

'Of course,' Paulie whispered, almost unable to speak around the ball of fury that was lodged at the back of his throat. Who the fuck was this prick to break into his home and help himself to his whisky? He would ask him, just before he broke his jaw and tore out his tongue with his bare hands.

The man on the couch twitched, and a gun appeared in his free hand.

'I must say, Mr King,' he said, with a smile, 'you must be a terrible poker player. Your anger is digging furrows into your forehead. Please, don't try anything stupid. This can either be civilised or vulgar. Your choice.'

Paulie's eyes were locked on the barrel of the gun, and the black void that was glaring at him. 'Fine,' he said. 'What is it you want?'

The man put the whisky glass on the table, then ran a free finger over his top lip, smoothing the neat moustache that nestled there. 'Come now, Mr King,' he said, cruel humour in his voice. 'I think we both know what I want. It's quite simple, really. I understand you visited Connor Fraser's office with him earlier this evening. I'd like to know what that visit was about, and whether Mr Fraser has in his possession any items relating to the late Danny Gillespie.'

'Like what?' Paulie asked. 'His ashes?'

The man's smile grew colder as the gun came up, moving from Paulie's gut to his head. 'Please, Mr King. Don't think for a minute I won't spray your brains over your wall if you fuck with me. My questions are simple. Does Connor Fraser have Danny Gillespie's research? If he does, where is he keeping it? I hope these are questions you can answer, Mr King. Or else your night is going to come to a very final, very unpleasant end.'

CHAPTER 39

Connor drove away from the care home in a daze, as though the staff's compassion and sympathetic understanding had punched him into a stupor.

When he had entered the home, he had been met by Aileen Black, the manager who had initially helped him set up his gran's accommodation when he had moved her in a few years previously. She took him into her office, explained that the on-site doctor had confirmed that Ida had passed away, most probably from a massive stroke.

'It would have been quick, Mr Fraser,' she said, her tone eerily like Jen's when she had called him. 'She wouldn't have suffered.'

There were forms to sign, accepting custody of the possessions in his gran's room. Then Aileen gave him the equivalent of a psychic hand grenade – a small, clear plastic bag holding Ida's wedding ring and the necklace she always wore.

'We took these off her before she was sent to the hospital,' she explained. Connor was about to ask, but she seemed to read his thoughts. 'For the post-mortem examination,' she explained. 'We can confirm end of life here, but as it happened with no one in the room, there has to be a post-mortem examination to confirm cause of death. I've put the phone number for the hospital in your copy of the property forms. You can call them in the morning, arrange to see her, if you want.'

He had staggered through the rest of their conversation in a numb stupor, his face feeling frozen into neutral repose. All the time Aileen spoke, all Connor could think of was that one, innocuous offer: *You can arrange to see her if you want.* Had the families of the two men he had killed in Belfast been offered the same courtesy, to see their bodies one last time? Somehow, he doubted it, thought instead that those men would be in a landfill site now, their families never given the closure of knowing exactly what had happened to them.

He drove on autopilot, heading for the only place he could think to go – the house just off Windsor Terrace in the King's Park area of the city. He tried not to stay there too often – when things had gone sour with Jen, staying there was like haunting the potential of the life that could have been with her. But it was the only place he could think of. A hotel would have been safer, more anonymous, but anyone who came looking for him that night would end up as a chew toy for the caged anguish coiling in his chest, and he would thank them for the distraction of violence.

He pulled into the driveway, felt his breath catch in his throat as his headlights played across the outline of the other car parked there. He pulled to a halt, skidding slightly on the gravel as he overworked the brakes. This couldn't be real. It had to be a dream, his mind's way of coping with everything the last few days had thrown at him.

He blinked, the hallucination stubbornly refusing to fade as he did.

Jen's car. Parked in the driveway, just as it always should have been.

He got out, walked towards the front door. Didn't know what to say when it swung open, Jen standing there, etched in the light from the hall, her face a mixture of hope and pain as she leaned awkwardly on her crutch.

'I'm sorry if this isn't okay,' she said, before he could speak. 'But I still have a key for the place, and after your gran and . . .'

He had her in his arms before he knew he was going to reach for her. Felt the anger and grief he had pushed down inside himself heave and come loose as he breathed her in.

He let her go after a moment, backed off awkwardly. 'Sorry,' he said. 'I know things haven't been right for a while. Just seemed . . .' He shrugged, unable to articulate what he was thinking or feeling.

'It's okay,' Jen said, her eyes bright with tears she refused to shed. 'That's kind of why I'm here. But why don't you at least come in?'

Connor followed her into the house, down the hall to the open-plan kitchen–living area at the back. Watched as Jen made her way to the breakfast bar, and the seats that had been adjusted to the perfect height to accommodate her injured spine and let her sit and stand easily.

'Look, Connor,' she said, rushing the words out before he had a chance to speak. 'Your gran, ah, your gran passing, it got me thinking. About you and me. I don't want this . . .' she waved at the air between them '. . . to go on any more.'

Connor felt as though he had been stabbed in the chest. 'Ah, I see, I—'

'Oh, God, no, no,' Jen said, panic rising in her eyes. 'I didn't mean that. I meant I want us to get past this, try to make us work. I blamed you for Dad's death, I see that now. But your gran dying made me realise none of that matters. We're both in dangerous lines of work, but if we're going to make this work between us, something has to change.'

Connor heard a vague alarm bell start to ring in his mind. 'Dangerous lines of work? Okay, I admit my job can get a little, ah, hectic, at times. But I'm not sure the haulage business could be described as dangerous – unless you're talking about your carbon footprint.'

She gave him a weak smile, acknowledging his attempt at a joke to lighten the moment. Then she held his gaze, jaw set, expression unreadable.

'Jen? What?' he said, feeling like a kid who had jumped into the deep end of the pool and remembered he couldn't swim.

She took a deep breath, then nodded to herself, as though confirming a decision. Then she started talking. She told Connor about Aberdeen, about her deal to distribute the drugs the Barrs brought into the country from Europe, and her attempt to blackmail Angela Barr with the threat of exposure to keep the deal on track when Paulie left for Belfast with Donna.

Connor stood, silently taking it all in, trying to remember the point at which the shy personal trainer with the dimpled smile and great laugh had become the woman in front of him. Felt a pang of guilt when he realised it was a journey that had begun the night they'd met.

'So what do you want to do?' Connor asked, after Jen had stopped talking.

'I – I don't know,' she said, naked confusion in her eyes. 'I thought I wanted this deal to save Dad's company. Convinced myself it was the right thing to do. But then your gran died, and I got thinking about you and me, the lives we lead. And I'm not sure this is what I want. I mean, me? Distributing drugs around the UK so kids can fuck up their lives? That's not me, Connor. Jesus, when did I think it was?'

He took a step forward, rested a hand on her shoulder. 'We all get lost sometimes, Jen,' he said. 'The question is, what do you want to do next? If you walk away from this, how will the Barrs take it?'

'I don't know,' she said. 'Angela wasn't exactly complimentary when I told her I was fronting the deal. I know Paulie's had dealings with her in the past, but I can't imagine you get to be one of Scotland's biggest drug-traffickers with a steady temper and a forgiving soul.'

'So we speak to Paulie,' Connor said, 'find out what we're dealing with. If he can persuade Angela to let it go, let bygones be bygones, great. If not . . .'

'If not?' Jen asked, a note of warning in her voice.

'If not,' Connor said, the fury in his chest growing restless once more, 'we burn her and her business to the ground. I'm sick of seeing the people I love hurt, Jen. I just want some peace. And if Angela Barr, or whoever is after me, is going to stand in the way of that, I go through them.'

Jen gave a small, almost shy smile. 'You do know how to woo a girl, don't you?' she said.

Connor laughed, felt some of the tension in his gut uncoil. 'Only the best for you,' he said. 'I mean, if the offer of the house wasn't enough,' he looked around the place, 'then the least I can do is go to war with a drug-dealer for you.'

She stood, Connor repressing the urge to help her as she adjusted her crutch. Then she took the two small steps towards him, laid one hand on his chest and kissed him. Pushed him away, reluctantly, as his phone began to vibrate in his pocket.

'The man in demand,' she said, her eyes glinting with humour and something more visceral.

'Sorry,' he said, reaching for his phone. He frowned at the display, no number recognised.

'Fraser,' he said, voice hard.

'Connor,' the reply came, slightly breathless. 'It's Flint. Gillian Flint. We need to talk. Now.'

'Look, Gillian,' Connor said, 'I told you in Belfast. I'll find your employer. And I will deal with him for what he's done. If you get in the way of that, I'll—'

'Paulie,' Gillian said, cutting across Connor. 'Connor, it's Paulie. I just got word. The people you pissed off in Belfast decided to go on the offensive. Seems Paulie was their first port of call. Which means—'

'Which means . . .' Connor said, terror forming in his gut as he looked at Jen. Could he do what he had failed to do before and protect her this time? '. . . that I'm next.'

CHAPTER 40

It didn't take Flint long to tell Connor what she knew. But listening to the call, watching Jen's helpless pleading to know what he was being told as she watched him, Connor knew one thing with absolute certainty.

This was his last case.

'I told you I didn't approve of that note being left with your gran,' Flint said. 'That was unprofessional and, knowing you the way I do, I told the people I was working for that it would only harden your resolve not to play ball with them. But to compound that error in judgement by grabbing Paulie, a man to whom I owe a degree of gratitude for what he did to Ryan Walsh last year, well, it was a step too far. I'm a professional, Connor, and this is starting to look like a vendetta.'

Connor blinked, pushing aside the memory of Ryan Walsh tied to a chair, Paulie putting a gun to his head and making a crimson scream of his brains on the wall behind him. Felt a wave of exhaustion wash over him. How much violence was too much? 'Okay,' he said, pushing the thought aside. 'Let's say for a moment I believe you, that you've suddenly grown a conscience and decided to help me, that this isn't some scheme of yours to get hold of the data everyone seems to want, it begs a very specific question. Who are you working for, Gillian?'

A sigh down the line, frustration and disappointment, as if Connor had been offered a gourmet menu at a Michelin-starred restaurant and ordered a burger and fries.

'I don't know,' she said. 'My contracts are vetted by my handler. I never know who I'm actually working for – it insulates me and them. All I know is why I'm hired. I have a, well, a reputation in a certain field. And this case falls right into that field.'

'The field of keeping US involvement in the Troubles out of the headlines, right?' Connor asked.

'Right,' Flint replied. 'It's no secret that US money and arms were funnelled to the paramilitaries during the Troubles. If you want to see how invested in Irish politics and patriotism we are, hell, we dye a river green to celebrate St Patrick's Day. It's a sensitive subject, and with all the political volatility here and in the US at the moment, the last thing either side needs is something like this coming to light.'

'Something like what?' Connor asked, voice sharp with frustration. 'Was Danny right? Was a double agent working for the military and the paramilitaries, coordinating certain attacks during the Troubles?'

'That's the working theory,' Flint said. 'And Dr Gillespie's research and the reports he found hold the key to identifying whoever that is. That was my contract – retrieve the information and plug any potential leaks of the data or its existence.'

'Leaks,' Connor said. 'Like Paulie.'

'My information is that he was, ah, approached less than an hour ago. To be questioned about what you and he were doing at Sentinel Securities, and what, if anything, you brought back from Belfast.'

'We just stopped in for coffee with a friend,' Connor said, his tone impassive, even as his mind raced with thoughts of Robbie and hopes that he was watching his back.

'Of course you did,' Flint said, her tone mocking.

'So what will happen to Paulie?' Connor said, feeling Jen's eyes fall on him again as he spoke.

'Initial questioning on site,' Flint said. 'If that doesn't yield anything significant, he'll be taken to a different location for more, ah, intense interviewing.'

'Any idea where that site might be?' Connor asked.

'Not yet, but I'm working on it,' Flint said. 'There are only a few suitable locations in the area. I just need to whittle them down.'

'How long?' Connor said.

'An hour, maybe more,' Flint said. 'I still have to be discreet. If whoever put me on this contract found out I was talking to you about this . . .'

'Understood,' Connor said. 'How long do you think I've got before they're at my door?'

'As long as it takes for them to finish with Paulie,' Flint replied. 'As far as I understand, this was a direct action, not a sanctioned scoop-up. It's one man, acting alone.'

'Which tells us he's rattled,' Connor said. 'Anything I can do in the meantime?'

'Wait,' Flint replied. 'As soon as I get word on Paulie, I'll be in contact. In the meantime, if you do have any information, secure it. I wasn't joking when I said this is sensitive, Connor.'

Connor ended the call, looked to Jen. Raised a hand when he saw the questions form on her face, her mouth opening to voice them. 'Got a call to make,' he said, giving her what he hoped was an apologetic smile.

He listened. The phone was answered after a few short rings.

'Robbie,' he said. 'It's Connor. Just had a call. That package I brought in to you earlier might attract a bit of heat. I take it you're somewhere safe?'

'I moved about five minutes after I started looking at the data,' Robbie replied, sounding distracted, as though he still had one eye on his laptop screen as he spoke. 'If you don't know what you're looking for, it's all innocuous eyewitness reports on terror attacks. But if you add context and Danny's suspicions . . .'

'What have you got?' Connor said, feeling excitement shiver down his back. 'A name?'

'Not yet,' Robbie said. 'But cross-referencing the dates of attacks with troop deployments and officers who were in Northern Ireland at the time gives me a place to start. I'm also compiling a list of what attacks were called in and tipped to authorities in advance – you know, like a car bomb being phoned in ten minutes before it went off. One thing is for certain. There definitely was someone who visited every one of the attack victims Danny interviewed. Someone was definitely pulling strings, boss.'

'Okay,' Connor said, looking at the clock on the wall. 'Robbie, I know it's late, but can you keep going on this? I don't think we've got much time, and I need a name or at least something we can use to fight back against these bastards.'

Amazingly, Robbie laughed. 'You think I could sleep with this in front of me? Don't worry, boss, I'm in a safe location, and I've no intention of stopping until I find something we can use.'

Connor thanked him and ended the call. Turned to Jen. 'I'm sorry,' he said, the words feeling inadequate, empty as he spoke them. 'Looks like I've dragged Paulie into this shitshow.'

A flash of panic crossed Jen's face. Then she nodded to herself. Decision made. She moved across to him, leaned into his chest.

'You're going to get Paulie back, aren't you?' she asked.

'I'll do everything I can,' he replied, not willing to taint whatever fresh start they had made with a lie.

He excused himself, made a sweep of the house, checking all the doors and windows. Stepped back into the kitchen area to find Jen sitting on the couch, a blanket over her knees.

'I can't sleep, but I need to get off my feet,' she said, patting the sofa beside her. 'Come, sit down. If all we can do is wait, we can do it together.'

Connor smiled, felt the weight of the day settle on his shoulders as he sat down beside her. Put one arm around her, then took a cushion and used it to cover the gun he held in his other hand. Felt the warmth of Jen as she relaxed into him, her breathing giving way to light snoring a few minutes later.

He closed his eyes, soaked in the moment of quiet.

He was startled awake what felt like a second later by the sound of scratching coming from the front door. He looked down, saw Jen was still curled into him. Then looked up at the clock on the wall. Found himself unable to believe he had fallen asleep, and been out for more than two and a half hours.

Another scratch from the door. Connor eased himself up, praying

Jen stayed asleep, at least until he could ascertain what was going on.

He moved out of the kitchen, into the hallway. Trained the gun on the front door as he approached it, the scratching noise getting louder as he got closer.

It was the lock. Someone was trying to pick the lock. Connor considered his options. Decided he didn't have time to play cat and mouse, to get out of the back of the house, circle round and confront whoever was at the door. Besides, he thought, with dread, he only had Flint's word that this was a one-man operation. How many hostiles could be waiting out there for him?

He kept low, took a deep breath. Reached up for the door handle. Unlocked it slowly, holding his breath as he prayed for it not to make a sound, then wrenched the door back with all his strength, stepping back and training his gun on the figure that tumbled into the hallway.

'Jesus, FUCK!' the figure roared, as he hit the floor.

Connor couldn't believe what he was hearing. He took a half-step forward, keeping the gun up, unwilling to give in to the sudden surge of hope he felt. 'Paulie? That you?'

'Well, it's no' the fucking Easter Bunny, is it?' Paulie rolled onto his back, his face a mask of blood from which his eyes glittered like dark jewels.

'Jesus,' Connor said, stowing the gun and grabbing Paulie by the shoulders to drag him into the house. 'What the hell happened to you? We heard you'd been taken by—'

Paulie barked a noise that was half grunting laugh, half blood-drenched gurgle. 'Taken,' he said. 'Aye. Fuck that. Bastard breaks into my house. Puts a gun on me. We had, ah, what do you call it? Oh, aye, a frank exchange of views. Fucker'll no' be doin' that again any time soon.'

Light spilled into the hall and Connor whirled to find Jen standing at the door to the kitchen. 'P-Paulie?' she whispered, sounding like a sleep-addled child who hadn't quite shrugged off the nightmare they had just been roused from.

'Aye, darlin',' Paulie said, dragging himself to his feet, leaving a trail of dark blood on the hall wall as he did. 'It's me. Sorry to bother you so late, needed a place to take a breath, and I needed a word with yer man here.'

'Come on,' Connor said, getting an arm under Paulie's shoulder. 'Let's get you patched up.'

Another laugh, this one causing Paulie to wince in pain. Connor knew the expression all too well. He'd pulled it a few times when he'd broken a rib or two.

'That can wait,' Paulie said. 'First, I need a whisky. A big one. And then, Fraser,' he turned to Connor, his eyes as dark and malignant as the bruises that tattooed his face, 'you and I are going to have a chat.'

CHAPTER 41

The flight from Belfast City got Simon and Donna into Edinburgh airport just before 8 a.m. They decided it was quicker and easier to swallow the cost and get a taxi back to Stirling. Neither of them spoke much during the drive. Donna called her parents to check how they were getting on with Andrew. Simon couldn't hear the other end of the call, but he could tell from the storm of emotions crossing Donna's face that her parents were playing the working-mother-guilt and long-suffering-grandparents cards to perfection. He knew Donna's job was a point of friction between her and her parents, especially her mother, who was firmly of the view that Donna should follow her path, give up work and concentrate on raising Andrew. Simon's arrival in Donna's life had only intensified that belief, solidified it into something almost feverish. After, all, a single mother working to provide for her son had a certain nobility to it. But now Donna had a man in her life, the missing piece of the nuclear-family puzzle, shouldn't she be concentrating on that? Simon couldn't understand Donna's mother's attitude: she had proven herself to be a strong, independent-minded woman who'd be damned if anyone could drown out her voice or opinion, yet her views on feminism and her daughter's right to choose her own path seemed grounded in some warped 1930s version of 'husband knows best'. But who was he to judge? Donna's parents had been married for almost forty years. Something must be working for them.

He wrenched himself from his thoughts, concentrated on his phone. There was a text from Connor, warning him that he and Paulie had been followed from the airport to Sentinel the night before, and suggesting they catch up 'over a bag of M&Ms'. Simon smiled at the code he and Connor had worked up for clandestine meetings. 'M&Ms' stood for Martyrs' Monument, a glass-encased marble sculpture of two sisters being watched over by an angel. Dating back to the nineteenth century, it was a memorial to sisters Margaret and Agnes Wilson, devout Covenanters who were found guilty of high treason for their beliefs. Sitting in the Old Town Cemetery, not far from Stirling Castle, the monument had the advantage of being in an area that gave clear lines of sight of possible attackers and several routes of escape. A perfect location for Connor and Simon to meet.

They got the taxi to drop Donna at her flat, then Simon went on to his garden flat in King's Park. He had the driver stop a street away, approached the flat cautiously, looking for anyone following him or any signs of surveillance. Finding none, he slipped down the stairs to the flat and let himself in.

The air was slightly stale, as though the flat had been holding its breath, waiting for him to return. Simon crossed to the patio doors that led out onto the walled garden at the back of the flat, and wasn't surprised when a tortoiseshell blur darted past his feet as the door slid open.

'Hello, Tom,' he said to the cat, which had jumped onto the breakfast bar behind him. 'How you been?'

Tom merely gave him an impassive stare, passing judgement on him in the way only a cat could.

'Let me guess,' Simon said, heading for the kitchen cupboard where he stored cans of tuna. 'You're hungry. How about I—'

He was cut off by the sound of the doorbell. Simon froze, eyes darting to Tom, whose only comment was an intensifying of her judgemental glare. Simon ran a quick calculation, cursed when he realised his own gun was stored in the bedroom safe, as much use as the gun he had dismantled and dumped around Belfast before he had boarded the flight home.

Another ring, somehow managing to sound more impatient.

Simon glanced around, eyes falling on the knife block. He grabbed for a knife, reversed his grip, keeping the blade tight to his forearm. Then he headed for the door, squinted into the spy-hole. Felt something between relief and dread flood through him as he saw who was standing there.

'Guv,' he said, as he opened the door to DCI Malcolm Ford. 'Pleasant surprise. Wasn't expecting to see you this morning. How'd you know I'd be here anyway?'

Ford shook his head as he stepped into the flat. 'Detective, remember?' he said. 'Knew you'd be wanting to get back now that Fraser's in town. Had a look at the flight schedules. First flight back from Belfast gets you in at seven fifty a.m. Factor in a taxi ride as I know you didn't have a car with you at the airport, and it wasn't difficult to guess.'

Typical Ford, Simon thought. His brain was as sharp as his manner. 'Hold on, though,' he said. 'How did you know Connor was back, and that I'd follow as soon as I could?'

Ford turned to him. 'Seems Mr Fraser is still of active interest to our friends in MI5,' he said. 'I got a call last night from the same people who called me when you huckled those two agents in Dundee. Told me that Fraser was back in the country, and wanted to be informed if he made any contact with me.'

'I take it he hasn't been in touch?' Simon asked.

'No,' Ford said, weariness creeping into his voice. 'But I really wasn't expecting it. After all, he'll have his hands full with his grandmother's death, won't he?'

'Ah,' Simon said, 'you heard.'

'I had officers watching the home after you let me know about the note being passed to her,' Ford said. 'They told me an ambulance had been called to the place. Didn't take much to get the rest of the details. You think that note had anything to do with her passing away?'

Trust Ford to cut straight to the important question. The question that would dictate how much damage Connor Fraser was about to do. 'I don't know,' Simon said after a moment.

Ford wandered over to the breakfast bar, took a seat. Reading the unspoken request, Simon got to work making coffee.

'What are you tied up with here, Simon?' Ford asked, as Tom approached him, nuzzling his arm for attention.

'Honestly, sir, I'm not sure,' Simon said, as he poured coffee. He told Ford about the files Connor had found, Danny Gillespie's suspicion that a double agent had been manipulating both Republicans and Loyalists during the Troubles, and his belief that the identity of that agent was hidden in his research somewhere.

'Christ,' Ford muttered, into his coffee. 'No wonder the Chief is shitting a brick over this. He must be getting his balls squeezed from on high.'

'Guthrie?' Simon said. Peter Guthrie, Chief of Police Scotland. A political animal with as much taste for real policing as a sommelier had for Buckfast, Guthrie was the man his political masters leaned on when they needed a friendly headline or a problem dealt with quietly. Neither seemed likely with Connor's current problems.

'Yeah,' Ford said. 'He's been breathing down my neck. Ensuring I offer "full and complete" cooperation with MI5, and demanding that we haul Fraser in the moment he twitches the wrong way.'

'Aye,' Simon said. 'Good luck with that.'

Ford gave a smile as bitter as his coffee. 'Guthrie can piss off,' he said. 'I don't answer to government agents, spies or whatever they call themselves. I'm polis, with one job to do – catch the criminals. If Fraser is doing something illegal, or against national security, that's one thing. But if he's been put in the middle of something because his friend got too close to something embarrassing for those in high office, to hell with them. That's their problem. It's strange, though.'

'What's that, boss?' Simon asked.

'The briefing Guthrie received. Seems the brief on Fraser has changed a bit. When you fronted down those two agents in Dundee, they said they were following Jen so she could lead them to Fraser as they needed to talk to him, right?'

'Right,' Simon said, a sudden flash of Paulie hosing a man with petrol jumping into his mind.

'Well,' Ford said, 'the parameters have changed. Now that they know Fraser is back in the country, they've changed it to a watching brief only. Reports on who he meets, et cetera. Whatever the reason, their desire to talk to him isn't as urgent. Odd.'

'Look, boss,' Simon said, having taken a moment to consider what Ford had said and found it made no sense, 'I don't want to put you in a difficult spot, especially with all the pressure you're getting from the Chief, but—'

'But you want me to do a little digging, see who was asking about Fraser in the first place?' Ford interrupted. 'The initial call I got, before you pulled those two officers off the street, was from the office of Walter Atkins, telling me that operatives were on the ground in my area, and Connor was the focus of their enquiries.'

'Atkins?' Simon said. 'You mean the Scottish Justice Secretary? But if this is national security and MI5, that's UK-government level. Why would he be involved?'

'Respect,' Ford said, his tone mocking. 'New government, new relations with the devolved nations, don't you know? It's all about respect now, working together as one team to deliver on this "national renewal" that the robot in glasses keeps going on about. None of this Tory "You will obey your imperial masters" shite any more. Or, at least, that's the spin they're keen to put on it. Seems he got a call from Westminster "as a courtesy" to tell him they would have agents working on his turf, and he filtered that down to me.'

Simon started, some vague memory flicking a switch on a light in a dark, forgotten corner of his mind. 'Imperial masters,' he muttered.

'What?' Ford said.

'Sorry, boss,' Simon said. 'Just thinking out loud.' He wondered how much more he could tell Ford. Decided to keep Gillian Flint's involvement out of things for the moment. 'Connor thinks there's a third party working here, independent of the official operation. He thinks they're the ones who left the note at his gran's care home.'

'Makes sense, I guess,' Ford said. 'A move like that would be seen as potentially hazardous to an official investigation. It could be construed as threatening an innocent third party to coerce cooperation.'

Another nag at the back of Simon's mind. Something about coercion. About . . . 'Exactly,' he said. 'So knowing who officially sanctioned action on Connor could help us find out why someone unofficial has been called in as well.'

Ford was petting Tom absently. Simon could almost see him playing with the pieces of the puzzle he had presented to him, assembling them into a picture he found acceptable. 'Makes sense,' Ford said. 'Okay, I'll look into it. But, Simon,' he turned to him, face blank, eyes dark, 'I can go only so far on this. If Fraser starts to make waves, or it looks like it's going to get nasty, I'll pull him in. And, remember, shit flows downhill, and the last thing you want is to be caught in that landslide. If Guthrie has a hissy fit, I'll make sure the pleasure of enduring it isn't just mine alone.'

'Understood,' Simon said, knowing that, whatever was coming at Connor, he would be right alongside him when it hit.

CHAPTER 42

Paulie complained about Connor's whisky collection, just loudly enough to tell Connor that he was in a lot of pain. He looked like he had been in a car crash; two black eyes, skin already turning the jaundiced purple-yellow that comes from deep bruising, lips bloodied and burst, blood drying on them like some obscene lipstick. It was obvious that his nose had been broken, again, and a cursory examination, to which Paulie only grudgingly agreed after some cajoling from Jen, revealed that he had at least three cracked ribs. Getting him comfortable on the sofa, Connor took a seat opposite him. 'You know,' he said, 'you should really think about the hospital, Paulie.'

Paulie reached for his whisky, almost managed to mask the grimace of pain as the alcohol touched his ruined lips. 'Fuck off,' he sneered. 'For this? Christ, I've had worse after a night out in Dunfermline. This is nothing. Besides,' his eyes locked with Connor's, gaze turning black, 'if I'm in hospital, who's going to settle up for me? You?'

Connor rolled his shoulders, let the insult slide. He needed Paulie cooperative. Getting into a pissing match with him would achieve nothing. 'What can you tell me about who attacked you?' he asked.

Paulie took another sip of his whisky, closed his eyes for a moment. 'Didn't look like much at first glance,' he said. 'Average height, slim build. Wore his suit like he'd been stitched into it. Wouldn't stop stroking his moustache when he spoke – think he was using that as a distraction, to split my attention between his tic and the gun.'

'Moustache?' Connor asked, remembering what Arthur Fielding had said about the man who'd visited him after the Carryduff massacre. 'Was he wearing a watch as well, always checking it?'

'Watch?' Paulie asked. 'No. No watch that I saw. He was a creepy fucker, though. Sat there like a fucking Bond villain, totally still apart from stroking his moustache. And then, when he did move . . .'

Paulie leaned his head back, groaning as he laid a hand on his ribs.

Connor couldn't get the thought of Arthur Fielding out of his head. Could this be the same man? It was possible, but how likely was it? Fielding had been visited almost forty years ago. Could a man in his sixties really do this much damage to someone like Paulie? It seemed unlikely . . . and yet . . .

'What type of age was he?' Connor asked.

'Late thirties, maybe early forties,' Paulie said. 'That was another part of what made him so fucking weird. He had a youngish face, but with that moustache and the suit, it was like he was playing at being older, if you see what I mean.'

'Oh, I see, all right.' Connor said, feeling pieces of the puzzle click together in his mind. The moustache. The fact that it was Paulie, not Connor, who had been targeted. The fact that Paulie was here, on his couch, rather than being tortured for answers or cooling in an unmarked grave somewhere. It made sense now.

'What?' Jen asked, startling Connor. He had been so focused on Paulie, he had almost forgotten she was there. 'What is it, Connor?'

'A message,' Connor said, his theory solidifying in his mind as he spoke it aloud. 'This was all a message. The moustache, the way he drew your attention to it. That's a message that he or whoever he's working for knows what Danny was on to, the man with the moustache who was pulling the strings behind attacks in the Troubles. And going for you? That's another part of it. Since this started, I've been the focus because whoever is after Danny's data knows he got it to me through the watch. But then we come back to Edinburgh, go to Sentinel, and they decide to go after you, Paulie, instead of coming straight for me?' He felt vaguely stupid for not having seen it before now. 'And letting you get away to come here? It's all a message. A way to put pressure on me, get me running to find the truth before they kick in my door. Which means I'm being used. Whoever beat the shite out of you wants to put pressure on me. Make me sloppy. That's what all this is about.'

'Hold on a minute,' Paulie said, gasping in pain as he hauled himself upright. 'What's all this shite about that guy letting me get away? What the fuck you think all this is, Fraser?' He gestured to his ruined face. 'That I tripped on the way up your driveway? Toughest bastard I ever fought. He let me away with nothing.'

'Sorry, Paulie,' he said. 'But think about it. He gets into your home undetected. Has the drop on you with a gun. Was smart enough to split your focus with the little moustache trick, which guaranteed you'd remember that one feature about him and tell me about it. How did you get away, anyway?'

'He started asking me questions, kept pointing the gun at me, threatening me with a bullet in the head if I didn't talk. Figured I had nothing to lose, so I charged him, got on top of him on the couch. Then we got into it.'

'And he didn't get a shot off as you lunged?' Connor said. 'You think that's likely? Sorry, Paulie, you've been played. We all have.'

Paulie said nothing, glaring at Connor as acceptance sank in, more painful than any bruise or cracked rib.

'Okay,' Jen said. 'Assuming that's true, why? Why play these games?'

'Like I said, to panic me,' Connor said. 'Whoever visited Paulie wants me to find this double agent, whoever he is, and expose him. This was just a way to flush the mark.'

'Flush the mark?' Jen asked.

'Old burglar's trick,' Paulie said, draining his glass and gesturing towards the bottle on the table. Connor nodded and Paulie refilled his glass. 'Say you're looking for a hidden safe in a house, or the most valuable item. Easiest way to find it is to panic the home owner with a fire or something similar. Nine times out of ten, they'll head straight for the thing they value most – the safe, the jewellery, whatever. You get them to lead you to the thing you want most.'

'Exactly,' Connor said. 'Which tells us something else. We've got another player in the game. Someone who's very, very keen for this to blow up publicly.'

'How do you figure that?' Jen asked.

'Think about it,' Connor said. 'DCI Ford confirmed to Simon that there were government boots on the ground – the two agents that Paulie and Simon took out on the road to Aberdeen. We know there's a private contractor on the scene. We thought they were trying to get to the information first to keep it quiet, but then Gillian Flint calls me to tell me Paulie's been targeted. But he turns up here. If everyone wanted this to stay quiet, Paulie wouldn't have been allowed to get away. No, whoever is trying to flush the mark wants us to get the answer, and make it public.'

'Makes sense,' Jen said. 'But who could that be? And why?'

Connor felt something snag at the corner of his mind, then slip away, as though carried away by the tide.

'I'm not sure,' he said, 'yet. But hopefully Robbie's analysis can help us with that. Paulie, probably best you keep a low profile here, rest up a bit. Jen, if you could stay with him?'

'No chance,' she said, shooting an apologetic glance at Paulie. 'This may be important, but I've still got the Barr situation to deal with, remember?' Paulie shifted at the mention of the name, as though it had poked him in his cracked ribs. 'It's all right, Paulie,' she said. 'I've told him about the Barrs and the deal. It's . . .' she took a breath, shoulders sagging '. . . I'm not going through with it. I'll tell the Barrs the deal is off.'

Relief and pride flashed across Paulie's face. 'Thank Christ for that,' he said. 'I'm too old to get back into the drugs trade. But, Jen, the Barrs aren't known for being the easiest people to disappoint. Angela Barr left a message for me, warning me about what would happen if this doesn't work out. May be better if I talk to her, see if—'

'No, Paulie,' Jen said, voice hardening. 'This is my mess. I never should have gone down this road in the first place.' She gave Connor a look. 'But I did. And it's my responsibility to sort it.'

Paulie looked ready to argue, then slumped back on the couch, pain winning the argument for him.

'Okay,' Connor said. 'I'll check in with Robbie, then meet Simon, tell him what we know. Hopefully we can get to the bottom of this sooner rather than later.' He lifted the whisky bottle from the table, inspected it. Almost two-thirds gone. 'If nothing else, I'm not sure I can afford to keep Paulie in whisky for much longer.'

CHAPTER 43

Connor could tell Robbie was enjoying himself just a little too much.

He had told him to meet him and Simon at the Old Town Cemetery in Stirling, so they could be updated at the same time. Being out of the office was a novelty for Robbie. His career as a security officer in the field had been short and fairly disastrous, ending with him letting an asset run away from him and through the streets of Edinburgh unprotected after a criminal case in which he was the key witness. But what Robbie lacked in street smarts he more than made up for in his abilities as an investigator. If there was a secret to be found, Robbie would track it down. He was, Connor thought, like a digital bloodhound – put him on the trail and he wouldn't stop until he found the answer he was looking for.

Simon was there when Robbie arrived, his head on a constant swivel, laptop bag clutched tight to him.

'Aye, here comes Super Agent,' Simon said, with a small smile.

'Boss,' Robbie said, as he approached them, eyes still darting around, making a show of covering all the angles.

'Robbie,' Connor said, 'thanks for coming. You got something from the files?'

Robbie gave a smile that was half innocent, half sly. 'I think so,' he said. 'Took a while to connect the dots, but I think I'm on to something.'

'Let's take a walk,' Connor said, gesturing to the neat gravel path that snaked through the cemetery. 'You can fill us in as we go.'

The cemetery wasn't overly busy, a smattering of tourists wandering around, glancing down at their phones or snapping pictures. It didn't take long to find a secluded area that looked back onto Stirling and the countryside beyond.

'Well, I think you were right,' Robbie said, walking between Simon and Connor. 'I think Carryduff is the key to all of this.'

'How so?' Simon asked. 'You find something in the statement Arthur Fielding gave to Danny about the attack?'

'Not Fielding, no,' Robbie said, his earlier smile returning. 'When you said Carryduff was the last incident he took a statement on, I went back. And Arthur Fielding wasn't the only person Dr Gillespie spoke to about the attack. It took a while, and the file kept on throwing up password challenges every time I opened a new directory or folder, but I got there eventually.'

'Got where?' Connor asked, hearing the edge of impatience in his voice.

'Gordon Sinclair,' Robbie said, Connor's tone doing nothing to dampen his pride. 'He was a PC on his first posting when the Carryduff massacre took place. He suffered third-degree burns to his face and chest, and the attack ended his career. But Dr Gillespie tracked him down to Ballintoy – it's a wee village close to Ballycastle. Anyway, he had quite the tale to tell.'

'Go on,' Simon said, exchanging a glance with Connor.

'Well, the way Sinclair tells it, he reported for duty as normal. At a police station during the Troubles, security was heightened. He was given his orientation, taught the drills on patrol and station protocol and the like, but then it got odd. He recalls being pulled into the Chief Super's office, only to be on the end of a grilling from another man.'

'Let me guess,' Connor said. 'A man with a moustache and a penchant for checking the time?'

'Exactly,' Robbie replied, eyes bright with excitement. 'Sinclair's statement says that the man was introduced as Lieutenant Kerr, a liaison between the RUC and the army on security matters. He took a real interest in Sinclair's background, good Protestant family, proud

Unionist roots, always wanted to serve Queen and country, that type of shite. Anyway, Sinclair didn't think much about it at the time. He was a new officer and there was a general fear that an attack could happen at any time. He says there was buzz about Carryduff, rumours that something big was coming.'

'But why Carryduff?' Connor asked. 'I never understood that. Okay, it was a police station so an obvious target, but why there? It was semi-rural, nothing major run from the station as far as we know, so why?'

'Because,' Robbie said, sliding a tablet from his back, 'all that "proud Unionist for Queen and country" shite I mentioned made hellish good copy three months later when the *Chicago Tribune* ran an article on the "barbarous paramilitary attack on the brave police in Ulster". Seems Sinclair had links to a big Irish family in Chicago, and they wanted to generate some headlines about what was going on back in Northern Ireland.' He passed the tablet to Connor, showing the news article from the time.

'Hold on,' Simon said, 'you're telling us that this Lieutenant Kerr vetted Sinclair so he was newsworthy and would generate some good headlines for the RUC in the US? That's a hell of a reach, Robbie.'

Robbie gave another smile: the magician about to saw his assistant in half. 'Aye, that's what I thought as well,' he said. 'Until I found a credible phone-in to the *Belfast Telegraph* about the attack two hours before it happened.'

'What?' Connor said, turning to Robbie. 'How the hell?'

'Wasn't easy,' Robbie said, 'but I went back and checked the cuts from the time, to see what other coverage the attack got. Found that a reporter at the *Tel*, a guy by the name of Liam Dunne, wrote a fair bit about the Troubles. When it was over, he wrote a book, *Reporting from the Front Lines, a Newsroom in the Troubles*. Took a while to find a copy – it's out of print now – but in that book, he details the moment of sheer terror when a newsroom would get a called-in bomb threat using a recognised codeword. He specifically mentions Carryduff.'

'But if the *Tel* got a bomb threat, they'd call it in to the police and the army. You telling me that didn't happen?' Connor asked, not liking the conclusions he was reaching even as he spoke.

'Not at all,' Robbie said. 'Dunne is clear in his book. No one ever fucked around with a bomb threat. They got it, they called it in. A headline is one thing, but sitting on life-or-death information is something else.'

'So the threat was reported and nothing happened?' Simon asked. 'They let the attack go ahead?'

'It looks that way,' Robbie said. 'I mean, add up the facts. Sinclair reports for duty. He gets a cosy little chat with this Lieutenant Kerr. There's increased chatter about a possible attack. There's a credible warning called in to the *Belfast Telegraph*. They pass it on to the relevant authorities. And nothing happens. What does that tell you?'

'That someone in the army or the police let the attack happen, even though they could have prevented it,' Connor said, the words bitter in his mouth. 'And we're thinking this Lieutenant Kerr is the man who let it happen, the one who was visiting victims after attacks, checking how his handiwork had gone?'

'It figures,' Robbie said. 'Think about it. The RUC and the army were deeply unpopular in parts of Northern Ireland, seen as an occupying, brutally oppressive force. To counter that, you needed a narrative, to put a face to the folk who are watching you go shopping down the barrel of a gun. So this guy Kerr provides that, lets an attack happen here, a killing there, massages the story, plays both sides against the other.'

'There's got to be more to it than that,' Connor said, mind reeling at the inescapable, coldly logical obscenity of what Robbie had laid out before them. 'I mean, Danny died for this. I . . . I . . .' He blinked away the thought of the two men he had killed on the Falls Road.

'Remember what Gillian Flint said?' Simon said. 'That this was something that would embarrass people in the US and here? Someone allowing acts of terror to garner favourable headlines and probably get financial support from the US? Yeah, I can imagine this would qualify. Especially if we find this guy Kerr. But how?'

'I had an idea about that,' Robbie said. 'Kerr is a name so bland it must have been fake, and I can't find any records of a Lieutenant, Captain or Major Kerr working in Ireland with the police at that time.'

'So how does that help us?' Connor asked.

'Well, just because I couldn't find him, it didn't mean that the liaison unit between the police and the army didn't exist. So, I went looking for that and . . .' He turned the tablet towards himself, tapped it a few times, then presented it to Connor again with a flourish. 'And I found that the RUC Special Branch was responsible for liaison with the British Army at the time. They had bases around Northern Ireland, and one of them,' he tapped the screen Connor was looking at, 'was at Thiepval Barracks, home of the 2nd Battalion, The Rifles.'

Connor felt his mouth fall open. 'Hold on, Thiepval Barracks? The Rifles? But that was . . .'

'Yup,' Robbie said. 'The unit Alasdair Gillespie, Danny's father, served in as a colonel. I checked, and the times match. He was there when Special Branch was operating out of the barracks. Bit of a coincidence, don't you think?'

CHAPTER 44

Jen wasn't sure what response she would get when she called Angela Barr, but 'I'll be there in an hour, and we will discuss this in person,' wasn't among her list of options.

Despite this, an hour after calling Barr to tell her that the deal was off, that MacKenzie Haulage vehicles wouldn't be used to transport drugs around the country after all, she found herself at the MacKenzie Haulage yard on the outskirts of Stirling, sitting at her father's desk, Paulie lurking in the corner of the room, like a malignant manifestation of the bruises and injuries that covered his body.

Barr was escorted in by Irene, the overly opinionated secretary Jen had inherited along with the business. Jen rose as Barr and a man she didn't recognise swept into the office as though they owned it. He was tall, wiry, dark hair fashionably erratic, something flat and dead in his eyes. His mouth creased into a smirk as he saw Paulie in the corner.

'Been in the wars, Paulie?' he asked, his voice a soft counterpoint to the sharpness of his features.

'Just a disagreement with my dog, Chris,' Paulie said, voice flat.

Barr flicked an appraising glance at Paulie, seemed on the cusp of asking a question, then turned her focus back to Jen.

'Mrs Barr,' Jen said. 'This is a surprise, I wasn't expecting . . .'

Barr took the seat opposite Jen, settled in. 'After our last call, I thought it was important that we met face to face, so you fully understand the gravity of your actions.'

Jen lowered herself into her own seat, propped her crutch beside it, then folded her hands in front of her, hoping Barr didn't see the slight tremor in them as she did so. 'First, I want to apologise for that,' she said. 'I hope you realise I would never do anything to expose you or the nature of your business with my father. I merely wanted to impress upon you that this is my company now, and I make the decisions. Not Paulie, not the memory of my father, me.'

'Ah,' Barr said, her eyes not leaving Jen's. 'I can respect that. After all,' she swept a hand behind her shoulder to where Chris stood, then pointed to Paulie, 'it's not easy being a woman in a world dominated by men like these. That being said, I hope we can discuss delivery logistics and move this deal forward.'

Jen took a deep breath, forced herself to hold Barr's gaze. Here it was. Moment of truth. She thought of her conversation with Connor, about their desire to live differently, to be different people. Held on to the thought. 'Actually, that's what I was calling you about,' she said. 'I'm sorry, Mrs Barr, but MacKenzie Haulage can't proceed with our, ah, arrangement after all. I thought it was something the company needed to do, something I needed to do, but after further consideration, I've concluded that it's not the direction I want us to go in. I apologise for the false impression I gave you, and I want to thank you for your time on this.'

'Thank me for my time?' Barr whispered, the temperature in the room seeming to drop, as though her words were ice tumbling into a drink. 'What the hell do you think you're doing here? Playing at gangster? This isn't a casual business, Ms MacKenzie. When arrangements are made, when product is shipped, I expect it to be delivered. If it is not, there are various people around the country who will be displeased. People who communicate in more, ah, direct ways than this cosy little chat.'

'Now, Angela,' Paulie rumbled from the corner of the room, 'Jen's trying to do this nicely. No need for threats, okay?'

'Threats?' Barr said, a cold smile slithering onto her lips, like a shadow playing across a headstone. 'Paulie, I thought you knew me better than that. I'm not making threats. I'm dealing in reality. Things are in motion – thanks, in no small part, to you vouching for

Ms MacKenzie here. This deal will go ahead, or I swear I will burn this pisspot operation to the ground, and your little girl here with it.'

'Little girl?' Jen said, anger sparking the nerves in her back. 'Mrs Barr, just who do you think you're talking to? I may be many things, but I am no one's little girl. I appreciate you coming here to meet face to face. But here is the reality, as you put it. I will not be party to drug-dealing. I thought it was something I could do, but recent events . . .' she paused, pushed the sudden image of Connor's gran from her mind '. . . have given me a new perspective. Now you can accept that graciously, or I can arrange to have your scrawny, over-Botoxed arse thrown out of this "pisspot operation" so fast your Jimmy Choos won't touch tarmac.'

There was an odd, numb moment, as though the room had been stilled by a crack of thunder. And then Chris was in front of her, leaning over the table, a knife glinting inches from Jen's face.

'You might want to learn a little respect, bitch,' he hissed, the sour smell of cigarettes on his breath. 'Otherwise I'll cut you from ear to ear.' His eyes darted left for a fraction of a second, falling on Paulie. 'And Paulie, you make a move, I will gut her, I promise.'

'You do, Chris, and I'll use that knife to feed you your eyes,' Paulie hissed. The desperation in his voice made Jen's stomach churn in a way the knife had failed to.

'You see, Ms MacKenzie,' Barr said, as calmly as though she was serving afternoon tea and asking if Jen took milk. 'This is what I meant by serious business. The deal is in motion. The shipment cannot be stopped. Your lorries will be at Aberdeen harbour tomorrow to move the shipments to various locations, and then we will talk about your . . .' she gave a small laugh, looked at Chris with an almost naked longing '. . . cut of proceedings.'

Jen moved her hand, eyes not leaving the blade. 'If you put it like that,' she said, 'all I can say is . . .'

She never finished the sentence. She threw herself back into the chair, seized her crutch and swung it at Chris's head with all the force she could muster. There was a sickening crack and his head snapped to the right, a gout of blood arcing from his cheek as he staggered back. Through the screaming, all-consuming agony in her back and legs, Jen barely heard the knife clatter onto the desk in front of her. She forced her eyes open, saw through tears of agony Barr lunging forward, scrabbling for the knife. And then Paulie was on her, a bloodied, vengeful god glaring down on a blasphemer.

'Stupid, Angela,' he said, grabbing her wrist and twisting it up. His voice was almost sad, wistful. 'I told you there was no need for threats.' He shook his head once, then wrenched Barr's wrist up again, the bone snapping, like a gunshot in the post-violence fragility of the room. She screamed, and Paulie clamped his other hand onto her mouth.

'Shut the fuck up,' he snarled. 'Jen, you okay? Get that knife, will you, and make sure Laughing Boy there is out for the count.'

Jen forced herself to move, trying to block out the agony in her back. How much damage had she done? What would the consequences be? The thought of more time in hospital, endless days of torturous rehabilitation and physiotherapy rose, nightmare-like, in her mind.

She got the knife, looked over the desk to where Chris lay, like a discarded dummy, on the floor. Blood was oozing from the gash in his cheek, dripping down his face and pooling like a crimson halo around his head. His eyes fluttered as though he was dreaming, and she could see the shallow rise and fall of his chest. She felt a momentary pang of guilt at the damage she had inflicted, smothered it with the memory of the knife in her face.

'He's out for the count,' she said, looking at Barr, whom Paulie had pinned to the desk. She could see one eye, a dark, poisonous marble of hate.

'Well, this could have gone better,' she said to Paulie. 'Now what?'

Paulie took a breath, grimaced as his ribs shifted painfully. 'Now,' he said, 'we send Irene home for the day, then escort Mrs Barr and her assistant to their car. Then,' he leaned forward, whispering into Angela's ear, 'you are going to drive yourself to the nearest hospital and get yourself fixed up. After that, Angela, you are going to fuck off back up the road to Sheep Shagger Central. And if I ever see you, Chris or anyone else from your part of the world again, I will take that knife and carve your face off your pretty little head. Are we clear?'

Barr gave the slightest of nods, her eye never leaving Jen as she did.

CHAPTER 45

Connor ended the call. 'Thank you.' Turned to see Simon standing at the car, face etched with concern.

'You all right?' he asked, tone telling Connor he knew the answer already.

Connor shrugged. 'Funeral home,' he said, the words feeling too small to hold the enormity of what they meant. 'Gran had her funeral all laid out and prepaid. There are a few things I need to do, but they've got the bulk of it sorted already.' He gave a short, bitter laugh. 'She's taken care of all the arrangements,' he said. 'Even in death, she didn't want to be a burden.'

'Anything I can do?' Simon asked.

'Nothing to do,' Connor said. 'I need to take an outfit in for her, arrange flowers, that sort of stuff. But the funeral isn't for a fortnight, so there's time.' He stiffened, anger hitting him like a caffeine rush. 'And I'd really like to make sure anyone who was connected with leaving that message for me with her is in the ground long before we send her off.'

Simon let the comment hang between them, the seriousness of Connor's intent settling on them both. 'Then let's get to work,' he said. 'Given what Robbie's found about Alasdair Gillespie and the RUC Special Branch, I take it he's our next interview.'

'Not yet,' Connor said. 'And not just because I don't really want to get on another boomerang flight to Belfast to talk to him.'

'Fair enough,' Simon said. 'So where do we go now?'

Connor considered. After meeting with Robbie in the cemetery, Connor had sent him back to whatever hidey-hole he had created for himself, with instructions to dig further into Alasdair Gillespie's military service and any possible links to the RUC Special Branch that liaised with the army. Which left Connor with an idea.

'We know that two groups are looking for this information,' Connor said, feeling the idea take shape in his mind as he spoke, 'official government, no doubt wanting to keep quiet the news of a double agent during the Troubles, and whoever hired Gillian Flint to find the data. So what does that tell us?'

'That a lot of people want this kept quiet,' Simon said.

'Exactly,' Connor said. 'Which means there's still skin in the game. That whoever Lieutenant Kerr is, he's still a player now, or he's connected to someone who has a very vested interest in keeping this quiet.'

'Right,' Simon said. 'But how do we find out who that is? Flint already told us she was hired anonymously. She knows why she was hired and what the contract is, but not who's paying the bills.'

Connor stared, the thought dropping into his mind, clattering and ringing through him like metal dropped down a mineshaft. He stared at Simon for a minute, his words echoing in his mind: *Who's paying the bills?* And, colliding with that, another thought, about his gran making her own funeral plans ahead of time – *she's made all the arrangements.*

'Stupid, Connor,' he whispered to himself. 'Stupid and slow.'

'Connor? What?' Simon asked.

Connor reached into his pocket. 'This.' He pulled out the page from *The Times* that Simon had found at the care home, with the message on it.

'But we checked that,' Simon said. 'It's a burner-phone number. Robbie traced it to a SIM card top-up, on the O2 network. Went dead after you called it and arranged our little chat with Flint in Belfast. We can't use it to trace whoever left the message.'

Connor shook his head. 'Not the point,' he said, looking down at the piece of paper. He took out his phone, fiddled with the screen, then turned it to Simon. It was a webpage from *The Times*, displaying previous puzzle solutions.

'This crossword was run in *The Times* the day you visited Gran and found this,' he said. 'Which tells us that whoever left it was in the area until recently. They bought the SIM card tied to this number when they were here. Robbie confirmed it was activated the night before the note was left with Gran.'

'So?' Simon asked, confusion clouding his face.

'So,' Connor said, 'we know they were in the area, and I bet they would have stayed around to see what happened, at least until after the twelve-hour deadline they gave me to get in touch with the number. But you got those government goons and Ford to put a watch on Gran's care home, make sure she was safe, so what would they have had to do?'

'Go dark,' Simon said. 'Keep their heads down, watch and observe, see if you came out of the woodwork.'

'Exactly,' Connor said. 'Gillian told me she'd advised against using my gran as a pawn in this, that it would only make me more determined to track them down. But they did it anyway, and they gave me a deadline. And then they attacked Paulie to get us moving. Which tells us what?'

'That they're desperate,' Simon said. 'Whatever's going on, there's a deadline involved in it. Something that's going to happen or, given the twelve-hour deadline has passed, has happened that they don't want you messing up for them.'

'Right,' Connor said. 'So they'd want to be close to Gran's care home, able to watch it inconspicuously, but at enough of a distance not to attract the attention of anyone official.'

'Okay, makes sense,' Simon said. 'But what does that get us?'

'Arrangements,' Connor said, cursing the grief over his gran's death for blinding him to what was now so obvious. 'If you want to keep an eye on someone, but can't get close enough, what do you do?'

'Get a disguise,' Simon replied. 'Or get someone anonymous to do it for me.'

'Right,' Connor said. 'And we know they had one person planted in Gran's home.'

'How do we know that?' Simon asked, brow creased.

'Because, Simon, just like Gran arranged her own funeral, I made arrangements for her as well. Like a copy of *The Times* being ordered into the home and delivered to her room every morning so she could do the crossword. And guess who I made that arrangement with? Guess who assured me they would personally hand that paper to my gran every day?'

Simon thought for a moment.

Then Connor saw recognition spark in his eyes. 'Right,' he said, thinking back to his visit to the care home after his gran died. About the condolences he had received from Aileen Black, the manager, who had helped him set up her accommodation in the first place. 'We should head out to Bannockburn. I'm betting Ms Black has an interesting story to tell.'

CHAPTER 46

After fending off the passive-aggressive tirade from her mother – 'Andrew was so proud of the story he wrote at school, you should have seen him', 'Your father's not as spry as he was, Andrew runs rings around him at the park' – Donna managed to get some time to herself in her office at the flat. As her laptop booted up, she sat, using the peace and the soft murmur of cartoons from the other room to calm her nerves and her anger with her mother. But she knew her mother was right – she was missing a lot of Andrew's day-to-day life due to her job. She did the best she could, making sure her time off was focused on him, ensuring Simon was part of what they did, whether visiting the zoo or, Andrew's current favourite, the trampoline park outside Ratho. But, still, she felt the sting of guilt for not being the twenty-four/seven mother to him that her own mother had been to her. As a single mother, it was unavoidable, but how much longer would that be the case? Simon was an increasingly significant part of her life, Andrew clearly loved him, and then there was what Simon had said in Belfast about 'what comes next'. What did that mean? Not just for her, but for bringing up her son?

She logged into the laptop. She could worry about the future later. Right now, she had a story to chase down. And that meant looking into the past.

She gave her password to the Sky database, thought about what she had discovered. According to Colm O'Brien, there were suspicions that a double agent had been working during the Troubles, manipulating events and playing off both sides against each other. It wasn't without precedent – Simon's reference to the Stakeknife case proved that – but where did that leave Donna?

She began a search, looking for public inquiries into the work of the security services during the Troubles. Found Operation Kenova, the independent inquiry set up to investigate the Stakeknife case. A few more clicks took her to inquiries into the Omagh bombings and the Saville report into the Bloody Sunday massacre. It didn't take her long to find the home page of the Independent Commission for Reconciliation and Information Recovery. It had been set up by the UK government to investigate deaths during the Troubles. She clicked through the site, paused when she found a press release welcoming a change to the NI Troubles Act, which repealed clauses that were in contravention of European law. What was it O'Brien had said? *The Brexit shite you blagged your way in here with is real. It's a threat to the Good Friday Agreement that ended the Troubles. If it was discovered that the Troubles had been manipulated for political or financial gain, can you imagine what that would do to the place?*

Was that what this was about? Something or someone who could destabilise the peace process? Donna leaned back in her seat, considered. Got out her notepad, skimmed back to the notes she had taken during her meeting with Paulie, Connor and Simon at the Crown in Belfast. Read their account of their talk with Arthur Fielding, the baker whose van had been stolen for the Carryduff massacre. A few clicks on the keyboard and she called up the front page of the *Belfast Telegraph* from 21 July 1987, the day after the attack. 'Horror in Carryduff,' the headline screamed, above a picture of the ruined police station.

Simon had told her of Robbie's belief that what had happened at Carryduff was the key to all of this. Was he right?

She clicked back on the ICRIR website, found the remit page. 'Crimes from 1966 to 1988'. So Carryduff, which happened in 1987, fell within it. Was that it? Had someone requested an investigation into Carryduff? Had Danny Gillespie, in interviewing Arthur Fielding, stumbled on something that threatened to derail almost three decades of peace? She thought again of what Simon had told her about his conversation with Fielding, about the hatred in the old man's eyes when he had talked about O'Brien threatening to rape his wife if he didn't give them the van. But what could one old man do for revenge against a now-successful businessman? He couldn't attack him directly, but other methods were available to him. Methods, for instance, like having a government inquiry crawl up his well-upholstered arse and look into his background.

Donna chewed her lip. Then, on an instinct, pulled up the online phone directory in the Sky database. Checked the spelling of 'Arthur Fielding', entered the name, added the suffix BT for Belfast, hit search, and hoped.

CHAPTER 47

They were sitting outside the care home, preparing to confront Aileen Black, when Simon's phone buzzed. He pulled it from his pocket, glanced at the screen, tension flicking across his face. 'Ford,' he said, with a glance at Connor, then hit answer. 'Guv.'

Connor could hear only Simon's side of the conversation, Ford's stern tones reduced to background static. But he knew from his friend's posture and the fixed glare out of the windscreen that he was taking in a briefing from Ford. Whether it was good news or bad, Simon's poker face refused to tell.

'Okay, thank you, boss,' Simon said, after a moment. 'Yes, I'll be sure to.' He ended the call, toyed with his phone for a moment, as though digesting what he had just been told.

'Well?' Connor asked.

'Interesting,' Simon said. 'I asked Ford to look into the official line on this – when you were first flagged for surveillance, why the alarm was raised. His first call was from the office of the Justice Secretary at Holyrood, Walter Atkins. Seems he was given the nod by his counterpart in Whitehall, told Atkins as a courtesy that UK agents were on Scottish soil.'

'How very collegiate,' Connor said. 'But how does this help us?'

Simon gave a small, tight smile. 'That's where it gets interesting. Seems Ford knows a few people at Holyrood, including those who sit on the justice committee and the civil service staff who support it.'

Connor nodded. It made sense for a senior police officer, especially one with a portfolio as wide-sweeping as Ford's, to have contacts high up in government. But what did that mean?

'Ford made a few discreet calls,' Simon went on, as if reading Connor's thoughts. 'It seems your name was first flagged in an information request from Whitehall five days ago. Late in the afternoon.'

Simon let Connor catch up. 'Five days ago?' he said. 'Hold on, that was the day of the funeral. And afternoon would be after the service, which means . . .'

'Yup,' Simon said. 'Someone saw you there, then tapped their friends in the civil service to get some background on you.'

'Who?' Connor asked, a suspicion forming in his mind.

'Not who,' Simon said, 'where. Ford's contact wouldn't reveal specific names, but the request came from the Special Operations Branch in the PSNI, based out of Knock Road. And here's an interesting wee fact. The RUC Special Branch, which was headquartered in the same barracks as Alasdair Gillespie, was incorporated into Special Operations when the RUC became the PSNI.'

Connor put the pieces together in his mind. 'So you're saying Gillespie saw me at his son's funeral, and called in a favour with his old pals in what was Special Branch?'

'It adds up,' Simon said. 'And it's another coincidence that puts Gillespie right at the heart of this.'

'Aye,' Connor said. Contrary to what Alasdair Gillespie had told him, he was very aware of his son's work. So much so that Danny had asked him for help in identifying a possible double agent. Then his son had been killed in a hit-and-run. Had he seen in Connor a possible ally, someone to help avenge his son's death, and looked into his background, or was it something more, something darker? Had he seen a potential threat, someone who would blacken his son's name by revealing what he knew and disgracing the army to which he had given his career?

'Something to consider,' Connor said, reaching for the car door. 'But later. For now, let's see what Mrs Black has to tell us.'

They walked into the care home, Connor feeling pressure begin to build in his head, as if a balloon of memory was being inflated with every step he took. The receptionist, a young man with a side parting so severe it looked laser etched, offered Connor a reserved expression of sympathy that was so smoothly practised it practically guaranteed the kid's future in politics. They loitered, then turned as Aileen Black descended the stairs.

'Mr Fraser,' she said, extending her hand. 'Again, I want to extend my deepest condolences over your gran. Ida . . .' she took a long, steadying breath '. . . was a remarkable woman. She'll be missed.'

'Yes,' Connor said, feeling the ice in his chest begin to splinter and crack. 'She will. I was wondering if my friend and I might have a moment of your time.'

'Of course,' she said, eyes flicking to Simon, then back to Connor. 'Nice to see you again, Mr McCartney. But I trust everything is okay with the arrangements for your gran? Her flat is paid up for the next two months, so there's no rush in moving her personal items, and she herself made preparations for her, ah, passing.'

'Absolutely,' Connor said, stretching an alien smile over his lips. 'It's just a couple of details. Won't take too long.'

'Please,' Black said, gesturing up the stairs she had just descended to meet them.

She led them up one flight and along a corridor, finally stepping into a room at the back. It was large, with floor-to-ceiling windows that flooded it with natural light and views of the gardens. Connor felt something hard catch in his throat as he thought of his gran in those gardens, how she had loved the light streaming into her room. 'Warms my old bones and does me the world of good,' she would tell him.

'So, Mr Fraser,' she said, taking a seat at her desk, 'how can I help?'

'You can tell me about this,' Connor said, laying the puzzle page on the desk in front of her. Out of the corner of his eye, he saw Simon tense, realised his voice had become hard with the promise of violence. Hated himself that the thought warmed him.

'I'm . . . I'm not sure what you mean,' Black said, adjusting her glasses as she slid the piece of paper towards herself. 'We both know your gran loved a crossword, made them a daily ritual. And that's—'

Connor slapped his hand down on the desk, hard enough for a

small pot of pens to jump as he did. 'Cut the crap, Ms Black,' he said. 'I've really had enough of it over the last few days. Look at the note on the puzzle. We both know you delivered the paper to my gran every morning, so you either wrote that note at someone's request or delivered it for them. So my only two questions are who, and why?'

Black slid her tongue across her lips. Glanced at Simon in some vain plea for help. Was disappointed.

She took her glasses off, the mask of indifference coming off with them. 'I'm sorry,' she said, voice strained. 'They contacted me. Said they knew about my mum, that they could help, if only I . . . I . . .'

'Your mum?' Connor asked. 'What about her?'

A sad smile twitched over Black's face, then faded. 'You're not the only one who has seen a family member ravaged by dementia, Mr Fraser,' she said. 'Unfortunately, we don't all have the resources you do. My mum has Alzheimer's-related dementia. It attacks short-term memory, leaves the long-term intact. So taking her out of her home, where she's anchored by a lifetime of memories, would be cruel. I couldn't put her in a place like this. So I pay for carers to visit her twice a day when I'm not there, keep her in the house. But that costs money, Mr Fraser. Money I don't have.'

'So someone got in touch with you,' Simon said, before Connor could speak. 'They asked you to deliver this note to Ida in return for a sum of cash.'

She nodded, defiance in her eyes now. 'Fifty grand,' she said. 'Fifty grand to deliver one message. It was too good to say no. After all, who would it hurt?'

'My gran died two days later,' Connor whispered. He could feel the rage building in him. 'Did you ever think that maybe the stress of that note, and trying to get it to me, might have been a part of that?'

Horror slackened Black's features, drained her of her colour. 'N-no,' she stammered. 'There's no way that that— No. Of course not. Surely . . .'

Connor glared at her, felt his hand curl into a fist, the urge to reach out and grab that long, slender neck . . .

'How did they contact you?' Simon asked, as he took a step closer, inserting himself between Connor and a clear path to Black.

She gave a short laugh. 'In the supermarket of all places. Asked about my mum, how she was. Lamented the cost of everything. Then they called me the next day, sent me a picture of my mum. Long shot, must have taken it through the living-room window. After that, they kept calling, offering the cash, wearing me down until . . .'

'Until you said yes,' Connor murmured. 'So, tell me, how did they get the message to you, and how did they pay you?'

Black's head snapped up, eyes wide, prey suddenly aware that a predator was near. 'They called, arranged to meet me at the King Robert,' she said, referring to a hotel not far from the care home and close to the Battle of Bannockburn visitors' centre. 'We met in the bar.'

'How many of them were there?' Connor asked. 'What did they look like?'

'Two,' Black said. 'Men.' She closed her eyes. 'Both late thirties, early forties, I think. Well dressed. Dark hair. One had a moustache. It really didn't suit him.'

Connor looked up at Simon, who gave the smallest of nods.

'So they gave you the note to be delivered to my gran and paid you,' Connor said. 'Did they say anything else?'

'No,' she said. 'Just to keep my mouth shut. And if you turned up, or anything else happened, I was to call them.'

'Call them?' Simon said, voice eager. 'They left you a number?'

Black hesitated, as if unsure she should breach this last confidence. Then she looked back towards Connor, and her resolve faded. 'Yes. They said they had other business in the area and could be reached on this number.' She produced her mobile, played with the screen, then slid it over the desk.

Connor picked it up, memorised the number and looked at Simon. 'Give them what they want?' he asked.

A cold, almost predatory, smile slipped across Simon's face. 'Why not?' he said.

Connor handed the phone back to Black. 'Call them,' he said. 'And tell them exactly what I'm about to tell you.'

CHAPTER 48

Using the address Simon had given her, Donna found Arthur Fielding's phone number easily. She dialled it, a small voice in the back of her mind telling her that, if she had just stayed in Belfast to chase the story down, she could have done this in person.

The ringing of the phone line sounded oddly fragile to Donna's ear. But how long had it been since she had dialled a residential landline? In the days of mobile phones, a landline that wasn't routed to an office, a call centre or some kind of public service was a rarity.

'Hello?' a voice answered, in a soft, Belfast lilt.

'Ah, Mr Fielding?' Donna said. 'My name is Donna Blake, I work for Sky News. I was wondering if I could have a moment of your time.'

'Oh, I'm sorry, love,' he replied. 'I've already got satellite. And I don't really want any of those sports channels. I see all the matches I want to in the pub. So if you'll excuse me—'

'I'm not calling from Sky TV,' Donna said quickly. It wasn't the first time she had run into confusion between the broadcaster and the news channel. 'I work for Sky News – I'm a reporter. I was wondering if I could talk to you about Dr Danny Gillespie. I believe you spoke to two friends of mine about him the other day.'

'Oh, aye, aye,' Fielding said. 'The guy who was built like a brick shite-house and his friend. Nice boys. Hell of a shame what happened to Dr Gillespie. They told me about it. He was a nice boy too. Always wanted a chat and a cup of tea.'

The word caught in Donna's mind. *Always*. So Gillespie had spoken to Fielding on more than one occasion. Interesting. 'Mr Fielding,' she said, 'the reason I'm calling is I've got a couple of questions that relate to what you talked to my friends about.'

There was an exhalation of breath at the other end, and Donna had a sudden image of Arthur Fielding lowering himself into his chair, settling in for a conversation. Simon had said the man had been talkative, if a little unfocused. She hoped she could use that to her advantage.

'Well, I'm not sure what you young things can get from hearing me tell the same story again and again, but since I've nothing else to do, go ahead,' Fielding said.

Donna hesitated, wondering how to proceed. Decided to be direct. 'I understand you spoke to my friends and Dr Gillespie about the massacre at Carryduff RUC station in 1987,' she said. 'Specifically about how your van was stolen and used for the attack.'

'Aye,' Fielding said, wariness chilling his tone and flattening the lilt. 'I did. Though I'm not sure how much use it was. It was all over the papers at the time.'

'Yes, sir,' Donna said, glancing at her screen. 'I've seen some of the stories. It was horrible what happened to you and your wife, ah . . .' a moment's pause, just long enough to sell Fielding the lie that she was looking at notes in front of her and hadn't memorised the details before the call '. . . Maureen.'

'Yes,' Fielding said, his tone chilling even further now. 'Yes, it was. But those were hard times, Ms Blake, and we weren't the only ones. Can you tell me what this is about, please?'

Donna heard the warning in the tone. She was on borrowed time. 'When you spoke to my friends, you told them how Maureen was threatened and you were shot in the leg by two men from the Provisional IRA. You said you knew those men, Colm O'Brien and Bobby McCandish. Tell me, sir, in the years after Carryduff, did you ever see them again?'

'No,' Fielding spat, hate in his voice. 'And I never wanted to. The Troubles were a bad, bad time. I'm no fan of the Brits, but those were just children at Carryduff, young lads and lassies who had been fed a line of bullshit about serving Queen and country, then marched onto the front line to take whatever was thrown at them. I was used as part of that. My van was used to hurt people. You think that's something I want to remember? I hope O'Brien and McCandish burn in Hell. But, no, I never saw them again. I had a sick wife to look after – she was never right after that night. Nerves were shot.' His voice faded, swamped by a fogbank of memory rolling over his mind. 'Now, if you'll excuse me . . .'

Time's up. Play the last card, Donna thought. 'Have you ever heard of the ICRIR?'

A pause on the line, just long enough for Donna to think Fielding had hung up, and then he said, 'The Troubles inquiry. Aye, I have. What about it?'

'Mr Fielding,' she said, sitting up in her chair. 'This is off the record, okay? I'm just trying to understand something and help my friends, who think Dr Gillespie's death might not have been a simple accident after all.'

'Fair enough,' Fielding said, impatience and sudden wariness greying his tone.

'Mr Fielding, there was a public call for victims of crimes during the Troubles, or their close relatives, to get in touch and request an investigation. The inquiry has refused to publish details of its case-load or the number of requests it's had. But you sounded angry about your van being used in a terrorist attack. They threatened your wife. Maimed you. Sir,' she took a deep breath, 'did you contact the inquiry and ask for an investigation into what happened at the Carryduff RUC station? Was that part of what you spoke to Dr Gillespie about?'

Another silence, longer this time. 'Yes,' he said at last, his voice a sigh of relieved resignation. 'Yes, I did. Not for me, you understand. For Maureen. And those kids who were killed. They deserved some justice for what happened. Christ,' he sighed, a shimmer of tears in the hitching of his breath, 'we all did.'

Donna swallowed her excitement. 'And you told Dr Gillespie you had made a request for an investigation?'

A laugh, strangely childish. 'Love, these days I have trouble changing the channel on the TV, and don't even get me started on that bloody air-fryer my nephew wanted me to use. The inquiry request for an investigation is online. Might as well have been in another world for me, no way I could understand how to – what is it you say? – go online and do that. But Dr Gillespie? Well, he understood it all just fine.'

'Hold on,' Donna said, 'you're saying . . .'

'Aye,' Fielding said. 'It was Dr Gillespie who helped me make the request for an investigation. Even let me use his computer to submit the form and everything.'

CHAPTER 49

Simon watched from a copse of trees that ran along the perimeter of the care home's gardens, saw them drive into the car park, their vehicle so bland it screamed for his attention. They parked close to Connor's Audi, then got out and circled the car. Two men, both stocky, the cut of their jackets telling Simon they were armed. They moved in the stilted, synthetic-casual fashion of men who had spent their lives being told to stand to attention and never quite broken the habit. So, ex-military, then.

He watched as they stood together, surveying the care home, then moved off as one.

The call Connor had had Aileen Black make was a simple one. She told them Connor had returned to the care home, highly agitated that someone had been into his gran's room and moved some personal items, In particular, he was worried about an old mantelpiece snuff box that 'meant the world to them both'. He had headed up to the room, with instructions that he was not to be disturbed.

It had taken less than twenty minutes for the car to arrive, which told Simon that Black had been speaking the truth about one thing at least: they were using the Bruce Hotel as a base. A lead to follow up later.

He gave the men just enough of a head start so he wasn't being obvious, then emerged from the trees. He crossed to their car and, once there, knelt down as though tying a lace. Grabbed the knife he had tucked into his boot, and stabbed the front and back tyres. No way they'd let these bastards get away from them.

Ida Fraser had lived in a self-contained flat on the third floor of one of the apartment blocks that had been grafted onto the main house of the care home. It was reached through a long, glass-fronted corridor that ran between the flats and the main house, like an umbilical cord. Simon watched as the men walked along the corridor, took out his phone, made a call to Connor. Watched as the men got to the lift and exchanged annoyed glances – the lift was out of service, thanks to Connor wedging the door open the moment Simon had called him. He watched as the men headed for the stairwell, then ducked through the fire door at the end of the glass corridor – which he had picked open and wedged when they were preparing this. Black had deactivated the alarm on the door. He called Connor again, then got into the lift.

Simon felt his stomach clench as the doors opened at the third floor, flattened himself against the wall, making himself invisible. Risked a glance into the hallway, saw no one, smiled. Slipped out of the lift and around the L-shaped corridor lined with doors to flats like Ida's. Watched the stairwell as the door swung open, the two men emerging warily. They exchanged a glance, then one of them, slightly wider and shorter than his companion, with eyes as severe as his haircut, consulted his phone. He glanced along the corridor, motioned towards Ida's door at the end. Simon watched for a moment, turned, grabbed at the item bracketed to the wall in a small alcove beside him. Watched as the men got to Ida Fraser's door, guns appearing in their hands as they stood off to either side of the door.

A hard knock. 'Mr Fraser?' one said, a Scottish accent that had been mangled by years abroad. 'John Stenhouse. I'm a member of the care team. Wonder if we could have a word?'

They listened, tensed as the door swung open a crack. Simon sprinted forward, raised the fire extinguisher and fired it at the men. They whirled, the door forgotten in the sudden onslaught. Simon brought the extinguisher up in a rising arc, catching the head of the man on his left and sending him careening sideways off the wall. Then, through the smoke, an arm appeared from within Ida's flat, stabbing at the other man's throat. He gagged, gun clattering to the floor as he staggered back, gasping for breath. Simon stepped forward, pushed him as hard as he could into the flat, swept up the gun, and turned to the man he had hit with the fire extinguisher. He was in a heap on the floor, blood seeping from his mouth. Simon grabbed his gun, then hauled the man to his feet and shoved him into the flat.

Connor was standing in the middle of the room, looking down at the two men collapsed in front of him. There was an absence to his face and eyes that chilled Simon. It was as if everything human had been drained from him, leaving only the cold fury of his grief.

'Well, that was easy,' Simon said, as he closed and locked the door behind him.

'Aye,' Connor said, eyes not moving from the men. 'Though it's about bloody time something went our way, isn't it?'

Simon handed a gun to Connor. He looked at it, as though surprised by its existence, then ejected the magazine and sprang the bullet chambered in the barrel. The message behind the movement was clear – we do this the old-fashioned way. No guns.

Connor knelt down, slapped the face of the man he had struck in the throat, just hard enough to get his attention. The man, who was still gasping, glared up at him, hate in his eyes.

'I see you've had a shave recently,' Connor said, pointing to a small cluster of cuts on the man's top lip. 'Take it you weren't a fan of the fake moustache your boss made you wear. Let me guess, too itchy?'

'Fuck off,' the man spat.

Connor gave him something that might have been mistaken for a smile, then jabbed him in the nose. It was a short rabbit punch, so fast Simon almost didn't see it. Blood exploded from the man's nose, and his head snapped back, a crimson arc tracing the move. 'I suggest,' Connor said, grabbing him by the collar and hauling his face upwards, 'you reconsider your attitude. I've had just about enough shit to last me a lifetime. So do yourself a favour. Answer my questions, and you might, just might, get out of here without the need for traction or a blue disabled badge for the rest of your life.'

A flicker of uncertainty infected the man's eyes. 'What do you want?' he hissed.

A reptilian smile slithered across Connor's face, and Simon felt a fresh wave of fear wash through his guts. He had seen Connor like this before. Focused, driven, possessed by a cold, calculating fury that would allow him to justify whatever actions he was about to take. He would hate himself for it later, take it as yet more proof that the character flaws his father had seen in him were real, but in that moment, Connor Fraser was devoid of pity or empathy, lethal and utterly ruthless.

'I want some questions answered,' Connor said. 'First, I take it you're part of the same crew who tried to jump me in Belfast a few days ago?'

Fear diluted the man's hatred, giving Connor his answer even before he nodded. So, he knew what Connor was capable of. That would make interrogating him easier.

'Good,' Connor said, as though praising a pet. 'And I take it I'm also right that you're the man who beat up my friend Paulie.'

Cruel humour pulled the man's bloodied lip into a sneer. 'Tough old bastard, I'll give him that.'

'That he is,' Connor said. 'But you were under orders to let him get away, weren't you? To make sure he got to me, his attack putting pressure on me to get to the bottom of what's going on?'

'I don't know about any of that,' the man said, defensive. 'I was just told to act posh, private school, like, give the old bastard a good hiding, make sure he thought he got away himself. The other stuff, no idea.'

'But you did know what you came here for?' Connor said. 'Tell me, what was that?'

'Files,' he said, wiping the blood from his nose. 'Boss said it could be a physical folder, a phone, a pen drive. Anything.'

'Know what's on it?' Connor asked.

'Don't know, don't care,' the man said, with a shrug. 'We were told you were in possession of some sensitive information. That was it. Boss tells us what to do, we do it.'

'Ah,' Connor said. 'And there it is. The real question. Now, take a moment, think about this. Trust me when I say it's important you get it right.' He reached into his pocket, produced a pen. Simon recognised it immediately. A Parker ballpoint. Silver top, blue body. It was the pen Connor's gran used for her crosswords.

'Who are you working for?' Connor asked.

'Fuck off!' the man spat. 'You think I'll tell you that? There's no way—'

Connor grabbed the hand the man was using to wipe his nose. Drove it down to the floor, pinning it there. Then he stabbed the ballpoint into the back of the hand. The man's head arched back, cords on his neck standing out, like over-tightened guitar strings. He gave a keening howl that was part sob, part scream. Connor silenced it by punching him in the throat again.

'Jesus, Connor!' Simon said, eyes wide. Connor's gaze didn't waver, just stayed locked on the man he had stabbed.

'Now,' he said, as the man collapsed forward, curling himself around his ruined hand, 'let's try that again. Who are you working for? Next time, I'll stab you between the ribs. Then it'll be the leg, the shoulder, the eye.' He grabbed the man's face, pinched both cheeks, forced him to look at him. 'Understand something. My life has been threatened. Your little note might have pushed my gran into an early grave. So your pain means fuck-all to me. You *will* tell me what I want to know. Understood?'

The man gave a stilted nod against Connor's grip and Connor let go of his face. 'Talk,' he said.

'Only met the contractor once,' the man gasped, skin paling as he looked down at the wound in his hand. 'We normally work for McGarry, Donald McGarry.'

Connor gave Simon a look, and he nodded recognition. Don McGarry worked out of an office in Hamilton, not far from Glasgow. Former soldier turned security operator, he ran most of the door operations on clubs and pubs from Milngavie to Shawlands. He was also known to take on more high-profile clients, providing them with former military contacts to ensure their safety. McGarry's men had a reputation for brutal professionalism. Which explained the two men Connor had faced in Belfast.

'Go on,' Connor said.

'Well, we were called into a meeting,' the man said. 'Don said that the man who had employed him wanted to inspect the goods, make sure we were up to the task. So we go into the office and there's this guy sitting there like he owned the place. Must have been in his seventies, but you could tell he was a hard bastard. It was him that looked at me, told me to wear that fucking fake moustache.'

Connor nodded, and Simon could see in his eyes an idea forming.

'This man,' Connor said. 'Let me guess. Greying hair combed back, three-piece suit? Sat like he was at attention?'

'Aye, that was him,' the man said. 'Creepy bastard. Barely moved, just sat there, glaring at me.'

On the floor beside him, Simon heard the groan of the other man as he started to regain consciousness. He stepped back, trained the gun on him. Unlike Connor, he wasn't averse to the convenience of using a firearm. 'Connor, I think we'd better wrap this up,' he said.

'Aye,' Connor agreed. 'Good plan.' He reached into his pocket for his phone, fiddled with it, then turned it to the man he had stabbed with the pen.

'This the man you met?' Connor asked.

The man glanced at the screen, then nodded enthusiastically, a puppy desperate to please.

'Yeah,' he said. 'Yeah, yeah, that's him. Bit younger, but that's him.'

Connor turned the phone to Simon. On the screen there was a picture, similar to a passport ID shot. 'Bloody hell,' he said, as he read the caption below the image.

'Oh, I'd say so,' Connor said. 'I think it's time we had that chat with Alasdair Gillespie now. Don't you?'

CHAPTER 50

Donna was already at the flat when Simon and Connor arrived. She had made coffee and was sitting at the breakfast bar, laptop open, Tom purring soft contentment on the chair beside her. Connor had a moment of vertigo as he walked into the flat, the comfortable familiarity of his former home made alien and new by Simon's different taste in décor.

Donna looked up as they walked in, smiled as she saw Simon, who crossed the room to kiss her. Connor thought of Jen, of the promise he had made to her to finish this case and try to live a more normal life. He fought back the urge to call her, check how her conversation with Angela Barr had gone. Part of him still had trouble believing she would go as far as arranging to be a drug-distributor to save her father's business. Yet what had he done over the past week when pushed to extremes? It was, he thought, only when you were on the edge of your preconceptions about who you truly were that you discovered what you were capable of.

It didn't take Simon long to bring Donna up to speed on what they had learned from the two men at the care home, who were, by now, licking their wounds and reporting back to Don McGarry. Which suited Connor fine. He wanted those who had chosen to attack him to know he was closing in on them.

After Simon had finished speaking, Donna spun her laptop round, showed them the home page of the ICRIR inquiry, told them about Danny Gillespie helping Arthur Fielding to make a complaint about the Carryduff massacre and his treatment at the hands of Colm O'Brien and Bobby McCandish. 'The question is where this all gets us. I mean, we've got bits of something – Danny Gillespie being killed after he helped to file an investigation request on the Carryduff massacre, his research that alludes to a double agent working on both sides of the fence during the Troubles, and his dad, a former army officer, being up to his balls in a private operation to get to you,' she pointed a pen at Connor, 'and the missing files. But what's the bottom line? Conspiracy? The murder of an academic to keep all this quiet? If so, why kill him after the report was filed with the inquiry? Everyone affected by it would know that the damage was done the moment Gillespie and Fielding hit send on their request.'

Connor poured himself a coffee. 'Code of silence,' he said. 'No one likes a grass. You go to the authorities, tell them what you know, no matter what it is, and you're dealt with. Street justice. It shuts you up, and sends a message. Do not fuck with us.'

'Okay,' Simon said, 'but a message to whom? Danny's father? Is that why O'Brien, McCandish and Walsh were at the funeral? To deliver the message? We killed your son. Make this go away or we're coming after you next? Is that why he asked his old military-intelligence friends to profile you, then got McGarry to try to take you off the board? Is it why Ford now has MI5 agents breathing down his and the Chief Constable's neck? And what's all this crap about getting the thug who beat Paulie up to wear a moustache?'

Donna arched an eyebrow. 'Moustache?' she asked.

'Gillespie senior had the guy who beat up Paulie wear a moustache,' Connor said. 'It was another prompt, just like letting Paulie go to try to force our hand. It was his way of telling me he knows who we're looking for – the man with the moustache who visited all the attack victims, including Arthur Fielding.'

'But why?' Donna asked. 'Who is this guy working for? He hires some private thugs to grab you in Belfast, then sends someone to beat up Paulie back here, all under the noses of government agents on the ground. Why? To help you find the men who killed his son, or to stop you getting to the truth.' She stopped, eyes wide. 'Jesus,' she said. 'You don't think he ordered the hit on his own son, do you?'

Connor thought back to the man he had seen at Danny's funeral, and the man he had met in Belfast a few days later. On both occasions, Alasdair Gillespie had been controlled, calm, almost impassive. Connor sympathised. He had ignored his grief over his grandmother, buried it under a veneer of calm that might make him look uncaring to some. Was that what Gillespie had done, or was he really that cold and repressed, so disconnected that he had ordered his own son's death? 'The only way we're going to know that is by talking to him,' he said.

'Christ.' Simon sighed. 'No harm to you, Connor, but I moved to Scotland to get away from Belfast, not jump back there a couple of times a week.'

Connor gave a smile. 'Don't worry,' he said, 'If I'm right, we won't have to go anywhere. Mr Gillespie will come to us.'

'Oh?' Donna said. 'And why would he do that?'

'Because,' Connor said, 'we're going to give him everything he wants.'

CHAPTER 51

Paulie cursed as his mobile vibrated at him from the coffee-table, insistent as an angry bee. He sat up from the couch, where he had finally found a position that accommodated his injured ribs, and leaned forward. When he saw the name on the caller display, he diverted his hand to the tumbler of whisky beside the phone.

'Iain,' he said, answering after taking a slug of whisky. 'Now why would you be calling me?'

'Paulie,' Iain Barr said, the fury in his tone flattening the normal Aberdonian sing-song lilt, 'you know damn well why I'm phoning. Angela's got a broken wrist, and Chris's cheek is broken. And for what? Because a spoiled little girl stepped into the real world and found she didn't like it? It's not on, Paulie, not on at all.'

Paulie closed his eyes, took a breath. He should have expected this. It wasn't that Iain Barr was a jealous, overprotective husband looking to avenge his wife. It was an open secret that their marriage was one of convenience, Iain unable to get over generations of Presbyterian guilt about who he was to come out and live as himself, but she was still his wife. Which, in Iain Barr's world, made Angela his property.

And Iain Barr protected his property. Jealously.

'No need for name-calling, Iain,' Paulie said, trying to keep his voice even. 'Look, I'm sorry about what happened at the office. But Chris pulled the knife first, and I had to make sure Angela knew that picking it up was a bad idea.'

'Bad idea?' Barr spat. 'No, Paulie. A bad idea would be you letting that little bitch fuck up this deal. We took a chance on you, Paulie, took your word about her. Now we've got a shipment coming in, and no way to distribute it. So talk to the little cow, make sure she understands that, no matter her qualms, this deal is going ahead, and we expect your lorries at the dock to collect the merchandise.'

Paulie reached for the whisky, held it to his lips. 'Iain,' he said, resisting the urge to drain the glass. 'Number one, stop the name-calling. It's disrespectful to Jen, and it doesn't suit you. Okay, so she got in over her head. My fault, I should never have arranged an introduction between her and Angela. But she's made her decision. Second, don't give me this you-can't-get-a-distributor bullshit. I know your network. You could get a fleet of lorries into that yard to pick those drugs up at the snap of a finger. This is you wanting to save face, show you're still the boss. I understand you need to do that, especially with the moves I pulled on Angela, and that's fine. But that's between me and you. You leave Jen out of this, clear?'

'Paulie, you know I can't,' Barr said. 'If people hear they can pull out of a deal with us, no consequences, what message does that send?'

'That you're a reasonable businessman who doesn't let dick-measuring get in the way of seeing when a deal isn't going to work,' Paulie answered. 'As I said, if anyone's at fault here, it's me. I got Jen into that room with Angela. If you have a problem, you talk to me about it, okay? But remember, Iain, if you do decide to visit me, or send some of your pals, you won't be visiting as a friend. We've known each other for a long, long time. You've seen me work. Do you really want to go down this road? We can work out some compensation, let it lie there. Okay?'

'I don't know, Paulie,' Barr said. 'I mean—'

'Get me a number,' Paulie said, sudden exhaustion rolling through him as his ribs began to snarl again. The whisky glass was looking increasingly appealing. 'Work something out for the inconvenience, and the injury pay for Chris and Angela. I'll pay it, no questions. Just leave Jen alone.'

'This isn't how I wanted things to go, Paulie,' Barr said.

'Me neither,' Paulie said, forcing himself to put aside the whisky glass. He would need to be clear-headed to drive after this. 'Me neither.'

CHAPTER 52

Getting in touch with Colonel Alasdair Gillespie wasn't difficult, but it was unpleasant. After his run-in with McGarry's men at the care home, and the confrontation in Belfast, Connor thought it was time to speak to Don McGarry.

'You've got a fucking cheek calling me after what you've pulled,' McGarry barked, after Connor had introduced himself.

'And you're lucky this isn't a personal visit,' Connor said, anger prickling the back of his neck. 'Trying to grab me in Belfast, then to use my grandmother to get a message to me? Believe me, Don, your boys at the care home got off lucky.'

'And what about the two in Belfast?' McGarry hissed. 'You think they got off lucky?'

Connor closed his eyes, pushed down the sound of the man on the ground in the alley gasping for breath, the roar of the gun as he blew the other's head off.

'We can discuss that later,' he said, voice like gravel being crunched beneath the wheels of a car. 'Right now, I need you to deliver a message to your boss.'

'My boss?' McGarry said. 'And just who might—'

'Alasdair Gillespie,' Connor said. 'The man who hired you to get to me. I'm assuming you can get in touch with him, and I'm guessing he's either with you in Glasgow already, or even closer, maybe here in Stirling.'

Connor took the silence on the phone as a confirmation. It made sense. As they had peeled away the layers of the case, Gillespie's involvement had become more obvious. And if there was some sort of deadline relating to getting to his son's files, he would want to be near to the person who had them. Which meant he had followed Connor and Paulie back from Belfast. Had probably been on Connor's tail since they had met in the Botanic Gardens.

'Go on,' McGarry said.

'Tell him he can have the watch back. And the files it was carrying. I've got what I need. I know who we're looking for. He can meet me at my offices in Edinburgh. Sentinel Securities, I'm sure you can give him directions. And give him my number as well. No offence, Donny, but I don't have the time or patience for middle men.'

McGarry took a breath that vibrated in Connor's ear. 'This isn't over,' he said at last, then ended the call.

'Can I assume that went well?' Simon asked, from across the kitchen counter.

''Bout as well as can be expected,' Connor said, laying the phone down.

'So now what?' Donna asked.

Connor shrugged. 'We wait.'

Donna shook her head. 'Not me,' she said. 'I need something I can report. I've wasted enough time digging into all of this without filing anything. Time to change that.'

Connor and Simon exchanged a look. 'So what's the story?' Connor asked.

Donna smiled at him, straightened as if looking into a camera. 'An investigation has been launched into the death of a leading British academic in Belfast, after it was alleged that his work investigating the Troubles in Northern Ireland uncovered a potential government agent working within paramilitary organisations during the conflict.'

'Nice,' Simon said. 'Only problem I can see is that there is no official investigation, and I'm not sure how much of that you'll be able to get on air before someone from the MoD or the Home Office shuts you down.'

'Which is why,' Donna said, packing her bags, 'the Scotland Office is my next step. Time to get them on the record, confirm there's an active operation in Scotland in relation to Danny's research. Give them a squeeze, and I guarantee I'll have the story by tonight. And as for getting D-noticed or shut down, our lawyers will challenge that faster than you can say "public interest" or "press freedom".'

She grabbed her bag, kissed Simon's cheek as she passed him, lingering just long enough to tell Connor that the casual act held a deeper meaning.

'Some woman,' Connor said, as she let herself out of the flat.

'Aye,' Simon replied. 'Which is probably why I'm going to have to marry her.'

Connor started as though Simon's words carried an electrical charge. 'Simon, I—'

He was cut off by his phone ringing.

'Later,' Simon said, a grin lighting his face. 'We can talk about it later. But, yes, you are the best man.'

Connor felt a blush colour his cheeks. Then he grabbed the phone. Answered it.

'I believe you have something for me,' Alasdair Gillespie said.

Connor's excitement at Simon's news curdled. He hated Gillespie for that.

'Colonel Gillespie,' he said, Simon tensing at the name. 'Good of you to get in touch. And so quickly, too. At least Don has proven efficient at one thing.'

'You told him you had the watch and the files,' Gillespie said, voice clipped and brisk. This was a man who expected results, not flippancy.

'Yes,' Connor said. 'And you can have all of it. And the name of the man you're looking for. But, first, we should meet. I've a couple of questions for you.'

'Now wait a minute,' Gillespie said, anger in his voice. 'I didn't agree to—'

'The alternative is that I take this information to the authorities, and give all the raw data, including the unedited reports, to a friend of mine in the press,' Connor said. 'Your call.'

'I'm close by,' Gillespie said. 'Where would you suggest we meet? Your office is obviously out of the question.'

Connor considered. A public location would discourage Gillespie from trying anything rash, but the flip side was that if he or McGarry decided Connor was more useful to them dead, innocents would be in the firing line.

'We're all friends,' Connor said, 'so why not make this cosy? You can come to my place. We can chat over biscuits and coffee.' He saw Simon's horrified expression, held up a hand.

'Give me the address,' Gillespie said, and Connor laughed.

'Come on,' he said. 'You've been ordering background checks on me. You're telling me you don't know where I live? Find out. We'll see you there in an hour.'

The call ended abruptly, and Connor turned to Simon.

'Your place?' Simon said. 'You lost your mind?'

'Nope,' Connor said. 'He's going to have to drive into the forecourt, right? Only way to access the house. So we can use the door camera, see who's with him, control the environment. We can block them in with the Audi if we need to, deal with any problems before they even set foot through the front door.'

'And when he does step inside?' Simon asked.

'We'll take him to the kitchen at the back of the house,' Connor said, referring to the large open-plan kitchen/living area that ran along the back of the property. 'And, trust me, we'll have more waiting there for Colonel Gillespie than coffee and cakes.'

CHAPTER 53

Donna first met Harry Dunn when she worked as a reporter for the *Western Chronicle*, a broadsheet that had served Glasgow and the west of Scotland since 1741. But as the bean counters moved in and started to squeeze the margins of the newspaper by asking questions such as 'Why do you need to report international news?', 'What's the point of proofreaders?' and 'Is formal journalistic training *really* more important than being able to get the story online first?', Harry had done what a lot of old newspaper reporters had done – he'd jumped ship. With his background on the *Westie*'s crime beat, Harry had had no problem landing himself a job in the civil service and, when the Tories were finally booted out of office at the general election, he was drafted into the Scotland Office to help detoxify the department's relationship with a press that was sick of being gaslit and fed whatever rancid, self-serving fantasy passed as government policy that day. Respected by reporters and feared by politicians, Harry was a perfect fit for the role.

He answered his phone on the third ring, his voice booming down the line like the verbal equivalent of a hug. 'Donna Blake,' he said. 'What's a glamorous TV reporter doing phoning a humble government-comms guy like me?'

'Hi, Harry,' Donna said, a smile spreading across her face. There was something about talking to Harry that always lightened the mood. It was as though he was a natural antibody to the cynicism that journalism and communications could foster. 'It's been too long since we caught up. I'll have to buy you lunch the next time I'm in Edinburgh.'

'Aye,' Harry said. 'You will. But that's for next time. Right now, you can tell me how big a favour you need, and how quickly you need it.'

Donna gave a short, embarrassed laugh. Typical Harry – always cutting to the top line of the story. 'Well . . .' she said, a moment of uncertainty on how to approach the question. Despite the confidence she had shown when talking to Connor and Simon, the spectre of having the story shut down due to security concerns was real. The moment she spoke to Harry, she was walking through a one-way door, taking theory into the realm of fact. Potentially legally actionable fact.

'Thing is, Harry,' she said, taking a deep breath, 'I've got hold of something that could be big. And given there are UK-wide ramifications, I thought you might have heard something at the Scotland Office.'

'Go on,' Harry said, an edge of wariness chilling his good humour just a little.

'Well, a friend of mine was across in Northern Ireland a few days ago, attending the funeral of a friend of his who was run over. Since that time, I've got reliable sources who tell me that not only has he been the subject of a background check by the UK Home Office but he's also been actively surveilled by government agents.'

'Agents,' Harry said slowly, as though tasting the word. 'You mean as in spies?'

'Come on, Harry, this isn't a James Bond movie,' Donna said, realising how ridiculous it sounded as they spoke. 'What I'm saying is that my friend is being actively investigated by the UK government, and followed by operatives acting in the government's name. I know the UK Home Secretary called his counterpart in the Scottish government to tell him what was going on, I just wondered if you'd heard anything about this. Given all the lines your lot have been getting out about mutual respect between Edinburgh and London and working together, I thought you might have heard something.'

A moment's pause, and Donna could see Harry sitting at his desk, tapping a pen softly against his top lip in the way he did when he was considering something. Then the soft sound of him shifting his weight, a grunt as he leaned forward.

'So you're asking if the Scotland Office is aware of an active UK intelligence operation in Scotland,' he said. 'And what, exactly, has triggered this hypothetical operation, Donna?'

Donna felt a moment of vertigo, as if she was standing at the doors of a plane and about to jump out. No going back now. 'There's evidence to suggest that the man who died had information relating to a double agent working for and against the government during the Troubles,' she said. 'My friend was given information that could identify that agent.'

'Jesus,' Harry said, his voice businesslike. 'You don't do anything by halves, do you? Why not just allege that he's got the address for Lord Lucan and Prince Andrew's missing deodorant stick while you're at it?'

Donna smiled. Harry's hatred of the monarchy had been legendary in the *Chronicle*'s newsroom. He despised giving it coverage in the paper, and railed against having to write about 'some toff playing at dress-up in a kilt' whenever any of 'them' visited the Scottish Parliament.

'Come on, Harry,' Donna said, 'I'm just going where the story takes me. You taught me that.'

'Aye, I did,' he said. 'Worst bloody mistake of my career. Okay, this is off the record, but I'll look into it for you. What's the name of your friend, and the man who you said died?'

Donna gave him Connor's name, and the details of Danny Gillespie.

'Right, leave it with me,' Harry said. 'I take it that this is you looking to stand the story up. You've got nothing to go on camera with yet?'

'Not yet,' Donna replied, thinking of Connor and Simon and their plan to meet Danny's father, Colonel Alasdair Gillespie, 'but I'd appreciate a fast turnaround on this, if possible. There are other lines moving that make it fairly urgent.'

'Other lines, eh?' Harry said. 'Do I want to know?'
'Not really,' Donna said. 'Thanks, Harry, I appreciate this.'
'Yeah, yeah,' he said, and ended the call.

Donna put her phone down. If Harry could give her a statement, confirming that an intelligence operation relating to Connor was under way, what did that give her? It gave credence to the theory that Danny Gillespie's research held a damning secret that the government wanted to keep quiet, but what else? If she wanted to stand this story up, she needed to go back to the start, to Danny Gillespie's death, find something, anything that might give a clue that it wasn't just a drunken mistake and he hadn't just staggered into the road at the wrong moment.

She logged into the press-cutting service, pulled up any stories relating to Danny's death. Unfortunately, in such a hyperactive news environment, it didn't rank highly, the story being reported in rudimentary, almost dismissive terms by all the main news outlets. 'Man dies after being hit by car' or 'Family's shock as "beloved" son killed in car collision' was the best she got, along with some cursory pictures of Danny.

She glared at the laptop, as though accusing it of failing her, then thought of something she had said to Harry Dunn: *I'm just going where the story takes me*. She typed in 'Dunmurry', the area of Belfast where Danny had died, then searched for news sites in the area. Sure enough, she found 'Dunmurry FM' a news page being run by a national broadcaster providing hyper-local content for listeners. She found the search bar, put in Danny's name, along with 'car' and 'fatal'. A moment later, a story popped up. It was longer and more detailed than anything the national press had carried, and the style of writing, the general mistakes and typos in the reporting told Donna it had been put together by a citizen journalist rather than someone who had trained in the profession. But it had the details, including an eyewitness account. She read:

> We were just coming out of the pub ourselves when we say the guy. Didn't seem that bad, was walking with the guy he had been in the pub with. But then they got to the junction,

stepped out. Wee van seemed to come from nowhere, clipped him dead on, threw him back into the pavement. The guy who was with him, old boy, gradnfather maybe, but he was gone by the time we got there. Called an ambulance, but it was too late. Dunno what happened to the old boy that was with him. Maybe staggered off it shock.

Donna reread the article. So someone had been with Danny at the time of the accident. Someone older. She thought again of what Connor had said, about the possibility that Danny's own father had targeted him because of what he had learned. Was it possible? But, no, the eyewitness said grandfather, not father. And the pictures she had seen of Colonel Alasdair Gillespie showed Donna a man who was thriving in his older years, unlikely to be mistaken for a grandfather. So who . . .?

She was startled from her thoughts by the buzzing of her phone beside her. She picked it up, hit answer.

'Harry,' she said. 'That was quick. You got anything for me?'

'I think the question is what have you got for me?' Harry replied, his tone flat, businesslike.

'Sorry, Harry,' Donna said, feeling a vague tendril of unease. 'I'm not sure what you're talking about?'

'I checked with some, ah, sources,' Harry said, 'at the Home Office and other channels. And I don't know what your "friend" Connor Fraser is smoking, Donna, but you might want to suggest he gets checked for delusions and paranoia.'

'What?' Donna asked. 'Harry, what are you saying?'

'I'm saying,' Harry said, suddenly sounding tired, 'that he's been feeding you a line. His name hasn't been flagged, there's no intelligence operation ongoing, and the last time Lord Hillerman talked to Walter Aitken it was about cross-border cooperation on race riots being held in the Borders.'

Donna took a breath. Held it for a moment as her mind raced. Then she exhaled. 'So you're telling me that the UK Home Secretary never made a call to the Scottish Justice Secretary to tell him about a security operation in Scotland?' she said at last.

'That's exactly what I'm telling you,' Harry said. 'It's fiction, Donna. A lie. The question you've got to ask yourself is who's lying to you. And why?'

CHAPTER 54

They watched as the car slid into the driveway, a huge black Range Rover with darkened windows and a personalised number plate, DO NM7.

'Subtle,' Simon muttered, eyes not leaving the screen that was showing the camera trained on the driveway.

'As a brick,' Connor agreed, watching as the front doors of the Range Rover opened, Alasdair Gillespie emerging from the passenger side and Don McGarry unfolding himself from the driver's seat. What he lacked in height he made up for in width, with huge shoulders and a barrel chest squeezed into a T-shirt that looked as though it had been shrink-wrapped over his body. For a moment, Connor thought of Paulie, but the resemblance stopped when you got to the head – where Paulie's was shaven, Don McGarry's was luxuriantly coiffed, his dark hair teased and tousled into a fashionable mess.

He and Gillespie exchanged words, then started walking towards the door. Connor got moving, back along the corridor to the front door. Reached for the handle, grateful for the reassuring weight of the gun in the pancake holster on his back.

He swung the door open before they could knock, McGarry standing in front, Gillespie over his shoulder. It was, Connor thought, like the Jehovah's Witness visit from Hell.

'Gentlemen,' he said. 'Come on in. But wipe your feet, will you? We've just had the floors done.'

McGarry gave Connor a contemptuous sneer, then squeezed past him into the hallway, followed by Gillespie. He looked somehow older than when Connor had last seen him, the rigid formality with which he had held himself somehow transformed into a brittle fragility. Was that what grief did? Connor thought. Or guilt? Would he end up the same way? Braced against the world, knowing that the next blow would be the one to shatter him?

He pointed to the door at the end of the hallway, not wanting to turn his back on either man. Simon rose from his seat as they walked into the room, eyes darting between Gillespie and McGarry. It was a quick, assessing gaze, and Connor could see Simon had decided McGarry was a threat to be watched closely.

''Bout ye,' Simon said.

Gillespie ignored him, turned on Connor, face tight with a fury and contempt that seemed to bleed from his pores. 'You said on the phone that you were in a position to return the watch and Danny's research. I see no reason to delay.' He held out a hand. 'Give them to me. Now.'

'I also said,' Connor replied, walking behind the island in the kitchen, 'that I had some questions. So,' he gestured to the sofa, 'take a seat and let's talk.'

Gillespie tensed, as though called to attention. 'I do not have time for these games, Mr Fraser,' he hissed. 'Let's just get this over with, shall we?'

'Sure,' Connor said. He reached below the counter, produced the watch. Gave it one last look, then handed it to Gillespie. 'You really did give that to Danny, didn't you?'

'Yes,' Gillespie said, glancing down at the watch. 'for his eighteenth. Just as my father gave it to me.'

'Hmm.' Connor nodded. 'Makes sense. Fine old antique watch, denoting military service. Nice touch of Danny's to hide the drive with his data on it in the watch, easy way to get it to me. Clever, very clever. The kind of thing a former military man with links to army intelligence would think of, isn't it, Colonel?'

Gillespie's head darted up, eyes locking on Connor. He opened his mouth as if to speak, then closed it.

'Thought so,' Connor said. 'It was you who told Danny to hide the drive in the watch, wasn't it? After he came to you with his suspicions about what he had found. Must have been a kick in the nuts for his mum to hand the watch to me rather than you at the funeral. Now why was that, Colonel? Was there a reason why your son wouldn't trust you, would turn to an old friend he had all but lost touch with instead?'

'How *dare* you?' Gillespie hissed. 'I did everything I could to help Danny. When he came to me with his suspicions, and all those people who had been visited by the same man, it was obvious he was on to something. So I did my best to help him, for his sake and for the sake of the army. I served in the Troubles, Fraser. I saw it first-hand. If there was someone working for both sides, someone who cost innocent lives, he needs to be found, and made to answer for what he did.'

'And that's why you advertised the details of Danny's funeral,' Connor said. 'Because you wanted O'Brien, Walsh and McCandish there to give you an update on what they had found. You went to them, didn't you, when Danny came to you with his suspicions? Tell me, Colonel Gillespie, how long did they work for you as touts?'

Gillespie twitched a small, bitter smile. Shook his head. 'I was right about you,' he said. 'You are good. You're right. I was charged with handling intelligence assets during the Troubles. I handled those men when I was based at Thiepval Barracks.'

'When you were working for the RUC Special Branch, as liaison between the army and the police.'

Gillespie gave a small, curt nod. 'Correct,' he said. 'Of course Danny didn't know I had worked with army intelligence when he contacted me, couldn't know how close to the bone he was when he asked for my help.'

'And what help did he ask for?' Connor asked.

'At first, he wanted me to confirm his suspicions, that he hadn't fallen down a rabbit hole and was seeing a conspiracy where there was none. But when I looked at the witness statements from people affected by attacks in the Troubles, the real ones, not the doctored ones that were online, it became clear that a man was visiting the families or the survivors either just before or just after the attacks. So he was either manipulating the attacks or making sure the job had been done right.'

'And when you found out that the Carryduff massacre was phoned in to the *Belfast Telegraph* and nothing was done about it, you concluded that this guy was real. That he had profiled the police station, found that it fitted the bill nicely as a target for the evil balaclava-wearing terrorists you were fighting, and let it happen to get some goodwill flowing to the Brits? That about cover it?'

Gillespie took a breath, glanced at McGarry, who was doing a passable impression of a statue. 'It wasn't just Carryduff,' he said. 'There were other attacks Danny uncovered, where witnesses and survivors said they had heard an attack was coming, and had gone to either the paramilitaries in their community with the information, or the police, and nothing was done.'

'So who is this guy?' Connor asked.

Gillespie's eyes narrowed. 'You said you knew,' he whispered. 'You said you had a name for me.'

Connor shrugged. 'I lied,' he said. 'I needed to get you here to talk to you. I'm close to cracking this, and Danny was convinced that Carryduff was the key to it. We've got a bomb warning that was never passed on to the station, and two of your intelligence assets being the men who facilitated the attack by stealing Arthur Fielding's van and terrorising him and his wife.'

Gillespie looked at Connor as though he had just slapped him. 'What?' he said.

'We spoke to Arthur Fielding,' Connor said. 'He told us how Colm O'Brien and Bobby McCandish asked him for the use of his van. When he refused, they visited him at home, threatened to rape his wife, took the van and blew out one of his kneecaps for the trouble. So how does that sit with you, Colonel Gillespie? Two men you admit were working for you as informants go off reservation and orchestrate one of the deadliest attacks of the Troubles. An attack the army could have stopped, but didn't? Did Danny find out about that? Did he hate you for it? Is that why he made sure his mother gave the watch to me, not you?'

Gillespie shook his head violently. 'You've got this all wrong,' he said. 'McCandish and O'Brien couldn't have been involved in the Carryduff massacre.'

'Oh, and why's that?' Simon asked.

'Because,' Gillespie said, his voice suddenly tired, 'the Carryduff massacre was in 1987, and in 1987 . . .' He trailed off, as though unwilling to finish the sentence.

'Go on,' Connor said, a surge of anxious anticipation making his voice tremble slightly. 'What were they doing in July 1987?'

'They . . .' Gillespie coughed, cleared his throat, as though the words were stuck there. 'In 1987, O'Brien and McCandish weren't in Northern Ireland. They were, ah, elsewhere, gathering support for the cause.'

Connor felt an almost physical shove as the revelation hit him. What was it Gillian Flint had said? *You've stumbled into something very sensitive, something people on both sides of the Atlantic have a vested interest in making sure does not enter the public domain.*

'America,' Connor said. 'They were in America, weren't they? Talking to people supportive of the IRA cause and the fight against the British. Who were they talking to, Colonel Gillespie? Who did you have them flushing out? Politicians? Businessmen with links back to Ireland? Who?'

'Both,' Gillespie said. 'It was a joint operation with the US government, a favour from Reagan to his girlfriend Thatcher. We ran the operation to flush out sympathisers, then cut off supplies and money to the IRA.'

'Okay,' Connor said, mind racing as he tried to process the new information. 'So why would Arthur Fielding lie? Or did he just make a mistake? Confuse O'Brien and McCandish with some others? And who is this ghost with the moustache that's pulling the strings?'

Gillespie opened his mouth to reply. But whatever he was going to say was devoured by the sudden roar that seemed to fill the world. His head exploded in a fountain of blood, sinew and bone. Instinctively, Connor ducked, grabbing the gun from the holster at his back. He took a deep breath, then stood up slowly, sweeping the gun around the room. To his left, Simon stood, his own gun in hand, trained directly on McGarry, whose weapon was still smoking from the shot that had taken Colonel Gillespie's life.

He smiled at Connor, the smile of a predator sighting its prey.

'Christ, he was a boring old fuck,' he said, voice casual, as though he was telling Connor the time. 'Now, Connor, tell your pal over there,' he jutted his jaw at Simon, 'to put the fucking gun down. You do the same while you're at it. And then we'll have a chat about those boys of mine you put down in Belfast. I owe you for their deaths, and I promise I'll pay that bill in full.'

'And why the hell would I do that?' Connor said. 'In case you haven't noticed, there are two of us and one of you. Even if you take out one of us, the other will put you down before you can say "headshot". So put your gun down, and then we'll talk.'

McGarry's smile became wider, colder. 'You're not going to want to shoot me, Fraser,' he said. 'Have a look at your door camera.'

Connor took a moment to glance at the monitor on the kitchen counter beside him, felt his stomach lurch when he saw four men approaching the house, weapons drawn.

'My men,' McGarry said. 'They find me dead, they're not going to take that very well. And, besides, you've gone to all this trouble to find the man with the moustache. Be a shame if I died before I can introduce you to him.'

CHAPTER 55

The men hustled into the kitchen, a tight knot of aggression. They spread out, relieving Connor and Simon of their weapons, then forcing them onto the couch.

'So you've been working for whoever is behind this all along?' Connor asked, glaring up at McGarry, whose eyes were glittering with a gleeful savagery that promised pain was only a few moments away.

'Not at first,' McGarry said. 'Gillespie contacted me, wanted me to get hold of you and the missing information, find out what you knew. But then I got a call from an old friend and he asked me to ah . . .' he chuckled to himself, as though remembering a private joke '. . . help out. I was more than happy to oblige.'

'This pal of yours, let me guess, you served with him in Northern Ireland?' Simon asked. 'He have a name? I'm getting pretty tired of referring to him as Moustache Man.'

'Actually, no, I was never in Northern Ireland,' McGarry said. 'I met Captain Hillerman when I was stationed at Dreghorn across in Edinburgh. You could say we hit it off straight away.'

Connor's head snapped up. 'Captain Hillerman?' he said. 'You mean Henry Hillerman? Now Lord Hillerman?'

McGarry nodded, smile widening as though he was delivering a punchline. 'Exactly,' he said. 'And he's very, very keen to meet you, Mr Fraser. Something about looking you in the eye before I deal with you for what you did to my boys in Belfast. As a former soldier, Captain Hillerman takes the loss of his men very seriously.'

'Jesus,' Connor whispered, the final pieces of the puzzle falling into place. No wonder Danny had been killed, and his father had been double-crossed. Gillian Flint had been right: this was something no one would want to see the light of day. That a lord, who was now a serving minister in the Home Office, had been manipulating terror attacks during the Troubles, letting some go ahead to whip up pro-Union support, while at the same time allowing Republican paramilitaries to raise cash in the United States? Yeah, that was one secret that was going to be kept quiet. And it didn't matter how many people had to die for it. One glance at Alasdair Gillespie's body on the floor in front of him convinced Connor of that.

'You're telling me that a government minister is going to open his doors to us for a wee visit?' Connor asked. 'That's one way not to keep a low profile.'

'Of course you're not going to meet him in person,' McGarry said, giving Connor a look that was at once sympathetic and hate-filled. 'But we do have this little thing called Zoom, these days. Became popular in the pandemic. We'll give him a call, you can say hello, and then he can watch as we gut you and your pal here.'

'Bastard!' Simon spat. He launched himself from the couch, aiming for McGarry. He pirouetted away, too quick, too graceful for a man of his bulk, and one of his thugs stepped in, smashing Simon on the back of his head with his gun.

Connor lunged forward, unable to grab Simon before he crashed to the floor. He knelt beside him, McGarry taking the opportunity to bury his boot in Connor's face. A bomb of agony detonated in Connor's head, his eyes tearing up as he felt his nose break. Blood surged up his throat and he spat a gob of it onto the floor as he caught himself. Kneeling on all fours, forcing himself not to pass out, he grabbed for the pain, concentrated on it. Held it close, something to fan his rage with, keep his fear at bay.

'Get them into the car, and then we'll come back for Gillespie,' McGarry said. 'We'll take them to the warehouse in Falkirk, deal with them there.'

Simon was lifted by two of McGarry's men and dragged out, the other two grabbing Connor and hauling him to his feet. He let himself be led, using the time to try to swallow the nausea and stop the world spinning. The light of day seemed to stab at his eyes as he was dragged out of the front door and towards McGarry's Range Rover.

Connor took a deep breath. Simon was starting to come around, his head lolling groggily from side to side, eyes open slightly as he was dragged towards the car. Connor prayed he was faking it, playing for time, and would be able to handle himself when Connor made his move. He knew that, if they allowed themselves to be bundled into the car, it was over.

McGarry stepped around them, approaching the car first, plipping the central locking. Connor tensed, took a sudden step back, grabbed the men on either side of him and threw them at each other. As they collided, Simon surged forward, smashing a vicious uppercut into the chin of the man on his left, while aiming a kick at the knee of the man on his right. The sound of the knee snapping was like a gunshot, and the man crashed to the ground, roaring animal-like in pain. McGarry whipped round, gun rising as he did, taking aim at Simon. Connor cried out, felt as though he was trying to run through setting concrete. Time seemed to slow down, and Connor could see everything with hellish clarity. The muzzle of the gun, McGarry's cold, dead glare, a bead of sweat glinting in the light as it rolled down his cheek like a tear. Simon staggering, off balance, nowhere to run, not enough time to get to cover.

And then, in an explosive instant, the world lurched into fast forward. There was a huge, rending boom, and McGarry was flying through the air, swiped off his feet by the Range Rover, which had suddenly shunted forward and collided with him. Connor darted to the side, grabbed Simon and pulled him away. They hit the ground, Connor rolling, trying to take the brunt of the fall. He whipped his head up, straining to see what had happened. McGarry was lying in a crumpled heap about three feet away from him, his legs at angles so unnatural they made Connor feel sick. He checked on Simon, dragged himself to his feet, staggered over to McGarry and took the gun that was lying out of his reach. He looked up, saw Paulie walking around the Range Rover, massaging his neck as he looked back to the twisted metallic sneer that now made up the front of his Mercedes where he had rammed McGarry's Range Rover.

He glared up at Connor. 'Can I no' leave you alone for five fucking minutes without you getting yourself into shit?' he snarled. 'Oh, and don't worry, you're going to be getting the bill for the car. And you'll be paying for it. Every bloody penny.'

'It'll be worth it,' Simon said, hauling himself to his feet. His eyes were dazed, unfocused, and Connor vaguely wondered if he had a concussion.

'Paulie,' he said, then stopped. What could he say? The man who hated him, who thought he would never be good enough for Jen, had just saved his and Simon's lives. And he had done it by sacrificing his most treasured possession – the car he kept in showroom condition.

Paulie seemed to read Connor's thoughts. Raised his hand. 'Now don't go getting sentimental,' he said. 'You're enough of a wanker as it is without that. Besides, I wasn't visiting for the sake of my health. Need a favour.'

CHAPTER 56

As Connor attended to Simon and his own broken nose, Paulie swung into action. It was, Connor thought, like watching an over-attentive dinner host obsess about clearing up between courses. A call was made and, ten minutes later, three men Connor vaguely recognised from previous visits to MacKenzie Haulage arrived in a Transit van. They busied themselves tying up McGarry and his goons, then bundling them into the van. From the groans Connor heard, they weren't being too gentle. A moment later, one of the men emerged from the house, what looked like a large binbag draped across his shoulder. Connor felt his stomach lurch as he realised it was Gillespie's body.

'Do I want to know what's going to happen to them?' Connor asked, as the van door swung shut.

Paulie gave Connor a level stare. No emotion, the sociopath he was peeking out from behind the disguise he wore to blend in with the world on a daily basis. 'About the same as what was going to happen to you if I hadn't turned up,' he said. 'Best leave it at that. Less you know, the better.'

Connor considered this. Was he prepared tacitly to approve the probable deaths of five men? So much for the new, quiet life he had promised to try to build with Jen. But then he thought of his gran, of the way those men had treated her as little more than a pawn to get to him, the men he had been forced to kill in Belfast. The reality of what was going to happen to McGarry and his thugs became more palatable.

He watched as the van drove away, followed by McGarry's Range Rover, leaving only Paulie's wounded Mercedes sitting in the driveway. Paulie studied the car, then shook his head sadly.

'I'm gonna have to get a tow truck in to move her,' he said to Connor, something almost like sorrow in his voice. 'You okay with it sitting there until I sort that out?'

Connor bit back the sudden urge to laugh. Paulie had just ruined his car to save his and Simon's lives, and now the man was worried about the etiquette of leaving a damaged car in the driveway? 'It's fine,' he said. 'Leave it there as long as you need.' He paused, then remembered what Paulie had said after ramming the Range Rover. 'You said you needed a favour?'

'Aye,' Paulie said. 'Can we talk about this inside? Need to speak to your pal as well.'

Connor nodded, the gesture reigniting the pain in his nose. Remembered the last time it had been broken – by the man he was now casually inviting into his house for a chat.

They convened in the kitchen, Connor grabbing ice for his nose and Simon's head and giving Paulie a whisky. Paulie took a long drink, then started talking, slowly and urgently, telling Connor and Simon about the call he had taken from Iain Barr and his concern that his offers of compensation for the aborted drug-distribution deal were unlikely to be accepted.

'What do you want us to do?' Simon asked, his tone telling Connor he already knew exactly what Paulie wanted to do next.

'You're a copper,' Paulie said, voice edged with disgust. 'I've just told you that there's a massive drug shipment on its way to Aberdeen harbour. So tell your boss, Ford, or anyone else you have to. Get the Barrs shut down. Just keep my name out of it.'

'You think that'll stop them?' Connor asked, dragging his eyes from the crimson explosion of blood trailing up the kitchen wall where Gillespie had been shot. 'From what you've said, they're big players. They'll know you gave the police the tip-off about the drugs. What's to stop them coming after you the moment they hear the first siren?'

Paulie gave a shrug of his massive shoulders. 'Let them come,' he said. 'Don't care what happens to me. But doing this will slow the Barrs down, keep their eyes on me, not Jen. And that's what I want. To keep her safe. Never should have involved her in this in the first place.'

'You didn't involve her in anything,' Connor said. 'Jen's her own woman, Paulie. She would have done this with or without you. I'm just glad she did it with you, so we can maybe sort it out quietly.'

'Okay,' Simon said, wincing as he moved his neck. 'I'll make some calls, get officers in Aberdeen to check it out.' He raised his hand as Paulie opened his mouth. 'Anonymously,' he added. 'No one will know where I got my information from.'

'Thank you,' Paulie said, spitting the words as though they were an obscenity. 'What are you boys tangled up in anyway? What were those jokers after you for?'

'It's a bit of a long story,' Connor said, reaching for his phone, 'but don't worry, you can hear all about it on the six o'clock news.'

Simon looked at him, smiled. 'You calling Donna?' he asked.

Connor nodded. 'I think she's going to have a few questions for our pal Lord Hillerman, don't you?'

'Oh, aye, I imagine she will,' Simon said. 'Look, you do that, I'll call Ford about Aberdeen. Just do me one favour, will you?'

'What's that?' Connor asked.

Simon rubbed the back of his head again. 'Don't tell her I got cracked over the head. She'll just worry, and you'll get the blame for not looking out for me.'

Connor felt a sudden stab of guilt. He knew Simon meant it as a light-hearted joke, but the truth was he had put his friend in mortal danger again. And now, from what Paulie had told them, Jen was in similar danger. Was he cursed? Did violence and pain follow him around, waiting to visit themselves on anyone he dared to care about?

'Go make the call,' he said to Simon. 'Let's get that sorted, ensure Jen is safe. I'll get Donna here. She can drop in on the way to Edinburgh and a chat with Lord Hillerman.'

CHAPTER 57

They met Donna outside the house, neither of them wanting her to see the recent redecoration of the kitchen wall with most of Alasdair Gillespie's brain. She parked her car beside what was left of Paulie's, her face etched with suspicion, then concern as she saw Connor's broken nose.

'Paulie do that to you for pranging his car?' she asked, aiming for humour and missing. One look at the way she was studying Simon, assessing him, told Connor Donna was seriously worried.

He gave her a sanitised version of what had happened with McGarry and Gillespie, leaving out Simon getting pistol-whipped. He looked pale, and dark circles were forming under his eyes as though he hadn't slept for a week, but other than that, he was managing to tough it out. If he wanted to play the hard man in front of Donna, then that was his concern.

'Bastard,' Donna hissed at the mention of Lord Hillerman's name, his military connection to McGarry, and Danny Gillespie's research.

'Name mean something to you?' Connor asked.

'Bloody right it does,' Donna said. 'I called a contact in government a while ago. He checked into the flag Ford told Simon was put on you, Connor, swore blind to me that there was no operation authorised, that Lord Hillerman never made any call to the Scottish government to tell the Justice Secretary about the operation.'

Connor nodded. It made sense. Either Hillerman had employed

government assets covertly to tail Jen in the hope she led them to him, or they had been McGarry's men all along. One call from Hillerman to the Chief Constable, full of authoritative bluster and threats of swift retribution if the Chief didn't give the men his full cooperation, and Hillerman had bought the two agents on the ground *carte blanche* to do whatever they liked, with no police interference. It was, he admitted, very neat, very professional work.

'So what now?' Simon asked. 'Edinburgh? Face Hillerman down with what we've found?'

Donna stood for a moment, chewing her top lip. 'Maybe,' she said, 'but I'd still like something more concrete. Other than what you claim Gillespie and McGarry told you about Hillerman's participation in the Troubles, we've not got much.'

'Ah, but we have,' Connor said, the thought striking him as he spoke. 'We've got Danny's research. He was right. Carryduff was the key to that. Now we know it was Hillerman who was involved, and O'Brien and McCandish were Colonel Gillespie's touts, we know what we're looking for. I bet there are more witness statements giving good descriptions of Hillerman, and I'm sure Robbie can dig up operational deployment records, either officially or otherwise, that put Hillerman in Northern Ireland at the right time. We've got him.'

'Aye, but hold on,' Simon said. 'One thing doesn't add up. Gillespie said it wasn't McCandish or O'Brien who were involved in Carryduff, that they were away drumming up support for the Republican cause in America at the time. So how does that fit?'

Connor thought back to Arthur Fielding in his sitting room. The way his eyes had darkened the moment he had heard O'Brien and McCandish's names. What was it he had said? *McCandish and O'Brien. Oh, I fucking knew them all right.*

'I need to check into that,' he said, the thought dancing at the edge of his mind. He could feel understanding creep into the darkness, like dawn breaking over a mountain range.

'Right, let's go,' Simon said, clapping his hands together. 'Donna, we can visit Robbie, see what he can tell us, then maybe head to Edinburgh, have a little chat with our pal the lord, maybe press upon him the importance of not fucking around with my friends.'

Donna gave a smile. 'You can do that on your own time,' she said. 'I'm still a reporter, Simon. Getting to Hillerman isn't going to be easy. He'll hunker down behind an army of spokespeople and spads, and you can bet they'll throw "national interest" in my face and try to shut this down.'

'National interest,' Connor said, feeling another rush of understanding.

'What?' Donna asked, eyes sharp, as though she were a tracking hound that had just scented prey.

'It's what Gillian Flint said,' Connor replied, fiddling with his phone to confirm what he suspected. 'About people on both sides of the Atlantic not wanting this to get out. About dyeing rivers green to celebrate the Irish. That's why Hillerman was in such a rush to get Danny's evidence back.' He turned the phone to Donna, showed her the news page he had found.

'St Patrick's Day,' she muttered, reading the article. 'Seventeenth of March. Three weeks away. Son of a bitch. If it broke that IRA men were raising funds for the Troubles in America and that a senior government minister was running both sides against each other . . .'

'Might take the shine off things a little, eh?' Connor said. 'Not just the parades, but the trade talks that go on around them. Mr Green.' He glanced at Simon, smiled at his confused look. 'Flint told us that was the name of her employer. *Let's call him Mr Green*. She was trying to help us.'

'Not sure I'd go that far,' Simon said. 'I mean, look what she let happen to Paulie. But okay, for now, benefit of the doubt.'

Connor shrugged. Remembered what Flint had said about keeping US involvement in Northern Ireland's affairs out of the public eye. But that didn't mean she wouldn't want to clean house. He had been wrong. She had pulled the strings, made him think someone wanted the story to go public. But it wasn't that. It was the threat of it going public that she wanted. Donna had said O'Brien had been hosted in New York by a politician with an eye on the Senate. Knowing him would be toxic, and the possibility of the story going public would threaten more than one career. Enter Gillian Flint, who would keep the story private. For a price. What had she said? *You'd do very well in the States working with me.* He hated the small part of himself that entertained the idea of working with someone so ruthless.

'Okay,' he said, checking his watch. 'Let's get moving. If we're right about all this, we just need Robbie to give you what you need. After that, you might want to head for Furryboot Toon.'

Donna gave Connor a glance that was half confusion, half concern. 'What?' she said. 'You sure getting your nose flattened didn't scramble part of your brain as well?'

Connor smiled. 'I'm fine,' he said, eyes coming to rest on Simon. 'Furryboot Toon. As in fer aboot ye from. It's how they speak in Aberdeen.'

'Aberdeen?' Donna asked. 'Why would I want to go to Aberdeen?'

Simon nodded to Connor, taking the conversational baton. 'We think there might be a story breaking up there soon,' he said. 'Could be big. Come on, I'll tell you while you drive.'

CHAPTER 58

Jen twisted in her seat again, agony washing through her back and down her leg in a cramping wave. She tried to get comfortable. Looked at the bottle of painkillers sitting on the table in front of her, tried to remember how long it had been since her last dose. Since the accident, she had been a regular user of co-codamol, which helped to take the edge off the pain. But when it was like this, and the pain transformed from a dull ache to a screaming lance of agony through her lower back down into her legs, on the days when she felt her body had betrayed her, the co-codamol wasn't always effective. She had considered something stronger, something, she thought with a wry bitterness, that Angela Barr could probably get her in bulk. But no. To do that would be to take the first step on the path to addiction. Jen knew she had a compulsive, addictive personality – her previous career as a personal trainer and her obsessive use of exercise told her that – and she already had enough physical crutches in her life without resorting to chemical ones as well.

She pushed the bottle aside, grabbed for the phone. Listened for a moment, then heard Connor's voice, the soft static in the background telling her he was driving.

'Hey,' she said. 'Where you heading?'

'Just got a bit of business to tie up,' Connor said, voice brisk, as though he was distracted.

'You sound like you've got a cold coming on, you okay?' Jen asked.

A brief laugh down the phone. 'Well, you could say my nose is running a little more than normal,' he said. 'Anyway, how you doing? Paulie told me things got a little, ah, heated with the Barrs.'

'Yeah,' Jen said, looking at the painkillers as she remembered the sound of her crutch crashing into Chris's face. 'You could say that. But I'm fine. I made a couple of decisions.'

'Oh?' Connor said, a note of wariness creeping into his voice. 'What kind of decisions?'

Jen reached forward, ignoring the fresh flare of pain in her back as she moved the tablets and grabbed the envelope they had been sitting on. She pulled it towards her, opened it.

'I've had papers drawn up,' she said. 'I'm going to ask Paulie to take over the day-to-day running of the business. It's not for me, Connor. I wanted to keep Dad's name alive like that, but doing deals with people like Barr is just too high a price to pay.'

There was a silence on the line, one Jen understood. Connor and her father had never seen eye to eye, and they had made no effort to hide that animosity. For Connor to comment on her decision to walk away from her father's business could be seen as either hypocritical or rubbing salt into the wound they had both tried too hard to heal.

'How you feeling about it?' he asked at last.

'Tired,' Jen said, the word out of her mouth before she had realised she was going to say it. 'I'm tired, Connor. Since the accident, since I lost the baby, then Dad, all I've felt is tired. I'm sick of losing the people I love, sick of seeing the world taken from me. So if this is how I get away from that, to find something for myself, then so be it. If Paulie will take over, that is.'

'I don't think that'll be a problem,' Connor said, with a kind of clinical certainty.

'You going to be able to come over later on?' Jen asked. 'Or I could meet you at the house?'

'Not tonight, sorry,' Connor said. 'I'll be away. But I'm back tomorrow, and then we can talk, okay?'

'Promise?' Jen asked.

'Promise.'

She took another breath, the pain in her back seeming to harmonise with the sudden heat she felt behind her eyes.

'Okay, then,' she said. 'Take care, Connor. Love you.'

'I love you too, Jen,' he said, with a simple honesty that made her breath catch.

She ended the call, then turned her attention to the papers in front of her. Looked around the room, which seemed to be infused with her father's presence.

'Don't hate me, Dad, please,' she whispered. Then she reached for a pen.

CHAPTER 59

It was dark by the time Connor got to Belfast, and the Falls Road. He hadn't intended to visit the pub alley where he had killed two men, but it seemed to have a magnetic pull he was unable to resist.

He stood there, listening to the sounds of laughter and music spill from the pub. Laughter and music that the two men he had killed would never hear. He thought of the first man, of the startled, wide-eyed terror in his eyes as he had clawed at his throat, trying to breathe through his crushed windpipe. And then there was the second man. Connor found he couldn't remember what he looked like, only the sight of his head snapping back, trailing blood, bone and brain after Connor had shot him.

Two men. Two lives ended in less than a minute. And all because Danny Gillespie had looked into the past, and found something – no, someone – there that no one wanted to be found.

Connor turned his back on the alley, got walking. It wasn't far to his destination, and he wanted the time to clear his head. Donna and Simon could deal with Hillerman and his involvement in all of this. Connor had one last duty to perform. For himself. And for Danny.

As he walked, he thought about the news article Donna had found. About the witness statement telling of a man with Danny at the time of his death, a man who had mysteriously disappeared after Danny had been run over.

Connor knew who that man was now. Cursed himself for not figuring it out sooner.

The door swung open before the echo of the bell had faded, light spilling out of the hallway.

'Yes?' the man behind the door asked.

'Mr Fielding,' Connor said, 'sorry to trouble you at this time of night. Connor Fraser. We met a couple of days ago, spoke about my friend, Danny Gillespie. Mind if I come in for a minute, ask you a couple of more questions? Don't worry,' He reached into his jacket and produced the bottle of whisky he had bought at the airport. 'I didn't come empty-handed.'

Fielding's blue eyes darted from Connor to the bottle, as though making a calculation.

'Aye, come on away in, son,' he said, after a moment. 'Television's crap tonight anyway.'

He led Connor into the living room, leaning on his cane as he went. 'Make yourself comfortable, son,' he said. 'I'll just go and grab some glasses. And will you be needing water?'

'Not for me, thanks,' Connor said, setting the whisky on the coffee table. 'Don't want it getting in the way.'

'Good man,' Fielding said, as he shuffled out of the room. 'Good man.'

He returned a few moments later, two whisky glasses grasped in one hand, his other on the cane. Connor had a sudden thought of Jen. Hoped Paulie was right, that his plan would stop the Barrs trying to take revenge on her for pulling out of the deal.

'So, son,' Fielding said, settling into his chair. 'What can I do for you? It's a funny hour to be visiting.'

'Aye, it is,' Connor said, cracking the cap on the whisky and pouring two large measures. Fielding took his in a hand that showed only the slightest tremor.

'*Slàinte*,' Connor said.

'*Slàinte mhaith*,' Fielding replied.

Connor took a sip of the whisky. It burned like the anger in his chest. 'To your good health,' he said. 'Tell me, Arthur. Is that how you toasted Danny in the pub before you pushed him in front of that car?'

Fielding froze, the glass almost touching his lips. He turned to Connor, his blue eyes suddenly chips of ice. 'What did you just say?' he whispered.

'The night you were in the pub with Danny,' Connor said. 'You know, after you got him to help you report O'Brien and Bobby McCandish for their fictitious part in the Carryduff massacre. The night you pushed him in front of a car to shut him up about what he found out. That night? Did you toast his good health then, too?'

Fielding gave a small, pitying laugh. 'Son, I'm not sure what the hell you're talking about. But I think this isn't your first drink of the night. You might want to be getting on up the road now.'

'See, I couldn't understand it at first,' Connor said, ignoring Fielding. 'After all, when we spoke to you before, you were so clear, so focused in your hatred of O'Brien and McCandish for what they did to you and your wife, that I couldn't see how you would get their names wrong, get them mixed up for other people. But then I remembered something else you said. Something about not being a fan of "those flag-waving, God Save the King arsehole Brits", and it got me thinking. About your true motives. About who you really are. So I had my friend, Robbie, do a little more digging, and do you know what he found, Arthur? I think you do. After all, it's why you killed Danny, isn't it?'

A flash of hatred twisted Fielding's face into a gargoyle grimace of cruelty, then softened into something Connor could almost believe was genuine sorrow.

'He was a good lad, was Danny,' Fielding said, taking a sip of his drink. 'He knew a lot about Carryduff, and about the Brit who allowed it to happen. Bastard. Letting us bomb the hell out of kids just to get some headlines that would make the Brits look better and not the murdering scum they were. But that was what we did. It was war. Christ, it still is, just fought a different way.'

'So you talked to him, tried to find out what he knew?'

'Turns out he knew a lot,' Fielding said. 'About how that moustachioed murderer Hillerman had one of his men running touts for him, giving him information on our operations and men. Hell of a surprise to find out it was Danny's dad doing it.'

'Our men,' Connor said. 'So I was right, you were IRA. This simple-baker line was all just a pretence to keep you off the police's radar?'

'Aye,' Fielding said, the pretence of the avuncular old man falling away, replaced by someone crueller and infinitely more dangerous. 'And that's what I told Danny. We had been talking one night, about Carryduff, and I admitted I approved the use of my van, but also approved the whole operation. Too much of this . . .' he lifted the glass in his hand '. . . and not enough of this.' He tapped his forehead with a finger.

'So that's why you put the report in asking for an investigation of Carryduff?'

Fielding nodded. 'Danny loved it. It was everything he had hoped for in his studies about the Troubles and healing from the scars they inflicted. Think about it. One of the men involved in a deadly attack on British soldiers reports his own operation, asking for it to be investigated and those involved, including himself, brought to justice? Talk about redemption and a journey of healing, Danny loved it. Practically pushed the laptop to me.'

'But why lie?' Connor asked. 'Why say O'Brien and McCandish were involved when they weren't? Why say they kneecapped you as punishment?'

Fielding smiled. 'Oh, they kneecapped me, all right,' he said. 'Just not for that. They were under orders to do me, punishment for an, ah, earlier infraction.'

'So that was it? Revenge? Name them, drag them into the inquiry, see how much shit you could spread around?'

'Not only that,' Fielding said. 'There was another reason. Something I didn't know at the time. Something I only found out when Danny gave me his laptop and access to his files.'

Connor sat back, remembering what Gillespie had told him in Stirling. 'You found out O'Brien and McCandish were working for the British as touts,' he said. 'Something you didn't know back in 1987 when Carryduff was bombed.'

'Traitorous bastards. The Troubles were war. Nothing more, nothing less. And the first rule of war is that you do not betray your own men or your cause. If I'd known about them back then, I would have fucking killed them myself. As it was, all I had was the weapon Danny gave me. That'll do for them. They won't be done for Carryduff, of course, but they've enough red in their ledgers to make sure they never sleep well again with the authorities climbing up their arses.'

'So you reported them to the inquiry,' Connor said, as the last pieces of the puzzle fell into place. 'But, let me guess, you got cold feet yourself, kept your name out of it? Which is why Danny had to die?'

Another slow, sorrowful nod. 'I submitted the report without him seeing it, but I knew it was only a matter of time before he found out. So I took him for a wee celebration drink. I wasn't planning on killing him – at least, I don't think I was,' his eyes lost focus as he looked into his own memories for some form of self-justification, 'just trying to make him understand. But then he got a little pissed, I saw that van coming and . . .'

'You took your chance,' Connor said.

'Aye,' Fielding replied, the gun appearing at his side. 'Just like you took a chance coming here tonight. Bad luck for you.'

'Let me guess,' Connor said, gesturing towards the gun. 'You got that when you fetched the glasses from the kitchen.'

'Aye, I—'

Fielding's words were cut off by the choking cry he gave as the whisky Connor had hurled at his face hit his eyes. Connor lunged forward, planted a knee on Fielding's chest, bore down with his bodyweight as he grabbed the gun from the man and twisted it from his grasp. He inspected the weapon, then pressed it hard against Fielding's temple.

'Go on,' Fielding hissed, eyes empty. Those of a man who knew death, and had no fear of it. 'You'll be doing me a fucking favour.'

Something in his chest was urging Connor to do it. He thought of his gran, of her dying alone in her room. Of the two men he had killed less than two miles from where he was. Of Danny, who had died because his only crime was looking into the past and trying to find some truth.

'No,' Connor whispered, withdrawing the gun. 'No more killing.

You don't deserve a quick end, Fielding. I'm going to make sure everyone knows who you really are, what you did.'

'Fuck off out my house,' Fielding snarled.

Connor flicked the safety on the gun, stuck it into his waistband. Backed out of the room and down the hallway, got to the front door. Opened it to step out into a night that somehow seemed brighter than before.

Froze when he saw Gillian Flint standing at the end of the pathway to the house.

'Evening,' she said. 'Fancy a wee chat?'

CHAPTER 60

Flint had a car waiting at the end of the road, complete with a driver who looked like he moonlighted as a body double for King Kong at weekends.

'So, where are we going?' Connor asked, as they slipped into the back, King Kong opening Flint's door for her while glaring at Connor over the roof.

'Well, you need a place to stay tonight,' Flint said, glancing at her watch. 'You've missed the last flight home. I take it you were planning on using that little bolthole your pal arranged for you on Glencairn Street?'

Connor opened his mouth, closed it. She gave him a smile that was packaged as shy but delivered as calculating.

'I think we can do a little better for you than that, don't you? How about a night in the Europa? The Titanic suite is nice.'

'You're offering to put me up in a suite?' Connor asked, vaguely wondering if she was offering to stay with him. 'Very generous of you. Why the special treatment?'

Flint's smile moved from calculating to you-know-better-than-that.

'I told you there are people who don't want any of what you've found out about Danny Gillespie, Arthur Fielding and Lord Hillerman coming out,' she said, streetlights making a patchwork silhouette of her face. 'They've asked me to extend some . . . courtesies to you, to make sure you're rested so you can think about what you're going to do next with a clear mind.'

'You're trying to bribe me to keep me quiet?' Connor said. 'Gillian, or whatever your name is, I thought you knew me better than that.'

Flint turned to him, her face set, eyes glittering jewels in the gloom of the car. She gave Connor a smile whose only purpose was to expose her perfectly white, perfectly American teeth.

'Oh, I do know you better than that, Connor. We're not trying to buy your silence. We already have that. We had it the moment you killed McGarry's two men on the Falls Road. We have witnesses, and I'm pretty sure you weren't in much of a state to clean up the forensics you left behind. Or there's Rory O'Connell, the thug you beat up then stole his car. Or the drug-dealers in Belfast you robbed to fund your time on the run. No, Connor, we're not trying to buy your silence with kindness. If I wanted, I could bring the hammer down on your life at this moment. You'll stay quiet. But, still, I want you to think of your next move very carefully. I told you before, you're good at this. You really should come and work with me. You'd have more fun in the US than in Stirling, I promise you.'

Connor took a deep breath, swallowed the surge of bile racing up his throat. They had him. For killing those two men, for everything he had done. But did it matter? Didn't he deserve to pay for taking two lives and hurting countless others? What had he said to Fielding? *I'm going to make sure everyone knows who you really are, what you did.* Did Connor deserve any different treatment? Were his crimes somehow nobler as they were committed in pursuit of the truth?

'It's not just me,' he said, his voice as cold as Flint's gaze. 'There's Donna Blake. She'll get the story out. Or Simon will.'

'Your friend Simon will keep his mouth shut,' Flint replied. 'Or have you forgotten he's a serving policeman? He'll keep his mouth shut, or he'll find himself facing a raft of charges, from withholding evidence to unauthorised use of a firearm. I think that might just cause a problem for his career, and his freedom, don't you? And as for Ms Blake, well, let's just say that a D-Notice and a court order ensuring the story is never run will keep her quiet. Knowing Donna she'll try to fight it, but I guarantee she'll lose.'

Connor glared at Flint. He felt a surge of impotent rage. Nothing. It had all been for nothing.

'What about Fielding?' he asked. 'Or O'Brien and Hillerman? They can't walk away clean from this.'

'Trust me,' Flint said, 'they won't. Hillerman's already drafting his letter of resignation, the usual crap about wanting to spend more time with his family. As for O'Brien and Mr Fielding back there,' she flicked her hand over her shoulder dismissively, 'don't worry about them. You'll keep quiet because I'll blow your life apart if you don't. And I like you. The others?' She flashed her teeth again. 'Well, let's just say I don't like them.'

They rode the rest of the way to the hotel in silence, King Kong the chauffeur not moving after he pulled into the forecourt outside the Europa.

'The room's in your name,' Flint said. 'Titanic suite, just as I said. All paid for. Seriously, Connor, sleep on my offer, then let me know what you decide.'

'You already know what I'm going to say. And, besides, I don't even have your number.'

'Oh, I think we both know that's not true,' Flint said, with another flash of her perfect non-smile.

CHAPTER 61

By the time Connor got to the airport the next morning. Donna was on the TV screens, hair whipping into her face as she stared into the camera. Behind her, perfectly framed to show off their official logos, a cluster of police vans was penned in behind crime-scene tape, two officers standing sentry-like, glaring at Donna's back.

'And it's here, at Aberdeen harbour, that police made the discovery of drugs worth in excess of eight million pounds after they were apparently smuggled into the country from Europe. It's understood that the class-A drugs were found in a storage facility operated by prominent members of the local business community.'

Connor smiled. Obviously the Barrs' lawyers had been quick off the mark, making sure their clients stayed out of the press for as long as possible. Connor didn't know how long that would be, but he hoped it would be long enough for the police to get so close to the Barrs that any thought of revenge on Jen for compromising their drug-distribution business would become a distant memory. If they did try to get to her, he would have to take a more direct role in discouraging them. And after last night's conversation with Gillian Flint, that was a path Connor didn't want to go down.

The Titanic suite had been waiting for him, just as Flint had promised. Connor had swept the room for any form of surveillance device, found none. He had slept fitfully, his mind racing with thoughts of Danny Gillespie, Lord Hillerman and Arthur Fielding. Flint had promised some form of retribution on Fielding, but Hillerman being allowed to walk free gnawed at Connor. He might have been acting on orders, he might even have thought he was justified in what he had done, but Connor couldn't accept that. He didn't know if Hillerman and Gillespie's actions had extended the Troubles, but he knew they had done nothing to shorten them or bring peace. People had died because of their actions, or inactions, their final victim being Colonel Gillespie's own son, Danny. He had known what he had discovered was dangerous, made Connor the custodian of that knowledge. And Connor would be damned if he didn't make sure Hillerman was exposed, no matter what threats Gillian Flint made.

The question was, how? How did he make a man who was seemingly untouchable, protected by a cloak of lies as ornate as the ermine robes he sometimes wore suffer for what he had done?

The answer came to him as he watched Donna on the screen in front of him. It was, he thought, strangely poetic and utterly apt. He would do what had, ultimately, got Danny killed. He would file a report with the Troubles inquiry, asking for an investigation of the activities of Colonel Alasdair Gillespie and Captain Henry Hillerman. The request for an investigation was open to victims of the Troubles or their surviving relatives. Robbie could deal with that, find Connor a name he could use. All he needed was to prise the door open a little, let the inquiry see what was behind it. And the information Danny had amassed, information Connor would give to the inquiry, would shine a bright light on what had happened. They might try to cover it up, might try to bury it just as Hillerman had with McGarry, but when he learned that he was being investigated, Hillerman would feel a moment of overwhelming, crippling fear. He wouldn't be able to stop himself thinking of what would happen to him if he was unmasked, if his carefully crafted life came tumbling around his ears because his darkest secret was exposed.

After his conversation with Flint the previous night, and the threat she had made, Connor thought that sounded like a kind of justice.

His phone buzzed and Connor reached into his pocket, smiled when he saw Simon's name on the screen.

'Simon,' he said, 'how's Furryboot Toon this morning?'

'Bloody cold,' Simon said, his voice warm with humour.

'Doesn't seem to be bothering Donna too much,' Connor said, glancing back up at the TV in the departure lounge.

'Nah, she's happy, like she just got her first splash,' Simon said.

'Really?' Connor said. 'I thought she'd be spitting bullets, what with the Hillerman story being spiked.'

'You heard about that?' Simon said. 'Aye, she got word last night, conference call with her editor and some big lawyer Sky brought in. She wasn't best pleased, but the drugs bust lifted her mood a bit, and I did my best to keep her distracted as well.'

'Simon, please, spare me your sleazy sexploit stories,' Connor said, rolling his eyes. A gentleman might never kiss and tell but, in Simon's case, that didn't mean he couldn't insinuate. Heavily.

'Oh, Christ, no, no!' Simon blurted. 'Not like that. Well, I mean, yeah, like that, but that was after.'

'After what?' Connor asked.

A pause on the line, and Connor could practically hear the smile growing on Simon's face. 'Well, after I made an eejit of myself and got down on one knee, of course,' he said. 'Told you I was going to have to marry her.'

Connor felt something he hadn't known was clenched inside him suddenly ease. It was like he'd filled with warmth after being immersed in an ice bath. 'Simon, that's brilliant! Congratulations! I, ah, I don't know what to say, man.'

'Say you'll get into the airport shop and grab a bottle of champagne. We've got some celebrating to do when you've . . .' Simon trailed off. When he spoke again, his good humour was gone, replaced by a raw awkwardness that made Connor wince.

'I'm sorry, Connor,' he said. 'I didn't think. Celebrating is the last thing you're going to want to be doing with your gran's funeral on the horizon.'

'Simon, it's fine,' Connor said, realising he was telling the truth as he spoke, not just trying to make his friend feel better. 'Gran loved you and Donna. She'd be as happy for you as I am. And you know what she was like. She'd have given me hell if I didn't raise a glass to you and Donna the moment I got home.'

'Aye, true,' Simon said. 'But I am sorry, Connor. Hopefully you being my best man will help make up for it.'

Connor was stunned into silence. His best friend, the man who had saved his life more times than he could remember, the man who was always by his side, no matter what the danger was, the man Connor wished he could be more like, was asking him to stand beside him on the most important day of his life? It was an honour he didn't deserve. And yet . . .

'Thank you,' was all he could say. 'You're a good man, Simon.'

'Away,' Simon replied, his previous good humour returning. 'I just do what I can. Now get your arse home safely, big lad, we've got some plans to make.'

Connor ended the call, stared up at the TV. Saw Donna there. She was wearing gloves against the Aberdeen cold, but Connor could have sworn he could see the bulge of an engagement ring on the finger of her left hand. He smiled. Thought of his gran. Of her insistence that he had to 'make an honest woman' of Jen. Connor didn't believe in the old-fashioned notion, thought Jen was already more honest and genuine than anyone he had ever met. He loved her, but would marrying her only invite more pain and suffering into their lives? He still wasn't sure he wasn't cursed to bring pain and misery to everyone he loved, and the last thing he wanted to do was bring more of that to Jen.

'One step at a time, Connor,' he muttered to himself. 'One step at a time.'

CHAPTER 62

Stirling

Three days later

Connor hated the room, felt as though it was trying to choke him with manufactured sincerity and cookie-cutter calm. The walls were a cool cream, dotted here and there with framed posters claiming that 'Grief is the ultimate loving tribute' or how the company was there 'to respect your wishes and ease your burden at this sad time'.

Connor wondered if tearing a few of the posters from the wall and upending the cheap Ikea table he was sitting at would ease his burden a bit. It felt like it would.

Jen rested her hand on his, as though sensing his thoughts. 'How you doing?' she asked him. 'Won't be long now.'

'I'm okay,' Connor said, looking around the small funeral-home anteroom they were sitting in. 'Just this place, you know? It's so . . . forced.'

'I get it,' Jen said, her eyes defocusing a little.

Connor felt a pang of guilt – it was selfish of him to be dwelling on his own grief without thinking of how much this would rake up painful memories for Jen of her father's death.

The door to the office swung open, and a small, bespectacled man with painfully slicked-back hair and ruddy skin that would have been more appropriate on a deep-sea fisherman than an undertaker bustled into the room. He took a seat opposite Connor, pushed a sheaf of papers towards him.

'There you are, Mr Fraser,' he said, in an accent that had resisted Scotland's attempts to tame it and remained broad Yorkshire. 'That's the plan your grandmother made with us. It's all there, the hymns, the readings, the musical choices, the floral requests. Just look it over, and let me know if there's anything you want to change.'

Connor took the papers, flicked through them. It was, as the man – Geoffrey, Connor suddenly remembered – said. But there was one item, after the first hymn, that made Connor stop.

'Reading and eulogy, Connor'.

He blew out a breath. His gran, requesting that he give her eulogy. A small request, and the least he owed her. But it terrified him. After all, what could he say about the woman who had been his third parent, the one who had understood him in a way his parents never had? The one who had been there when his mother had been withered and husked out by cancer, while his father lost himself first in his work and then in a bottle? How could he sum her up, do her justice in a five-minute speech in front of a roomful of people he hardly knew?

He didn't have the answers to those questions. Not yet. But he would find them. For his gran, and for himself.

They were in the office for another ten minutes, time that passed Connor by in half-heard conversations and a blur of document signing. And then they were back outside, in a day that seemed too bright and cheerful after the synthetic serenity of the funeral director's office.

Jen looped one arm around Connor, leaning on her crutch with the other hand. They were on Forth Street, the funeral director's office a small, squat, harled building that sat across the road from a bowling alley. *Bless me Father,* Connor thought suddenly, *for I have sinned and bowled a strike.*

'What are you thinking?' Jen asked, squeezing his arm.

Connor turned, smiled at her. 'Ack, nothing really. Just about Gran, and what the hell I'm going to say at the funeral. Why would she do that to me anyway? Ask me to speak for her?'

'Because she loved you,' Jen said. 'She was so proud of you. You're the only person she would want to speak for her.'

Connor thought of the men he had killed in Belfast, of the threat Gillian Flint had made to expose those murders if he didn't keep quiet. Hardly the actions of a man to be proud of. He wondered what Flint would do when she discovered he had reported Lord Hillerman to the Troubles inquiry. Pushed the thought aside. If Flint came for him, if he had to answer for his crimes, he would do it without complaint. He would take responsibility for his actions. And maybe, in doing so, he would make his gran proud and live up to her sense of him.

They got to the car, which was parked a short distance from the funeral home. Connor plipped the central locking, opened the door for Jen. He had just taken her crutch when there was a sudden blur of movement and he was shoved back, staggering away as he tried to stay on his feet.

'Fucking bitch!' a tall, wiry man with dark hair spat. His face was slashed open at the cheek, the wound nestling in a mass of gangrenous-looking bruises. He darted forward, lunging towards Jen, who was off balance and staggering back to get away.

'Do you know what you did?' he hissed. 'Aberdeen is fucked. Angela's in prison, and the polis are looking for me. All because you—'

Connor grabbed the man's arm, whirled him around, away from Jen. He lunged forward, and Connor felt a heavy punch to his chest. He folded over with the force of the blow, then leaned in, snapping his head up to crash into the underside of the man's jaw. As his attacker staggered back, Connor landed a savage straight right to his face, felt a sudden satisfaction as bone broke against his knuckles and the man crashed to the ground.

'Friend of yours?' he said to Jen, who had regained her balance and was walking towards him.

'Name's Chris,' Jen said. 'One of Barr's goons, he . . .' Her voice trailed off as her face went pale and her eyes became horrified, tear-filled, glittering like jewels. Connor tried to step forward, suddenly afraid she had been hurt. But as he moved, the world lurched sickeningly around him. He stumbled, fell to his knees.

He could hear Jen shouting his name, but it was like he was underwater and she was at the edge of the pool. He tried to get to his feet, felt the world lurch again. And why was he so cold? Chris hadn't hit him that hard, had . . .

Connor felt his breath catch in his throat as he looked down at his chest, where Chris had punched him. His T-shirt had been turned into a glistening bib of blackening blood. He blinked, felt the blood scald his cooling hands as he grabbed his chest and toppled over.

Stabbed, he thought, with a strange mix of panic and calm acceptance. *I've been stabbed.*

He blinked, and then Jen was filling his view. She was looking down on him, tears streaking her face. Saying something he couldn't hear. He tried to lift his hand, stroke the tears away, tell her it would be okay. He just needed to catch his breath. But the effort was too much for him – it was as if he had been secured to the pavement, glued there by the blood that was pumping from his chest.

He swallowed, closed his eyes. Warm now. Finally.

From what sounded like a different planet, he heard the first faint wail of a siren. So far away. So unimportant. All that mattered was Jen. She needed him. He closed his eyes, the darkness seeming to engulf him. Forced his eyes to open. Focused, willed his body to work for him, just one more time.

Heard Jen's hitching sobs. Grabbed onto the sound, a beacon to follow, a cry for help to answer. If he could summon the strength, the courage, for one last fight.

Thought of his gran. Of her request that he speak for her at her funeral. Of Simon, and his invitation to Connor to be his best man. Heard Jen's cries again, louder this time, sharper.

Started to rise . . .

ACKNOWLEDGEMENTS

This was the hardest book I've ever had to write. I lost my mum about two-thirds of the way through the draft. If you've read the other Connor books, you'll know I lost my dad while writing *Violent Ends* two years before. So coming back to this, and finishing Connor's story, has been utterly exhausting.

To all my friends, especially Joe, Lou, Vic, Ed and Derek, thank you. You got me through. And to Mark Leggatt, who made sure the wheels stayed on, especially when I tried to get back on the bike after Mum died, you have my eternal thanks.